Desert Son

First paperback edition June 2023

Cover design by GetCovers
Edited by Hannah Gokie

ISBN 978-0-9996012-4-2 (paperback)

www.fjtalley.com

Desert Son

F. J. Talley

Table of Contents

Chapter One

"Shift to mark 277!" came the shout of the commander. "Come about into attack position!"

"Aye, ma'am!" The helmsman punched in the course and shifted his gaze to the commander, who glanced at him, then barked, "Ahead two thirds." She turned to tactical, adding, "Train pulse weapons on their weapons array."

"Aye, Ma'am."

"Command to Spark."

"Aye, Ma'am."

"Lead on our next run."

"Understood," said the dark-haired man on the screen. He glanced at his helm. "Prepare for maneuver Shaw Alpha 4 on my mark."

"Wait," said the other commander. "That would put us in direct opposition."

"And that's a problem how?" came the voice of still another colleague.

"That's a valid question, Minty," came a fourth female voice. "Stop exercise. That's enough for today. We'll debrief at 0800 hours tomorrow. Rest up. Wolfe out."

* * *

Raina Wolfe and Tucker McLeod sat to review the recording of the exercise once more before leaving the commandant's office. The joint operations academy for the Star Alliance and Central Federation had been in operation for four months, and while they had enjoyed some success with their students, they had a long way to go. McLeod was particularly impatient with the progress of the officers and NCOs in the academy's first class.

"I think you're more frustrated than you need to be, Tucker," Wolfe said. She knew Sr. Captain Tucker McLeod better than most, and could read his expressions like an astral chart.

"Probably, but that doesn't make me feel any better. I thought I was a better teacher than this."

"Oh, please." Wolfe laughed. "You're the best. But you're also the most impatient man I know." She pointed to the vid screen. "They're coming alone fine: they're gaining a better understanding of tactics and operations than they ever had in their fleets. And they're good people overall."

"True. We asked for the best, and they are impressive, in tactics, operations, even decision making. What bothers me is that they're doing everything by rote—there's no instinct or response, they're just reacting. That won't help them in real battles."

"I understand that, but the only way they'll develop those instincts is by training and giving them the chance to fail—without taking their heads off."

McLeod shrunk in his seat. "Have I been doing that?"

Wolfe smiled. "No. Quite the opposite. You've shown admirable patience with them. You just vent a lot to me before and afterwards."

"Oh."

Wolfe laughed again. "We're a team, Tucker. I've vented to you on more than one occasion about their flying and reactions."

"Fine." McLeod was almost dismissive. "What are your plans for tomorrow?"

"Additional maneuvers. Goody has the two corvettes ready so the federation flyers can practice more basic Alliance maneuvers."

"At least that's going well."

"It is."

McLeod turned to her. "They're just not like us, are they?"

"That goes without saying."

"Which reminds me, what's the latest on *Axon*?"

"She's coming along fine," said Wolfe, referring to her first full command, a Densen-Class cruiser in the Federation. "We'll be ready in time for our recommissioning date."

"Great."

At that moment, they heard a hail and were shocked to see the logo on the vid screen. Before answering the hail, McLeod sealed the office, then pressed the pad. Fleet Marshall Sinclair's face filled the screen.

"I hope you two weren't getting too comfortable," Sinclair said. "It seems we have *Raven*'s first assignment."

McLeod and Wolfe straightened in their chairs, as the focus on the vid pulled back revealing Minister Demeter Long and Fleet Marshall Morgan North of the Star Alliance.

"I suppose we should ask more about the progress of your students, before we get started," said Sinclair.

Wolfe and McLeod looked at each other before McLeod turned back to Sinclair. "On track and doing well, sir. We believe our training methods are making a difference."

North's face broke into a smile. "And I would guess not as quickly as you would like, eh, Tucker?"

"You might say that."

"Well, it's been a matter of weeks," Sinclair said. "And they won't develop your instincts and understanding of each other in such a short time. I know both of you and I'm sure they're working hard."

"They're also committed," Wolfe said. "The interaction among the students is admirable and is making the process much easier than we anticipated."

"Excellent," Sinclair said. "Though we may have to jump start that process."

"So you implied," McLeod said. "What do you have?"

McLeod and Wolfe noticed Sinclair turn to his left and nod. A planet came on the screen and turned slowly on its axis as Sinclair continued. "This is the planet Amaeus. It's in the Alpha Quadrant."

"I don't know it," McLeod said. "What's our interest in it?"

"What *Raven* was created for, Tucker," said Demeter Long, Interstellar Minister for the Star Alliance. "They've applied for Federation membership."

Wolfe turned to McLeod. "One for our side."

"Not exactly," Sinclair said. "In fact, we have doubts about their suitability for Federation membership, at least at this time."

"What's the hold up?" Wolfe asked.

"There are several small points, but the biggest has to do with the government and energy." North turned again to his left. "Take us to the central desert." The globe turned, then the focus zoomed in toward a large, arid area that easily covered twenty-five percent of the planet.

"This is the central desert," Sinclair continued. "The planet overall is class seven, so relatively good natural resources, though the concentrations of water are uneven. The same goes for their concentrations of specific minerals such as tullarium."

"They have tullarium?" asked Wolfe, her eyes widening. "Are they using phase weapons?"

"At the moment," Sinclair said. "They understand the Federation and Alliance strongly discourage the use of such weapons. But tullarium has other industrial uses, too. Tullarium is located throughout the planet, but the largest deposits are concentrated in the central desert."

"How concentrated?" McLeod asked.

"Estimates are that close to eighty-five percent of their reserves are in the central desert, and those resources go at a premium to the metropolitan and agricultural areas of the planet. In effect, the people who control the natural resources have a great deal of influence on the planet overall."

"That's hardly surprising or unusual in the galaxy, sir," Wolfe said. "What's different about this planet?"

"What's different is this man," said Long, pointing to the screen which revealed a handsome middle-aged man with dark hair and grey eyes who had an aloof expression on his face. "This is Thorian Crist. He is the main reason we are skeptical about Amaeus's membership in the Federation."

"How so?" McLeod asked.

"Crist is a mineral tycoon who controls forty-five percent of the tullarium and other minerals in the central desert and has the capacity to take over much more given his substantial army of mercenaries. He is resisting the Federation application and could cripple the planet if he embargoes his resources and takes over more facilities and stores within the central desert."

"How quickly would that become a problem for the people of the planet, sir?"

"Within weeks," Sinclair said. "And the Planetary Collaborative is aware of that."

"What is Crist's problem with the Federation, assuming he has a problem with it?"

North sat up straighter in his seat. "That is a long and complicated story, but he has a strong belief in self-determination, and further believes—"

"That Federation membership subsumes self-determination," McLeod said. "How many times have we heard that?"

North smiled. "Most days. The difference is that Crist has made his opposition crystal clear and has made direct threats against the Planetary

Collaborative; he is immovable both on resisting membership and preventing it with all his resources."

"Which are considerable?" Wolfe asked.

"They are," Sinclair replied. "He could strangle the planet by assuming greater control of the central tullarium fields—something he's capable of doing." Sinclair paused before continuing. "But we believe there are clear strategic interests for the Federation and the Alliance in Amaean membership. We'd like to have them as members, but only if Crist is neutralized."

"And that's where Raven comes in," said McLeod.

"Correct. And neutralized means exactly that: removing his influence so that the planet can make its own decisions about membership in the Federation. By the way, the planet voted decisively for Federation membership, also supported strongly by the Planetary collaborative."

Wolfe frowned. "And how is the collaborative organized?"

Sinclair held up his hand. "I'll send you all of the background information so you're prepared. Our question is this: is Raven ready for this assignment? It's not the same as their ability to work between the Federation and the Alliance; it's a straight covert mission."

McLeod and Wolfe exchanged glances before Wolfe said, "We believe we're ready now, Fleet Marshall, but we'll need to look over the background information first to assemble the proper team."

"Agreed," said McLeod. "We may ask for clarification on some points, but we'll choose the team based on the specific tasks we design." McLeod frowned again. "May we assume that the board needn't know our chosen approach or method?"

"That's preferable, Tucker," Sinclair said, and he smiled. "That's how *Raven* was designed to perform."

McLeod returned the smile and turned to Wolfe. "Then let's get to work."

Chapter Two

"We will have order!" said Zahara Ali, chair of the Planetary Collaborative. The gray band in her black hair glowed as her chest rose and fell. "We have much to discuss today, and it won't do for us to argue."

The four collaborative members looked sheepish as they relaxed into their chairs, but only for a moment. Ian Anoki, the minister from the northern region broke the silence. "I agree, Zahara," he said, casting a small smile around the table. "There is much for us to do if we are to avoid a crisis."

"Good. Then let's discuss more about our application for Federation membership."

"That's where I have questions, Zahara," said the collaborative's oldest member, Leyla Hill. "I was under the impression that the Federation was looking favorably on our application. Has that changed?"

"Not so much changed, Leyla," Ali began, "but Federation membership is not the simple process it was thirty years ago. Now the

Federation looks at each candidate world very carefully looking for a reason to deny membership."

"That doesn't make sense," Hill said. "Their purpose is to encourage cooperation across the galaxy. How can they do that if they exclude worlds?"

Anoki hmphed. "Do you really want me to answer that, Leyla?"

Hill sat back and stared at Anoki. "Why don't you do that, Ian?"

Sensing the mood, Ali rapped her gavel. "Please, let's not start already." She looked up serenely at Hill. "Leyla, as the Central Federation has grown, it finds itself unable to provide the support services and development it could before. Therefore, they are very cautious in their expansion, particularly with planets experiencing volatile internal struggles."

"Are the struggles on Amaeus so different from other worlds?" Hill asked.

"I don't believe so," came the quiet voice of Kyla Crist. "When the Federation representatives traveled here for their last visit, they told me that our challenges were like those of other worlds."

"Then you must have been listening to a different representative than I did," Anoki said. "They told me we have significant issues to deal with before they would consider our application." Anoki leaned forward in his seat. "Are you saying you heard differently?"

Before Crist could answer, Ali rapped her gavel again. "My impression was the same as Ian's. The chair of the Federation delegation told me that membership in the Federation must reflect the will of the people of our planet, and without a clear mandate, Federation membership is unlikely."

"Then what was the last vote for?" asked Takoda Marten, minister from the eastern government. "We put it to the populace and received a significant majority. What does the Federation want?"

"They want the will of all the people to be reflected in the vote," Ali said, and turning toward Crist, she added, "without the threat of terrorist or rogue action if membership were granted. The last thing they want is to provide membership to a planet and have that spark a civil war. Once that happens, they lose any assets or contributions of that planet until the crisis is averted. They also don't want to be drawn into a civil conflict on either side."

"In other words," Anoki said, "they want worlds that can be an asset to the Federation, rather than a burden."

"And do you really feel that Amaeus would be a burden to the Federation?" Crist asked.

"Your brother seems to think the opposite," Anoki replied. The board room fell silent and Crist's eyes momentarily diverted so she couldn't see the ever-so-slight movement in Zahara Ali's lips as she suppressed a smile.

Crist clenched her teeth. "This is not about my brother, Ian. It is about—"

"I respectfully disagree, Kyla," Ali said, bringing the attention back to her. "Your brother had made his opposition to Federation membership known for years. And he has flexed his muscles in the central region to show his displeasure."

"The will of the people is clear, Zahara," Crist countered. "And regardless of family ties, I stand with the majority."

"But how strongly, and how loudly?" Anoki said. "You have made your support of Federation membership known and helped campaign for it, but have you ever severed yourself from your brother's actions and statements?"

"Have you?"

"He's not my brother."

"And I am not his *mother*. Are we to be held hostage, not by Thorian Crist, but by our fear of the unknown and empty bluster?" She looked around the table. "I, for one, will not."

The sound of drumming fingers at the head of the table brought the ministers' attention back to Ali. "Well, you may have the luxury of ignoring your brother and his control of so many of our natural resources, but as the representative of the central region, I don't. Thorian has more than once held millions of families as economic hostages with his control of tullarium and other mineral resources. We can't afford to have that control threaten not just my home, but our entire planet's future."

"And do you believe Kyla can control that, or her brother?" Marten asked.

"Well, she's the only one of us who doesn't seem concerned about him," said Anoki. "Does she know something the rest of us don't?"

"Don't start, Ian."

Anoki smiled. "Then let us in on the secret, Kyla," he said, his arms reaching wide at the table. "Let us in on the secret of your calm when a terrorist in your family threatens the future of our entire planet. Just how can you be so serene with that threat hanging over your head?" He leaned forward, staring at Crist. "Or maybe it isn't hanging over your head, is that it?"

Crist's fingers splayed as she tensed her entire body. "Just what are you implying, Ian? If it is in any way a conspiracy, I suggest you remember my legal reputation."

"Reputation?"

"As one of the best lawyers on Amaeus. With a strong desire to win."

"Are we finished posturing here?" Ali asked, amused by the exchange. "You're acting like little boys fighting over some foolish toy." She waited for half a minute, then looked at Crist. "Though you must admit, Kyla, that you are the only person who doesn't express fear about what Thorian Crist is doing now or has done in the past. Can you explain that?"

Crist sighed. "It certainly isn't because we're close as siblings. And nothing Thorian has done can explain the disturbances around the planet that threaten all of us."

"Don't try misdirection, Kyla," Anoki sneered. "The actions of your terrorist brother are the subject here, and your inability to either control or condemn him."

Crist rose. "I will not accept attacks on my character or integrity here, Ian, from you or anybody else. If you have something specific you want to accuse me of, say it and say it now."

"Kyla," said Hill. Repeating, she said, "Kyla." Crist turned to the older woman. "Kyla, please sit down. We are a team here."

Crist sat, but kept her eyes glued on Anoki, who sat back with a satisfied grin.

"We should understand that it is not only specific actions that might be suspect for any of us, as you suggest, Kyla," Ali began, once more in charge. "It is also the appearance of impropriety that we must guard against." To this, Anoki smiled, but said nothing. "And that may compromise our Federation membership as much as anything your brother can do. You understand that, don't you?"

"I do, Zahara," said Crist. "And I also understand that we will not accomplish our goal of Federation membership if we continue to launch barbs at each other, thus weakening our collective hand." To this, Anoki shrugged and backed away from the fight.

"I believe we should take a break now," said Marten. "We must present a united front to our people."

If only that were possible, Crist thought, as she looked around at the table.

Chapter Three

The eyes of McLeod, Wolfe, and their principal covert operations personnel were glued to their personal vid screens. McLeod saw signs of stress as Gordon Shaw, chief engineer and designer of *Raven*, rubbed his temples. McLeod also noticed Mark Carnahan, covert operations specialist, shifting through pages on his screen in rapid succession, and wondered what he was thinking.

Wolfe ended the speculation by convening the meeting. "People. You've seen the same things Tucker and I have seen, and I don't want to minimize what we're being asked to do." She turned her attention to the larger vid screen. "Let's look at the tasks ahead."

"Wait, Raina," McLeod said. "Let's examine the general challenges first, then the details."

"A good idea. Let me pull that up on the screen." As the screen came to life, Wolfe continued. "We need to envision the entire operation, not just the covert part in the Thorian Crist compound; we may have to act in other locations planet-side."

"There it is," said McLeod, as the screen focused on a wide view of Amaeus. "A rather pretty little planet, but also a mess. They have wonderful scientific advances, little poverty, and fine natural resources. There are five regions as part of the planetary government. Each of the prime ministers of those regions serves as a member of the planetary collaborative, essentially their executive council."

"How well does that work, captain?" asked Araminta Ross, the only full Terran at the academy. "Are there any nasty regional squabbles?"

"Don't know that at present, Minty," McLeod said. "We'll look into that before making any final decisions."

"As you consider the objective, captain," Carnahan began, "is this a simple extraction, or—"

"There's nothing simple about it, Mark," Wolfe said. "In fact, getting into the compound alone will be difficult."

"And the mission isn't an extraction exactly, though that is an option," McLeod added. "We were told to 'neutralize' the offending party, a Thorian Crist. Let me put him on the screen." McLeod pressed a few buttons and the face of Thorian Crist filled the screen.

Trevor Scott looked up. "He looks nasty. I wouldn't want to meet him in a dark alley."

"I agree," said Wolfe. "And 'neutralize,' as Captain McLeod said, gives us several options."

Shaw frowned. "Any reason some other covert team couldn't take care of this?" He directed his questions to Wolfe, who glanced at McLeod before answering.

"All we can tell you, Goody," she began, using Shaw's nickname, "is that the council has assigned this to *Raven*."

"We believe there are too many details and complications for another team to take this on, commander," offered McLeod. "Plus, Amaeus is an applicant to the Central Federation, and sending a formal team to Amaeus might cause more trouble than it's worth."

"But isn't that *Raven's* mission?" asked Ross. "To lower barriers to Federation or Alliance expansion?"

"So they tell us," McLeod said, smiling. "And in either case, there has been a clear mandate by the Amaean people to apply for Federation membership." He pointed again to the vid screen. "It is Crist and his people who are making that difficult."

"How much flexibility do we have in defining what 'neutralize' means, sir?" asked Scott.

McLeod smiled again. "The council offered that term for a reason, Trevor, though if you were to ask me, they don't want a surgical strike that simply removes him, because it won't stop his operation from continuing to wreak havoc on the planet. That would not be in the interests of the Federation."

"And to be honest," Wolfe added, "the council doesn't want to know exactly how we do this."

"Oh."

"Exactly." Wolfe turned her attention back to the group. "Let's review more about the political environment and about Crist himself." She pressed two controls. "Here is a photo of the planetary collaborative, so you can see each of the members. I won't go over them individually except to tell you that the one complication we have with the collaborative is this woman." The screen shifted to focus on the youngest member of the collaborative. "This is Kyla Crist, the prime minister of the southern government. She is a lawyer by training, in fact, a formidable one."

"Any relation to—" Shaw began.

"Younger sister," Wolfe said, cutting him off. "And as far as we can determine, they are not on good terms. Crist—Kyla Crist that is—enthusiastically supported the Federation application, whereas Thorian has made several threats against the planetary collaborative opposing Federation membership."

"For what reason?" asked Ross.

"He says he wants to ensure Amaean sovereignty," McLeod began, "but most believe he wants to solidify his power over the planet both economically and politically."

"A real piece of work," said Scott.

"But why is the situation with the sister such a complication?' Shaw asked. "Sibling rivalries happen all the time."

"That's harder to explain, commander," McLeod replied. "But as best we're able to determine, the Amaean people are having difficulty separating Kyla Crist from her brother."

"News agencies have reported divisions within the planetary collaborative focusing on Kyla Crist," Wolfe said. "There is nothing to the accusations against Kyla Crist, as far as we know, but things are heating up for her."

The table was silent, with Carnahan finally leaning back in his chair. "Could she be an ally to us?"

Wolfe smiled. "That's what Tucker and I were thinking, Mark. In any case, we don't want her to be an enemy."

"Though we also can't expect her to support actions by outside forces like *Raven* on Amaean territory," McLeod added.

"Thought that out, did you?" Shaw asked, looking directly at McLeod.

McLeod smiled. "I'm not just a pretty face, commander."

"We have several tasks to complete as we plan this mission," said Wolfe. "And we must be precise about this: it has to be a clear and convincing accomplishment of objective as this is our first mission."

"That means Captain Wolfe will not allow me to engage in my normal improvisation," McLeod said. "And in that vein, here are your temporary assignments as we develop the plan: Trevor, focus on approaches to Kyla Crist and the planetary collaborative. Raina and I have our doubts about involving members of the planetary collaborative other than Crist, but we still need to determine both physical approaches and cover stories to work with her—if she's willing." McLeod turned to Ross and Carnahan. "What we need from you two are an analysis of approaches and operations within the Crist compound in the central desert: that won't be easy, as the place is incredibly well-defended. That's why two of you are working on it." McLeod turned his attention back to the group. "Captain Wolfe and I will evaluate academy personnel and assemble the full crew."

"What about me?" asked Shaw.

McLeod smiled. "Commander, you will determine how we configure *Raven* both in transit and during the operation for maximum efficiency, and make sure we can pull it off. This is, after all, your baby."

Shaw rose from the table. "Glad you recognize that."

* * *

The desert's heat and aridness were a blanket that enveloped even the inside of the Crist compound. Crist sat at an oval table with his most trusted associates, picking his fingernails.

"Please continue your report, Wen," Crist said, studying his hands.

Wen Bokari consulted his pad. "The latest news reports are showing more unrest and unease among the people after the latest energy price increase, sir." Bokari was a tall man with a youthful appearance. "I believe we are having the impact we wanted."

"But is it quickly enough?" asked Elvin Cordell, a former military general. "I'm still getting used to these slow civilian operations." He turned his attention to Crist. "Is this how you want this to go, Thorian?"

Crist raised his head for the first time. "We go soft at first if we can, Elvin. You'll get your time to play later."

"I wasn't asking to play."

"I know that, Elvin. But if we can get the collaborative to the negotiating table, everyone wins. Using military power too early compromises that."

"And negotiating is what we want, right?" asked Bokari, smiling.

Cordell looked at Bokari with lidded eyes. "I suppose someone has to be the idealist, here." Cordell and his colleagues laughed.

"The short answer to your question is 'yes,' Wen," Crist said. "We keep our strikes directed toward property, not people, and hope they see the wisdom of negotiation." He shook his head. "I will never understand this opposition to profit that so fascinates the planetary collaborative, and their naivete about that profit if we join the Federation."

"Not everyone understands that fact of life," said Victor Ansara, Crist's principal lieutenant.

"True. But we must convince them otherwise." Turning to Walker Menzel, Crist added, "Status of our money operations, Walker."

Menzel scratched his head. "On track, sir. We've recruited new partners in Bank of the Lowlands and the Real Estate Association. That should allow us to clean Anson of several holdings over the next four to six months."

"What about our total for the year?"

"Hard to say that, sir. We're still unsure of the capacity of the Eastern Star Bank, so that may be under our projections. We're safe in saying 308mil for the year even without them, however."

Crist turned for the first time to the only woman at the table—Cole Maddox—chief engineer. "Is that enough for your toys and personnel, Maddox?"

Maddox suppressed a smile. "Easily."

"Good. What about our covert people, Victor? Are they ready?"

"Definitely, sir. I spoke with several of them in the news services, and they're fomenting plenty of agitation among the people and within the collaborative. I wouldn't want to be your sister."

"I don't think she wants to be her, either. Serves her right: all this crusading and advocating is a waste of time." Crist thought for a moment then looked again at Ansara. "Make sure she lasts long enough to be a distraction: we can't have her off the collaborative too early."

Ansara raised his hands. "Under control, sir. She will be in place as long as we want her in place."

"Even taking into account her colleagues on the collaborative? I wouldn't put it past that woman Ali or the other one, what's—"

"Anoki."

"Yes, Anoki," Crist continued, "to go off too early and spoil our work."

"I monitor work with the news services personally, sir," Ansara said. "We should have no problem, and we'll adjust as necessary with additional news reports or commentaries." He smiled. "They have no idea how well they're being played."

"Good. Let's keep the music going."

Chapter Four

McLeod looked around the seminar room and smiled. Besides the small permanent crew of *Raven*, he and Raina Wolfe had assembled an excellent team for this first mission. He was pleased with the energy in the room and the tone of the chatter and almost didn't want to bring it to a close.

"As much as I enjoy our discussion," McLeod began, "we need to focus on the mission at hand."

Raina Wolfe sat to his left at the head of the table. "Great. As we begin, let's review the purpose of this operation." She turned on the vid screen showing the planet Amaeus. "Amaeus is a candidate planet to join the Central Federation of Planets, and while the governing council of the Federation is favorable toward their application, there are some hiccups. This man," she pressed a button, "Thorian Crist, controls a significant part of the central energy fields and is ruthless about getting what he wants."

"Pardon me, Captain," Ava Driscoll interrupted, "but if he's so bad, why hasn't he been arrested or in some other way been held accountable?"

Wolfe smiled. "A fair question, and the answer is: 'it's complicated,'" to which the group laughed.

"The fact is," McLeod began after the group grew quieter, "that Thorian Crist acts at the edge of the law by supporting dissident groups that oppose any kind of affiliation with the Federation or the Alliance. They further believe any such affiliation threatens the sovereignty of the planet."

"Is that the real purpose?" Max Serrano asked. "I mean, there might be another motive."

After a brief glance at Wolfe, McLeod replied, "We think so, Max. Crist is perhaps the richest person on the planet and he wants nothing to threaten his wealth. He may believe his economic power would be compromised by membership in the Federation, or that the taxes to support Federation membership compromise his business interests."

"But that doesn't have to be the case, Captain," Serrano offered. "I mean, you could look at lots of examples like that, but that has more to do with the ineptness of those planets' governments, and—"

"You don't have to convince me, Max," McLeod said. "And it's not the point. But your original question is valid: we believe Crist has plenty of personal stakes in this, including family relations, and they are his motivations." McLeod turned to the screen, changing the picture. "This is the central desert of the planet, Crist's backyard. That's also where most of the planet's mineral resources are located, at least the most valuable ones. Crist has been moving ever so deliberately to acquire more and more of those resources.

"We think his ultimate objective is to control so much of the planet's resources that the planetary collaborative—the governing body—will have to negotiate with him."

"Something tells me that wouldn't be good for this planet," Driscoll said.

"Exactly, Ava," McLeod agreed. "And it's Crist's refusal to accept the planet's vote to affiliate with the Federation which is prompting our involvement."

"How strong a vote, captain?" Serrano asked.

Raina Wolfe consulted her notes. "Upwards of eighty percent of eligible voters supported affiliation. Well over sixty-five percent supported it in the central region, which is Crist's stronghold. News reports say he was livid after the election and raised prices on several important minerals right afterwards."

"He *is* a piece of work," Driscoll said. "What is our precise mission?"

"Let's hold for a while on the details of that, Ava," McLeod said. "Suffice it to say that we are to neutralize Crist—and we get to define what 'neutralize' means." The room grew quiet again and McLeod exhaled. "People, our ultimate purpose is to support self-determination in the galaxy in the context of our forces, the Central Federation and the Star Alliance. Crist represents a direct threat to the planet and to the cause of self determination."

"And by applying for Federation membership," Wolfe added, "Amaeus has come under the protection of the Federation. We are here to help them make their dreams a reality. Were they locked in an internal battle where the mandate wasn't as clear or where there was a healthy opposition to membership, we wouldn't be here."

Driscoll nodded her understanding, and Wolfe turned back to McLeod. "So beyond the general objective of removing this obvious thorn in the side of the planetary government, we have to do that with minimal disruption."

"Which is why *Raven* is here rather than another vessel?" asked Crystal Gunderson.

"That's it, Gunny," Wolfe said. "And we are to do this with minimal disruption, using the planet's own conditions and situations to make that possible."

Driscoll exhaled. "That's a tall order."

"It is," McLeod said. "And as it is our first mission, we need to make it happen. Sr. Altern Scott and Chief Carnahan have analyzed our access to the Crist compound on Amaeus, while Commander Ross will review more about the planetary collaborative. Let's get to work."

* * *

Trevor Scott began the discussion by focusing on the key terrain features and other issues that made access to the Crist compound so difficult. Having reviewed those with Scott the night before, Wolfe found her attention waning. She scanned the group as Scott spoke: her personnel were focused, making notes and otherwise showing their clear attention. *Good*, she thought. *We have almost no margin for error in this mission.* Scott was discussing the avenues of approach when Wolfe looked up again.

"Captain, how much detail should I go into on the approaches, since we already know our preferred routes?"

He spoke to Wolfe but McLeod answered. "Give them the entire package, Trevor, including obstacles, cover and concealment—the works. We all need to know the issues we're dealing with, especially if we have to change during the mission itself."

"Understood." Scott turned back to the screen. "In terms of terrain, this is a desert, with very few oases. The compound is near trees that indicate substantial tullarium deposits." He pressed a button, and the visual changed to the Crist compound. "This place is well-defended, as you'd assume."

Carnahan rose and pointed out several small low buildings. "These are the more obvious buildings of the Crist compound. They cover an area of about seventy-five thousand square meters." Carnahan heard a whistle from someone at the table. "Exactly. And we estimate that's only about twenty-five to thirty percent of what's there. Plus, he locates many of his security forces in a ring of buildings distant from this compound, but connected through an underground network."

"This must have been a bitch to construct," Serrano said.

Carnahan shrugged. "When you're the richest person on a planet, you can make anything happen. As we said previously, it's well-defended with very little cover. There are also very few obstacles, but that's a double-edged sword. There are also three avenues of approach, each presenting its own challenges."

Wolfe stood and approached the screen. "The available intelligence from previous expeditionary forces shows entrances at several locations around the compound to the underground tunnels. The only other way into the area is by air, but that's tricky because they have anti-aircraft batteries. It's also too overt for our purposes. Using the trees and the cover of night is our best bet."

Driscoll shifted in her seat. "Night time operations are not my forte, ma'am."

"Doesn't have to be, Ava," Shaw said. "Someone has to be on *Raven* with me to keep the operation going. You're here because of what you can do, not what you *can't* do."

"A good point," McLeod agreed. "If you like, I can tell you each privately why we chose you for this mission: trust me, we need every one of you for your expertise, either on the ground or in this vessel."

"Speaking of the vessel, sir," Serrano began, "what about configurations for the mission?"

McLeod turned to Shaw. "We can go out of order for this one, Goody. Why don't we address that now?"

"Aye." Shaw approached the screen and shifted to a picture of a Toshino freight vessel. He turned back to the group. "You know this is a standard configuration, correct? Well, we propose shifting to this configuration as we reach six clicks from the planet, since it's unlikely they're using any kind of sensing equipment that extends beyond four."

"Will that configuration give us the maneuverability we need?" Ross asked.

"It should," said Lily Kono, the chief helmsman. "The engine placement is a little different compared to that of a standard Toshino freighter, so we have greater ability to shift on the fly." She grinned. "But Commander Shaw said we didn't have to be a freighter the whole time, right, commander?"

"Correct, Lily," Shaw said. "You'll get your chance for fun before we enter Amaean space." Shaw pressed another button and *Raven* shifted. "Captains McLeod and Wolfe have agreed that our transport to Amaeus can be in config three, the starfighter."

Kono smiled again. "Oh yeah. Pedal to the metal."

"It's not a race, Lily," McLeod countered. "But I'm looking forward to it, too." He nodded again to Shaw, who continued.

"The freighter—config one—is our least threatening configuration and the least likely to prompt any curiosity. And if you're ever had a visual on the exterior, it looks pretty beat up. I'd be surprised if people take a second glance at us."

"Perfect for a covert operation," said Carnahan.

"Correct," Shaw agreed. "Which is the point."

Wolfe stood by Shaw. "The third element of the operation involves the planetary collaborative, the governing body for Amaeus. Since that only involves a select team of people, we'll hold off on that part of the briefing until either tomorrow or while en route. In the meantime, Commander Shaw will work with the skeleton crew to ensure *Raven*'s preparation for launch." Before the group could leave, Wolfe added, "The remainder of you have several specific items in your folders that require your attention. Chief Carnahan and Sr. Altern Scott will coordinate supplies and equipment for the covert operations."

McLeod checked his chron and smiled. "Very well. We launch in forty-two hours: let's be ready."

Chapter Five

With officers and enlisted personnel scurrying around the bridge, it's a wonder anything got done on *Raven*. The bridge was smaller than on most Federation or Alliance vessels the personnel had served on, but McLeod was both confident and comfortable in his chair. He looked to his right as Wolfe conferred with Shaw, before the chief engineer and designer of *Raven* returned to his station by the engine room. Shaw exited the bridge and Wolfe turned to her friend.

"They're comfortable," Wolfe said. "But not too comfortable."

"We chose a good team for this mission. And we have a great deal to do." McLeod called up his personal vid screen. "When do you want to continue the briefing on Crist and the planetary collaborative?"

"Goody is already in place," Wolfe replied. "So we can start when you're ready." McLeod looked to Kono.

"Lily. What is our estimated time to the second junction?"

"Seventy-seven hours, more or less, sir."

"With the way you drive?"

Kono laughed. "Just obeying the speed limit, sir. And once we confirm astrogation at the junction, we can increase speed about twenty times."

"Fine," McLeod said, and he smiled. "Now wipe that silly grin off your face, commander."

"Aye."

McLeod opened his com link. "Let's review Thorian Crist's background and those of his lieutenants." He nodded to Driscoll, and the image of Thorian Crist came up on the screen. "Thorian Crist is the central character in this drama. He had a brief career as a military officer—by all accounts a formidable one—and left the military to strike out on his own in the energy industry. Don't assume that's all he does, however. He is equally impressive as a businessman and explorer. Crist is not someone to be ignored. He objects strongly to the Federation application and made that clear when the planet chose affiliation with the Federation with such a strong mandate. Crist has issued several demands to the planetary collaborative, primarily by asking for delays in the application, but he's also proposed several other actions to the planetary collaborative, including a second vote." McLeod changed the photo to a group of six, with Crist at the center. "These are Crist's primary lieutenants; you can see more of their backgrounds in your briefing materials."

"Pay special attention to the smaller man on the far right," said Wolfe. "That is Wen Bokari. He is young and idealistic, and our reports say that he is uncomfortable with the more extreme elements of Crist's inner circle. In fact, he is often the butt of jokes by the man next to him,

Elvin Cordell. He's a former military officer who enjoys war far too much."

"Again," McLeod said, "they are a complicated group. We believe we have the greatest chance with Bokari, but will monitor that along the way." He turned to Driscoll. "You'll be working overtime on this one, Ava: that's the only way we'll be able to track whatever happens while the team is planet-side." McLeod looked up. "Questions?" McLeod saw no reaction from the bridge nor through his com link, so he turned to Wolfe.

Wolfe changed the photo to members of the planetary collaborative. "You've already read about the planetary collaborative in your materials. What you need to know is that the leader of the group, Zahara Ali, is rather in love with herself, and runs the collaborative as her mutual admiration society. When she has conflicts with people over policy, she takes it personally. And one of the people she is in conflict now is the sister of Thorian Crist, Kyla Crist. They are related in name only, it seems: they've never gotten along, and have been on the opposite side of many governing issues for years. Kyla Crist is head of the southern government, while Thorian has called the central region home for most of his life. Our intelligence is that Ali is piling the pressure on Kyla Crist, as is the man in the center of the photo, Ian Anoki."

"But don't assume that Anoki is one of Zahara Ali's people," McLeod said. "He's as power hungry as she is. They are both people to watch."

"Chief Carnahan and I will contact Kyla Crist to enlist her in our efforts," Wolfe said. The bridge was silent after the statement. "Questions, anyone?"

"No, ma'am," said Francine West, the weapons officer. "It just seems risky when we don't know what Kyla Crist's reaction will be."

"Captain Wolfe and Chief Carnahan have worked missions like this before," McLeod said. "If anyone can pull it off, they can."

"We know that Kyla wants her brother's influence reduced or eliminated so Federation membership can go forward," Wolfe continued. "Whether she agrees with outside assistance is another issue altogether."

McLeod had spoken with his colleague more than once about the risks she was taking with Kyla Crist, but Wolfe wouldn't budge. "The bigger challenge," McLeod continued, "is to penetrate the Crist compound in the central desert. In fact, Commander Shaw will change both the temperature and humidity of *Raven* to simulate the conditions in the central desert. While they don't vary too much from the conditions of the central city, we need to acclimatize ourselves. We will reconvene the briefing for the desert team at 2000 hours in the ready room, meaning Virgil, Minty, Altern Scott, and me, with Frankie as the backup. See you in two."

* * *

McLeod sat back in the chair and shrugged. "I told you it was a tight compound."

"You didn't tell us it was a fortress," Ross said. "I'm not complaining, mind you, but it is a little challenging."

"Understood," McLeod said. "But it's what we've got to work with. Are we clear on the basic plan Trevor has outlined?"

"Just a need for clarification, sir," said West. "We don't know much about Crist's defensive capability. I don't want to head in there with weapons that won't get the job done."

"That's a challenge, Frankie. We know he has projectile rifles, pulse rifles and cannon, and other standard munitions." McLeod looked down and pressed several controls to call up his notes. "Our intel indicates Cordell leads a small army, so anti-aircraft missiles, cannon—the typical arms for a light army. We have what we need on *Raven*."

"A better question is about their detection and sensor ability in the desert," Scott said. "And on that we have far less intelligence. Either the planetary collaborative hasn't bothered to attack him, or they feel they can't."

"We believe they could take him on in a fair fight, but have been trying to avoid that to maintain planetary unity," McLeod said. "Apparently, Crist has enough allies—if you want to call them that—that taking aggressive action against him might cause pushback and action against the collaborative: they couldn't afford that in advance of the Federation application."

McLeod shifted to a previous screen on his vid and projected the photo on the large screen behind him. "As Chief Carnahan said earlier, we identified these three major access points close to the compound center, but we need more information and will be flying over the compound upon arriving planet-side. Without at least a cursory sweep of that compound, we'd be going in blind."

"Got that right," said West. "Can't say I like that, captain."

"No one does, Frankie." The door chime shifted their attention to the ready room door, and Wolfe and Carnahan entered and took their seats.

"I hope you have good news for us," McLeod said. "We're still trying to make sense of the Crist compound."

Wolfe shot a glance to Carnahan and smiled. "I can't say we're in any better shape, Tucker. The area around the planetary collaborative has fewer defenses, but it's in the middle of the city. Getting to Kyla Crist will not be easy."

"We think we have that licked, sir," Carnahan said. "We'll need to monitor more reports and study more while we're en route to select the best plan."

McLeod eyebrows rose. "How many plans do you have now? My guess is three."

"On the button, sir." Carnahan smiled. "It's clear you've worked with Captain Wolfe before."

McLeod passed the controller to Wolfe. "Can you fill us in, Raina?"

Wolfe took the control and called up several new files. First an aerial, then a ground-level photo of the planetary collaborative complex came on the vid screen. "I'll use the pointer from here. There are several entrances around the main building: it's an oasis off the center of the city so there's a land buffer around it."

"Smart," said McLeod.

"Which also makes access more complicated. We have a plan, though." Wolfe moved her pointer, circling around three points on the photo. "Here, here and here are public access points for people who want to speak to government officials." Wolfe looked up. "The planetary collaborative ministers maintain contact with their home regions when they're not in session, which is during the middle days of the week. When they're in the city center, they have extensive staff in place to answer critical concerns and requests from their home regions. These are the places where the access is more lax."

"Unfortunately, that only gets us into the complex," Carnahan said. "It's more complicated getting close to the ministers themselves."

"What have you found out about identification and security systems?" McLeod asked.

"Our intelligence is spotty, sir," Carnahan said. "But we're confident we can create convincing materials: it may just take us a day or two after arriving planet-side."

"If there's sufficient time," McLeod said. "Let's ask Ava about news reports: we can't afford having some explosion in the desert while we're figuring things out."

Wolfe smiled at her friend. "Always the patient one, aren't you, Tucker?"

"That lack of patience may serve us well this time, Raina. This planet is too valuable to leave this to chance."

Chapter Six

"Come in," Thorian said. Victor Ansara opened the door quickly and entered. "You're early."

Ansara shrugged. "We have important work to do today, sir. It wouldn't do to wait too long."

"What's the hurry?

Ansara sat in his normal seat, immediately to the right of Crist. "We need to keep the collaborative off their game, sir. We can't do that by delaying action and allowing public opinion to build in their favor."

Crist made a dismissive gesture. "And yet your previous reports to me indicated public opinion was steady. So long as it doesn't build in the collaborative's favor, why rush?"

"You misunderstand me. I'm not interested in being rash, but decisive." Ansara grinned. "That's what you've been known for all your life: why change?"

"Understood. Perhaps we should step up our plans." Hearing a knock at the door again, he said, "Come in," and welcomed in the rest of his inner circle. They entered and took their usual seats, then turned their attention to their leader. "I'd like reports on our progress. Victor believes we should speed up our activities to keep the planetary collaborative off their game. Do you agree?"

Elvin Cordell laughed. "I've said that for weeks, but people kept raising objections to it."

"Not to the idea, Elvin," said Maddox, a stark woman with sharp features and blazing red hair. "Just to avoid pushback from the collaborative for inciting violence. Once we cross the line to being seen as a terrorist organization, we lose public support."

Wen Bokari turned toward the window and lowered his eyes.

"You can't get out of speaking so easily, Wen," said Crist. "You've often preached care. Do you agree with it in this case?"

Bokari exhaled slowly and raised his eyes. He glanced at Cordell before speaking. "I support direct and decisive action that doesn't cross the line, sir. I believe we must guard against being seen as simply in this for the violence and power." Bokari gained confidence as he spoke, adding, "We've preached self-determination and autonomy for Amaeus and the economic power that comes from independence. If people only see violence from us, we've lost." Bokari sat back in his chair, not realizing he had been sitting so straight. Crist noticed the smile forming on Cordell's face but ignored it.

Crist leaned forward onto the conference table. "Our original plans focused on remaining quiet for two more days before our operation against Anson Corp and their tullarium fields. Is that on schedule and is there any reason to change our plans?"

"It's on schedule and our people are ready," Cordell said. "But we haven't settled on the distraction for the capital city." He looked around the table at his colleagues. "How is that going?"

"Victor?" Crist asked.

"We've been feeding reports to the news outlets on the personal agendas of the planetary collaborative, sir. It's kept them off balance and caused elevated tension among the ministers. It's been fun to watch."

"You are a nasty man, aren't you?" Maddox asked.

"Problem, Cole?" asked Crist.

"No, sir. I continue to believe caution is the best course of action for us."

"Noted." Crist sat more erect. "Now let's get to the meat of this discussion: what are we to do with the collaborative?"

"The key is creating and managing instability," Cordell offered. "Our strike teams can take out any of the ministers at will, and we can do that either in their home regions or in the central city."

"Taking action in the city is too risky," Crist said. "They go home often enough: take out one of them there."

"Do we have to take one of them out? Really?" asked Bokari. "Isn't some other direct action better?"

"Like what?" Cordell said. "This is our own version of war, Wen."

Bokari, who usually backed down from Cordell, sat up straighter. "It's war for the hearts and minds of the people, General. I thought we were interested in building support for governing, not for starting a civil war."

"The pup's grown up!" laughed Cordell. "All right, Wen, how would you do it?"

"There's the new housing project in the west," said Walker Menzel, usually the quietest of the group. "The project is siphoning up too much tax revenue; we've agreed to that. Taking out that project would be a strong blow against the collaborative."

"If we take that action," Crist said, "how do we ensure that it reflects poorly on the collaborative and not on us?"

"We've never taken action against any target in the west," Ansara said. "And that was the region with the second lowest approval for the Federation application. It's a perfect target."

"Perhaps." Crist turned to Cordell. "How well equipped are we for the attack, Elvin?"

"Well enough," Cordell said with a wave of his hand. "It's a simple operation: we have several crude weapons and bombs that will direct the blame to others, such as Pulliam, Inc. We can issue statements after the attack that focus on the stability in the central region as opposed to the chaos in the west. It should work perfectly."

"He's right, sir," Ansara said. "That will continue to chip away at the collaborative's support overall. When the people see our superior stability and economic power, public opinion will shift to us."

Crist sat back and nodded, letting his mind wander. He knew the government and economic system that would benefit the greatest number of people on his home world, and he bristled as he remembered the many times Zahara Ali had rebuffed his offers of assistance. *I hope you're ready for this.* "Very well. Elvin, prepare for the attack. Victor and Wen, keep feeding the proper information to news sources so this operation gives us the greatest impact.

"Victor, Elvin, stick around so we can discuss the operation and how we want to handle it. The rest of you have your assignments." Almost silently, Bokari, Maddox, and Menzel left the room.

The door had just closed when Ansara spoke. "This needs to be a precise operation. We can't afford for anything to suggest that we're the ones destroying homes for the poor."

"I agree," Crist said. "We must show the damage that occurs when the government engages in these social experiments and show how they're unnecessary in the central region where we have economic freedom and lower taxes." He turned in his seat. "And that's the challenge: I don't know how we spin this so that another group will be blamed. We also can't guarantee that Pulliam will be blamed: it's not that simple."

"I have that, sir," said Ansara, his eyes twinkling. He took out his pad and found what he was looking for. "Two other builders competed for the housing project contract. They both proposed larger and more expensive designs than the one approved by the western government. We can pin this on them, so it would deflect the blame to one or both of them, two groups that proposed a more expensive design."

"And more expensive equals higher taxes," Cordell said. "And we have just the opposite: no need and lower taxes. This is the way to win."

Crist smiled. "I agree, and thank you for reminding me about those two competing organizations on the housing project, Victor. It is a blatant misuse of public resources that Hill should have stopped. As an elected prime minister, she should have known better, and stopped such a blatant misuse of public resources. Just make sure it doesn't reflect on us, Elvin."

Cordell sat back in mock horror. "I'm a professional, sir," he said. "I know exactly how to do this."

"Heaven help us if you were just an amateur."

Chapter Seven

A comfortable distance away, the starship *Lance* and its crew awaited its next action. Tyrus Landau, its commander, was a study in contrasts. Known by many as a ruthless leader and commander, he looked like a favorite uncle, with his glasses, round appearance, and kind eyes. His reputation as an effective commander with little heart preceded him.

"Are you as bored as I am, sir?" asked Jolon Reed, his executive officer.

"I've learned when to become excited and when to allow myself to be serene, Jolon. This is a time for steadiness. We have a day before we have to act." He turned to his friend. "Let's just savor the moment, shall we?"

Reed laughed. "Very well." He leaned back in his seat and stretched. "I don't suppose taking a nap would be a good idea?" His voice trailed off when he heard no response from Landau.

"Incoming communication for you sir," said Cleve Rubinco, *Lance's* communications officer. "It's labeled confidential, sir."

Landau stood. "My ready room, Cleve."

"Aye."

Turning to Reed, Landau said, "You have command, Jolon." Without waiting for a response, Landau walked to his quarters and once inside, he called up his communication. He was surprised to see it was in form of a document rather than a recording. He glanced at the document first, then studied it more carefully. Nodding several times while he read it, Landau made a few notes on his personal pad, then closed the document and rose. He reentered the bridge to the surprise of his crew.

"That was quick, sir," Reed said. "Sure you don't want me to stay in your chair a while longer?"

"No need, Jolon. I have additional information we can use." Reed shifted to his regular seat and waited.

As Landau was getting settled, Celia Kane, *Lance's* tactical officer, interrupted him. "I have to ask, sir, Amaeus is a small planet, comparatively speaking. Is their staying out of the Federation that important?"

Landau smiled. "I imagine we haven't made that clear enough to you, Celia. Besides the normal concerns about both Central Federation and Star Alliance expansion, there are higher deposits of tullarium and klocutin on Amaeus than on almost any other planet in this sector, or in fact in the whole quadrant. We're not interested in Amaeus's autonomy; what we care about is our ability to conduct normal trade with them and having easier access to their mineral deposits."

Reed sniffed. "Still, they are more remote than I'd like."

"Understood," Landau said. "And I agree. However, both Enov and Ceriria may seek Federation or Alliance affiliation in the next few years.

Were that to happen, our access to Amaeus and other planets in this sector would decrease significantly. If we can slow the expansion on Amaeus, our efforts to stem affiliation on those planets will be more successful."

He turned again to Kane. "Does that answer your question, Celia? The real importance of Amaeus is its role as a gateway to even greater penetration of the Federation and the Alliance in this sector. If they affiliate, we'd find it more difficult to advocate free trade and movement."

Kane sensed that her audience was over. "Yes, sir. Thank you, sir."

It was only then that Reed noticed a flash on Landau's personal pad. He shifted his chin, and Landau took notice of it. Landau glanced at it, scrolled down, then looked up again. After a minute, he turned again to Reed.

"Our intelligence has given us some valuable information, Jolon. And it may give you the chance to stop being bored."

Reed's eyes flew open as he sat up. "Something big or small?"

"Small but significant, Jolon. We have the chance to make directed strikes against two targets on the planet. You recall we were trying to identify targets so we could continue causing instability on the planet?" Landau held up his pad. "This is the information we need."

* * *

"Position relative to junction, Lily," said McLeod, growing impatient.

Kono consulted her panel. "We're there, sir. Shift to core positions?"

McLeod nodded not to Kono, but to Driscoll, who pressed a button.

"All-com open, sir."

"Ladies and gentlemen," McLeod began. "Return to core positions and report." He shifted his attention again to Driscoll, adding, "Let me know, Ava."

"Aye."

As he turned his attention back to his control, McLeod sensed Wolfe next to him.

"You're having far too much fun here, Tucker."

"You should talk."

Wolfe laughed. "You didn't say I couldn't have fun, too." She lifted her chin toward Kono. "What's your assessment?"

"She's about the best I've ever worked with, and that's saying something." McLeod leaned forward. "That's not even taking into account her delightfully irreverent attitude."

"I knew you'd like that about her. When I trained and worked with her wing years ago, it was uncanny: she anticipated things no one else did. She's probably the pilot I trust most in the service."

"I'm not surprised."

"All personnel in core positions, captains," Driscoll said.

Wolfe rose and walked toward Driscoll. "This is Captain Wolfe. Commence shift to Configuration 1, on my mark. Engage." The hull made a soft humming sound, and the lights dimmed for a fraction of a second as *Raven's* hull made the shift from the stealth starfighter to a replica of a freight vessel.

"Port screen, Ava," said McLeod. He sat back to watch the collapse of the port wing and weapons ports revealing the bumpy, weathered hull of a freight vessel. He heard chuckling and looked back to Wolfe.

"I don't tire of it either, Tucker." Wolfe turned to West. "Frankie, how would you rate our preparedness in this configuration?"

"You mean weapons, attack ability, that sort of thing?"

"Yes."

"We lose little, ma'am. Our primary cannon can still be deployed, and our sensor capability is unchanged."

"Shift complete, captains," Driscoll said. "Took about forty-five seconds."

Wolfe whistled as she shook her head. "Goody is a genius."

"That he is," McLeod said. "Standard beacon, Ava. Let's present ourselves as a safe, unobtrusive freighter, shall we?"

"Aye."

"Check on personnel and be sure to feed any relevant weather and communications info to Su-Commander Kono." He turned to Kono. "Lily, you have the flexibility to make the immediate changes as you need, but let us know if you do."

"Aye, sir. So I suppose I can't do any loops when I get to the atmosphere?"

"No, Lily. Sometimes even I have to be serious. Raina, I'm going to confer with Goody."

"Got it."

McLeod left the bridge as Wolfe returned to Kono's station. "How is she moving, Lily?"

Kono couldn't suppress her smile. "Smooth as anything, ma'am." She turned to Wolfe, looking serious. "How long did you say I could serve on *Raven*?"

"As long as you want, Lily, but remember we're still building the crew for *Axon*, and I had you in mind for her."

"True. And that would give me only you in command, right?"

Wolfe frowned. "I thought you liked Captain McLeod."

"He's great, ma'am. It's just that you and I go way back."

Wolfe smiled. "I'll take that under advisement."

* * *

"Are you sure your sources on the planet are reliable?" Jolon Reed asked.

"I'd say so," Landau said. He turned Reed's attention to the map on the screen. "There are three organizations, or alliances, on Amaeus that oppose Federation membership. We are to create unrest so the blame falls on those three entities."

"I thought our primary target was Thorian Crist's organization."

"It is, because it's by far the best organized and most powerful. We can't afford to ignore the other organizations, but when Crist's organization folds, none of the others have the imagination or the resources to put up much of a fight. If we discredit Crist, we're home free."

"What's the progress with the governing group, the—"

"Planetary Collaborative? They aren't budging, though I believe there are more cracks in the eastern and western regions now. Our operatives on the ground are working very hard, and they assure me that our actions can strengthen local opposition to the Federation." Landau called up a topographical map of Amaeus. "So we can make two strikes: one in each of those regions."

"Just point me in the right direction."

* * *

McLeod's appearance in the engine control room surprised Shaw, who rose to his feet.

"No need for that, commander," McLeod said. "This is a social call."

Shaw remained standing and tipped his head. "Social call?"

"Yes. We should get to know each other better."

"Understood."

"But first, I want to tell you how impressed I am—this goes for the whole crew by the way—with your design of *Raven*. This is an incredible vessel and people can't stop talking about it."

"Thank you, sir."

McLeod shifted to sit on the edge of the table. "So I was wondering: who from the Star Alliance did you expect to be in command of this vessel?"

"I don't know what you mean, sir. That wasn't my decision to make."

"Perhaps not. But you must have had *some* notion." McLeod gestured with his hand. "Please sit, Goody. You're making me nervous."

Shaw laughed. "Nervous? I should have thought that was impossible."

"Then you've never seen Raina and me in an argument: that woman can scare the living daylights out of me."

Shaw regarded McLeod for a moment, then sat. "I suppose I had some ideas . . ." Shaw said, as his voice trailed off.

"And?"

"Well, I thought *Raven* would be solely a Federation vessel, which suggested several strong commanding officer candidates."

"Including Captain Wolfe?"

"I believe that now, though at the time I was thinking about officers who already held captain's rank: this was before her promotion."

"Not a big fan of the Alliance, or just me?" McLeod leaned forward again. "I don't have many hurt feelings for you to worry about, Goody."

"I don't know many Alliance officers, sir."

"I understand. But whether my old reputation bothers you—emphasis on the old—that's not who I am anymore." McLeod stood again. "And if there's anything you want to object to or talk about, please speak freely with me, or if you prefer to, with Captain Wolfe. She can and will tell me anything. You are perhaps the finest engineer in the active services, and you've designed an outstanding vessel. This mission is important, and I plan to be a partner with you as well as your commanding officer, but I *will* be in command." McLeod held out his hand, which Shaw took.

"Understood, sir."

"Good." McLeod smiled. "Now let me get back to bridge before Lily Kono does something crazy and wrecks your baby before we complete our first mission."

"Aye, sir."

Chapter Eight

"I do not think we should be holding this meeting," Leyla Hill offered. "We've never done this before, and I, for one, don't like it." The collaborative members—minus Kyla Crist—were seated in Zahara Ali's private office. The chair of the collaborative kept her office cold, adding to the sense of unease among the assembled people.

"Necessity sometimes requires us to do things we find distasteful, Leyla," said Ali. "Our ultimate responsibility is to the people of Amaeus and not to convention." She turned to Anoki. "This is your meeting, Ian."

Anoki leaned forward onto the conference table and spoke slowly. "We are at a point of crisis within the collaborative, and for the sake of the planet, we must make some very crucial decisions today if we are to be in a good place tomorrow."

"That doesn't tell us why Kyla was excluded from this meeting," Hill said. "Or did you invite her, and she refused to come?"

"Don't be naive, Leyla," said Takoda Marten. "We know why Ian didn't invite Kyla, so let's get to the point, shall we?"

Marten looked again at Anoki, who sighed. "There have been rumors, and I—"

"Rumors from where?" Hill asked. "*You?*"

"Leyla!" screeched Ali. "You know the rules of—"

"The rules don't apply here," Hill snapped. "Or did you forget that the rules also require proper notice to *all five* members of the collaborative before holding official meetings?"

Ali's lips pressed into a thin line as she acknowledged Hill's logic. *Why had she listened to Anoki?*

"I'm waiting," Hill said.

Another ten seconds passed before Ali turned to Anoki. "Perhaps we've gone about this in the wrong way." Ali returned her gaze to the entire table, then continued. "What Ian meant to say is that we must guard against not only wrong doing but the appearance of wrong doing or bias by collaborative members, as I've said. The relationship between Kyla and her brother suggests the possibility of bias, so we must to be on guard that Kyla does not hurt our credibility."

Both Hill and Marten shook their heads, Marten resting his chin in his hand.

"Zahara," Hill began, "we have never had reason to doubt Kyla's loyalty to this body or to her constituents in the southern government, though that is not our primary concern. She has always supported our decisions and helped develop strong support around the planet for the Federation application and for the worker benefits agreement. Are we to ignore this good work because of," she turned to face Anoki head on, "unsubstantiated rumors?"

"Leyla," Ali began, in a much more soothing tone than earlier. "Whether there are rumors or not, we must be conscious of how the people are feeling, and what they're afraid of. They are clearly afraid of Thorian Crist, and I'm not the only one who has heard statements connecting Thorian to his sister. How much of a leap does it take before someone accuses Kyla of profiting from Thorian's work in the central region?"

"You mean *your* region?" asked Marten, taking up the fight. "That's where he's most active. Has anyone tried to connect you with him? You are as close to Thorian Crist as Kyla is."

Ali rose out of her chair gripping the edge of the table. She stood for a moment, then relaxed her hands and resumed her seat. Her voice was quiet, but burned with anger. "No one would ever make that connection, Takoda, because there isn't one. Blood is for life."

Anoki waved his hands, trying to wave away the tension. "We are not here to debate the challenges of the central region, but," he said, glancing at Ali, "to discuss whether we should ask Kyla to step down as head of the southern government until the tension and unrest in the central region has passed."

"But that isn't even her region!" Hill cried. "We're trying to hold her responsible for something that is out of her control! And you consider that fair?"

Ali sighed. "What is fair and what is proper for the time being are two different things, Leyla, we—"

"No, Zahara," Marten said. "I will not support this action or the suggestion. It is not our job as ministers on the collaborative to ask one of our own to step down. What of the people in the southern region? They are her constituents: have *they* asked for her resignation?"

Hill, angry at the suggestion regarding Crist, was shaking her head at her seat. She raised her eyes to speak, but Anoki cut her off. "Our work on the collaborative is to support the will of the people. And that—"

"And the will of the southern region is for Kyla Crist to be their prime minister," said Hill. "Or are you trying to foment rebellion in a region not your own, too, Ian?"

Anoki rose and pointed his hand at Hill. "I am not the one whose brother is trying to hold the government hostage for his own gain, and I—"

"But you plan to benefit from it, don't you, Ian?" Hill smiled. "Is that what this is really all about?"

"Madame chair," Marten began, "We're not getting anywhere in this discussion without all the players at this table." Ali looked at the gathering and started to speak, but realized Marten's point. She sat back in her chair, and Marten continued. "And we will not get anywhere until we can have an open discussion about our concerns regarding the central region and Thorian Crist's work—*together.*"

Hill laid her hand on Marten's arm as he sat back, willing him to stay seated. "I agree that we should hold a frank discussion about this once we are all assembled." Hill spoke deliberately. "We don't have the authority to remove a regional prime minister from her post: that is for her own government to do." She turned to face Ali. "And it's not our job to suggest that to her government, either."

Ali put up her hand to ward off further objections. "Very well. If we will not ask Kyla to step down or at least consider doing so, how do we handle the public relations nightmare if she remains?"

"How would we handle the nightmare if we stick our noses into the southern government's activities?" Hill asked.

"Touché," Marten said. "You know, we talk a lot in this body about the will of the people. It's the will of the people to affiliate with the Central Federation, and it's the will of the people to strengthen public education throughout the planet, and so on." Marten looked up and scanned the faces of his colleagues. "It is clearly the will of the people in the southern region that Kyla serve as their prime minister, and as I recall the vote electing her prime minister wasn't even close. I've heard nothing—not a peep—about her regional government being concerned about her relationship with her brother. They're concerned about her brother—who wouldn't be—but not about Kyla."

Anoki smiled and gave a chuckle. "All right, Takoda. You don't have to say anything else—I get it." Anoki pressed his shoulders down to smooth out the tone of his voice. "So how much do we tell the planet about Thorian Crist's activities in the central desert, and how his work threatens our overall peace and prosperity?"

"That's a discussion that should be held with all five of us in attendance, wouldn't you agree?"

Anoki shrugged, then turned to Ali. "Your move, Zahara."

Ali looked at the conference table, focusing on the gavel. "Perhaps that would be best." She laughed to herself. "Since the only person who could have broken our stalemate would have been Kyla. How ironic is that?"

* * *

"Nearing central desert, captains," said Kono. "And it's as bleak as the reports said." Kono guided *Raven* to an acute flyover angle to bring her oblique to the Crist compound.

"Time to Crist compound?" McLeod asked.

"Three minutes, sir," said Kono.

"Good." McLeod turned to Serrano. "Ready for the sweep, Max?"

"Aye, sir. Already started."

"Of course you have." McLeod smiled. "How long should we hover here, Raina? I want an effective sweep, but not enough to raise the interest of Crist or his people."

"Hard to say. Given our configuration, we can probably loop through at least two times at different angles." She looked at Serrano. "Can you direct the sweeps so that Lily can fly in any pattern she wants, Max?"

"Aye, ma'am. We could do it in two straight shots with a 360 degree sweep each time." He turned to Wolfe. "Do you have a preference?"

"Your choice, Lily," Wolfe said.

"Aye." *Raven* lowered to six hundred meters from the surface and slowed to one hundred forty kilometers per hour. Kono kept the flight smooth as she sensed an explosion of lights on the operations panel to her left.

"Whoa," Serrano said.

"Commander, we try not to 'whoa' even on a freighter like this one," Kono said.

"That's not it," Wolfe said, already scanning the lights on the operations panel. "Are you getting everything, Max?"

"Yes, ma'am, but I can't analyze it now: there's just too much."

McLeod left his seat and approached operations. "I don't like the sound of that."

"You will eventually, sir," Serrano said. "But we may need another twelve hours minimum to rethink our access points and plan. There's a lot more here than any previous sweep has shown."

McLeod began flicking his middle and ring fingers across his thumbs, creating a muffled flicking sound. Wolfe noticed it and smiled. "Any particular reason we've been in the dark, Max?"

"I can't say, ma'am. My best guess is that no one has been this close to the compound before."

"We may also have far better and more sophisticated instruments than anyone else," Wolfe commented.

"That makes sense," McLeod said. "Score another one for Goody." McLeod returned to his seat. "Continue sweep, Lily, then let's head for the central city."

"Aye."

"And Max, any sense now if our work will be easier or more difficult because of what you've seen?"

"Both: we'll have more things to watch out for or to avoid."

"That was your good news?"

"No, sir. But it also means we'll have fewer surprises once we choose a course."

"Thank heavens for small favors," Wolfe said.

Chapter Nine

"Come in," McLeod responded to the door chime. His door opened and Wolfe strode in.

"They're assembling now, Tucker. Are you ready?"

"I am. Let's head down."

They left McLeod's quarters and turned the corner, when Wolfe pointed to his chest. "What's that?"

"What?"

"On your chest. That animal."

McLeod was dumbstruck "Are you *serious?*"

"Yes. What is it?"

"It's a raven."

Wolfe stopped walking and frowned. "A raven?"

"Yes, a raven—as in this vessel."

"A raven is a *flyer*?"

"Bird."

"Right." Wolfe shook her head. "A bird." She paused. "But that's what it is?"

"Yes. It's a Terran bird."

Wolfe shook her head again. "So that's why you always used the name raven; it actually meant something to you."

"Exactly." McLeod smiled. "And since we're not in uniform for this mission, I had this made up. A good idea, no?"

Wolfe kept walking and opened the door to the ready room. Their officers and key enlisted personnel were seated at the oval table. Around the table were Amos DuBois, *Raven* astrogator and instructor at the academy, and Virgil Kelly, tactical officer. Joining him were primary officers for covert operations, weapons, and communications, Araminta Ross, Ava Driscoll, Francine West, and Gordon Shaw. Lily Kono, Mark Carnahan, Max Serrano, and Trevor Scott completed the group. Wolfe and McLeod walked to the front of the room and sat, noting the aerial photos of the Crist compound on the screen.

"You all look ready for this," Wolfe said. "That's good. We have a lot of work to do." She turned to Scott. "What's your evaluation on the access to the Crist compound, Trevor?"

Scott stood and walked to the front. A tall man, Scott often stooped to avoid towering over his colleagues. He scanned the photos before pointing to the central structure. "This may surprise you, but this is not the command structure. It's actually an atrium for his people to gather in as they wish. The atrium is decorative only."

"How can you be sure?" asked Kelly.

"Because the radiation and signals all emanate from this portion to the west: this is the control center and command module. Now follow as I trace along this outer ridge." Scott ran his fingers along the sand in the photo to a spot outside of the spider-like arms. "The limit of the tunnels is about half a kilometer from any of the arms, and there are tunnels connecting the arms themselves, like concentric circles. It's an elegant design."

"Can you map this for us?" McLeod asked.

"We're on it, sir. We're creating a complete sense of where everything is in this spot—as best we can figure it, that is."

"What we're trying to determine," Carnahan began, "are the security features, armaments, and personnel, captain. To say it's difficult is an understatement."

"What about intelligence from other sources?" Wolfe asked.

"Oh, we have lots of that," Scott replied. "We have little from within the outer rings, however. I won't say we're going in blind, but I'm not comfortable yet."

"Give me a minute." McLeod rose from the table and approached the screen. Wolfe smiled as she noticed McLeod's thought processes taking over. She received glances from Serrano and Shaw, but waved them off with a brief shake of her head. Finally, McLeod raised his head.

"What other ways might we gain entrance with minimal exposure? And while we're at it, what do we know about Crist's military forces in the compound?"

"Got it," Ross said. "Total estimated personnel in Crist's organization are eight thousand, but these are spread throughout the central desert, most defending his energy and mineral holdings. The military personnel are split among infantry, armory, and artillery. He has very little in terms of aircraft except about twenty rotaries."

"How about in the central complex, Minty?" Wolfe asked.

"We can only speculate, but we estimate he has four hundred troops in the central complex, again divided among infantry, armory, and artillery. The remainder of his employees are miners, research scientists, and support personnel."

"Not very much," Shaw said.

McLeod laughed. "Perhaps not, but more than an extraction team of five or six people."

"It depends on how we support that operation from the air, captain," Shaw said. "*Raven* has capabilities they won't be expecting."

"Agreed. But we need those capabilities hidden unless absolutely necessary. Going from covert to overt doesn't work for this vessel or its mission unless we have lives to save."

"True," Shaw said. "But we can figure out ways to deploy *Raven* without losing our anonymity."

"Good. Work on that with Captain Wolfe." McLeod returned his attention to Scott. "Continue planning this operation, Trevor, and include any specific recommendations for team members, keeping in mind we need to keep some covert operations people on *Raven* along with helm and engineering and so on: they may be needed to make last-minute decisions or changes in the plans."

"Yes, sir."

"Chief, what about the operation with Kyla Crist? That's more delicate, since it's in the central city."

"Yes, sir," Carnahan said. "Captain Wolfe and I have outlined the primary objective and procedures, but wanted to review them here."

McLeod returned to his seat and sat back. "I'm all ears."

* * *

An hour later, McLeod was drinking coffee in the ready room when Wolfe joined him.

"You seem lost in thought, Tucker. I'm not used to that with you."

"Perhaps. Tell me that this is the best plan and I'll stop complaining."

Wolfe rolled her eyes then sat at the table. "Perhaps not the best plan, but Carnahan and I believe it's best in the short term. All reports are that Kyla Crist is desperate to stop her brother, but she holds no sway with him."

"You're sure of her loyalty to the collaborative and support for the Federation?"

"Aren't you?"

"Yes, but I was asking for your assessment."

"I'm sure. And everything we've seen from news reports and intelligence sources says that's true. We needn't worry about that."

"But we do have to worry about how she receives you once you're in the central city, with minimal weapons."

Wolfe slapped McLeod on his arm. "Now you're being silly. You know what might happen if they found weapons on us, Tucker. The entire operation would be at risk, to say nothing of our lives."

"Don't remind me. Are Ava and Goody sure their communications methods will work in that shielded environment?"

"Only one way to tell. But I trust them both and—" Wolfe noticed McLeod's slight reaction.

"Goody shouldn't worry you, Tucker: he's loyal to the mission and to our overall objectives, and certainly to me." She laughed. "He'll get used to you in time."

"I'll hold you to that. But it isn't a matter of trust: we're asking them to do things they haven't done before and putting their lives at risk in the process."

"Been there, done that. And you're one to talk: the operation at the compound is even more dangerous."

"But having weapons makes all the difference in the world, Raina." McLeod shook his head. "No matter: we're here to do a job, so let's stop worrying." He looked up again. "Are they ready for us?"

"Have you finished your coffee? We're not starting again until you've had your coffee."

McLeod took his last sip. "Aye, ma'am."

* * *

McLeod and Wolfe reentered the ready room, noting two small groups in active discussion that fell silent as they entered. McLeod spoke once he and Wolfe were seated. "What can you tell us, people?"

Carnahan passed over an ID card to Wolfe. "What do you think of this, ma'am?" The card had a picture of Wolfe with a fake name and a press affiliation inscribed on it. Wolfe ran her hand around the edges and felt the thin chip within.

"It certainly appears valid. How did you create it?"

Carnahan took the items back. "We accessed several intelligence sources within the news media. One of them has a very fluid staff list with people always coming and going, so the government agencies can't keep track of them. They just figure anyone with an ID must be legitimate."

"This agency?"

Carnahan nodded. "Yes, ma'am. And we have examples of their cards from the recent past. These should work."

Wolfe frowned and inhaled. "They may have changed their IDs or the chips, chief."

"Well, um," Carnahan began, "well, we, that is Chief Driscoll and I, thought if there were questions about the currency of the IDs, that your more seasoned appearance would make it okay." McLeod laughed until he saw Wolfe's reaction.

"So what you're saying," said Wolfe, "is that I look old enough that I might have an older ID, is that right?"

"That's what I heard, Raina," McLeod said. "And it's probably as good an excuse as any, don't you think?"

"Never mind," Wolfe said. "Chief, how about the location for our drop and our access to the complex?"

"Yes, ma'am," said Carnahan. "Chief Driscoll and I worked that out. We also recommend conducting more on the ground reconnaissance prior to approaching the collaborative."

"Of course," Wolfe said. "That's standard procedure. When is the collaborative next in session?"

"They went into session again today, ma'am," Driscoll said. "They remain in session today, tomorrow, and the following day before recessing."

"Good," McLeod said. "That may give you a day to secure the proper access to the collaborative and to Kyla Crist."

Wolfe smiled "Agreed. Though given what's at stake, I hope that won't be too long."

Chapter Ten

"—mirror those of Crist and his organization in previous actions. This is believed to be the first such attack by Crist on a non-business entity or in response to a direct attack on his holdings in the central desert."

All eyes in the ready room turned to McLeod as he lowered the volume on the recording made fifteen minutes earlier. "Captain Wolfe worried earlier that we wouldn't have enough time to prepare for this operation: she may have been right." McLeod returned his attention to the screen, advancing to a different news service report.

"The Planetary Collaborative has issued a statement regarding the attacks in the western region, calling for heightened vigilance by security authorities in the region and pledging the support of all ministers in this effort. Head of the central government and chair of the planetary collaborative, Zahara Ali, also indicated that the collaborative would be discussing its membership to determine if there are any interim actions that should be taken to ensure the full integrity of the collaborative in this troubling time." The broadcaster faced the camera. "Experts see this as a veiled attempt to censure the head of the southern government, Kyla Crist, estranged sister of Thorian Crist." McLeod stopped the report, and turned to Ava Driscoll. "Have you any more on this, Ava?"

"Yes, sir. We've heard that Kyla Crist may be asked to step down completely as a member of the collaborative, or at least absent herself from their current work."

"That wouldn't work for our plans," Wolfe said.

"Perhaps not, ma'am," Carnahan agreed. "But we can still approach her in her private residence, where there is less of a security risk than in the collaborative."

"Unfortunately, chief, it also means she may wield less influence with her colleagues on the collaborative."

"But if our aim in seeking Kyla was to wield influence with her brother, that's not compromised at all," McLeod offered.

Wolfe pressed her hands to her temples. "I don't know. The problem is any instability regarding Crist—Kyla Crist—means she has less influence or position overall." She turned to Carnahan. "What do you think, chief?"

"Right on the money, ma'am. But I still think we're right in going directly to her first."

"Agreed." McLeod rose. "Though we'll need additional intelligence before proceeding. Let's land in our current configuration close to the collaborative and begin our latest reconnaissance."

* * *

"All decks prepare for landing," Driscoll said. "Report status."

McLeod was pacing on the bridge, making Driscoll jittery. McLeod checked the time and noted they had spent two hours organizing themselves for the landing team's departure toward Planetary Collaborate Headquarters, known on the planet as PCH. Carnahan and Scott appeared on the bridge in common sector garb and approached Wolfe.

"Ready, ma'am," Scott said. "Chief Carnahan has identification documents for us as Belaran shipping workers. We'll fit in."

"Very well. And a good choice, since you won't be expected to know the local languages too well, other than sector basic." Wolfe left her seat in the center of the bridge, avoiding McLeod, who was still pacing and walked toward the operations station, motioning for Carnahan and Scott to follow her. "Pay close attention to the mood of the people there and spend time around the common citizens. We want a sense of the overall mood of the planet and their opinion of Kyla Crist."

"That might be difficult to assess," Carnahan said. "We're in the capital city with lots of government employees: they're bound to be biased."

"A good point," McLeod agreed as he stood behind Wolfe. "But make the effort to sit or listen in on several conversations. There is a cold beverage, called—let me see—"

"Jangulo," Kono said. She turned to McLeod. "I had it once; it's pretty good."

"There you go," McLeod said. "There are little shops all over the place, so if you can stand drinking two or three of them in the next couple of hours, that may be your best shot. Same goes for little cafes by the river."

"All decks prepared for landing; all personnel ready," said Driscoll.

"Complete final approach and land, Lily," said Wolfe.

"Aye."

* * *

The news reporter on the screen spoke with little inflection, but her words were a body blow to Thorian Crist.

"There is little doubt that this is the work of Thorian Crist or his people," the broadcaster said. "Government sources say that the weapons and methods used in this attack mirror those of Crist and his organization in previous actions. This is believed to be the first such attack by Crist on a non-business entity or in response to a direct attack on his holdings in the central desert."

The voice continued, but Crist had slammed the screen off. "How dare they! When I attack, I want credit, but when I do not, nothing—nothing should come back to me!"

"Sir, I am sure—" began Ansara.

"They will pay! They will pay for this insolence!"

"Sir, without knowing who they are, how can we hold anyone responsible?"

Crist turned to him snarling. "And I don't want excuses or defenses: I want action!" The loud voices had attracted Bokari, Maddox, and Menzel.

"Find out who, how, and why," Crist continued. "I want the person responsible for this taken down and destroyed: not hurt, not just killed, but completely, utterly destroyed, do you hear?"

"We just heard, sir," said Bokari. "How—"

"You already know! Find out who attacked the housing project in our name and destroy them: that's all you have to do!"

"I don't understand," began Menzel, "Isn't that the same project we were going to attack and lay the blame—"

"You are wasting time! We know that! Find and destroy: is that so hard to understand?"

"No, sir," Menzel said. He stole glances at his colleagues, then shifted his head toward the door. "We'll go now."

Crist sat heavily into his seat as Menzel, Bokari, and Maddox left the room. He was silent for a minute, then turned to Ansara. "Find out, Victor. And find out how they chose the same facility we were targeting. I do not believe in coincidence."

"Neither do I, sir." Ansara started toward the door, but stopped and looked over his shoulder. "Should I find and send in Cordell?"

"Where is Cordell?"

"With his people, I imagine; planning the attack on the housing project."

"Then he has time for another operation, doesn't he?"

"Yes, sir."

"Have him come to me."

"Yes, sir," Ansara said, as he closed the door behind him.

* * *

"You aren't yourself, Tucker," Wolfe said in McLeod's private quarters. She looked at the bare walls, noting that her own quarters held small decorations, and wondered if McLeod's starkness indicated something troubling about him. "And we haven't even started the operation yet."

"True. There are just too many factors in this operation I can't figure out, like this whole attack in the western region: it makes no sense to me."

"Really? Is an attack by a known economic terrorist such a surprise?"

"I get that. My problem is that the news reports said he's only attacked opponents in the central desert, generally those involved in the minerals and mining industries."

"What did you tell me once about your ancestors? Something about the west?"

McLeod smiled. "The wild west. A short period of Terran history where everyone was fighting and firing at everyone else, and not just over mineral rights. But I don't see how that applies here. We know Crist is trying to build support for his view that Federation membership is a bad idea for Amaeus. He can't do that if he's attacking projects everyone on the planet wants."

"How do we know everyone wanted this housing project?"

"I don't; that may be a poor example. But my problem is, it's hard to view this attack as anything positive. How is Crist going to build support if he attacks a public project in another region of the planet? That would build support *against* him."

Wolfe began pacing the room and found she could only take four steps in one direction before hitting the wall. "I'm not used to quarters like these for a commanding officer."

"Lean and mean, Raina."

"But assuming that you're correct, do you think the attack was by someone else and made to look like Crist?"

"Always a possibility."

"But with no evidence."

"Nope. But that's what we'll be investigating while you're having tea with Kyla Crist."

Chapter Eleven

"She's the nicest one of the bunch, if you ask me," said the man, a lean factory worker who lived north of the central city. "I watch them on the vid screen, you know, and half the time the other ministers aren't even listening when people complain to them."

"This is during open meetings?" Scott asked, sipping his jangulo. He was enjoying the flavor.

"Yes. They hold those once a month. I don't know if it's just for show or not, but Kyla Crist always asks really deep questions and takes notes. The other ones don't even pay attention. I don't much like politicians, but she's okay, I think."

Scott placed his hand onto his chin and shook his head. "We just ask because all we've seen on the vid reports since we got here is about this Crist woman and her brother; we were just curious." He leaned forward, adding, "I don't much like politicians, either. They're the same anywhere you go in the galaxy."

"Got that right," Carnahan said, acting bored with the conversation. "This is our first time on-planet: what do you have for sport around here?" The man smiled and started talking sports with Carnahan as Scott pondered their last five conversations. Most of the people they'd spoken with shared the vid reporters' opinions of Thorian Crist's reputation on-planet, but were also concerned about the implications of Federation membership. They feared losing autonomy and local decision-making authority and the increased tax burden that Federation membership might require. Many also opposed population-based Federation military service, imposed on planets with more than one billion citizens.

Where they were split was on their opinion of the collaborative. Many felt, as the man in the café did, that Kyla Crist was an innocent and perhaps naive member of the collaborative, especially given her relative youth of thirty-eight years. Others felt she should do more to distance herself from her troublesome brother. Few had a high opinion of the Planetary Collaborative in general, preferring to focus on the prime minister from their own region. The last man they spoke to was from the eastern region, whose prime minister Takoda Marten had been in the job for almost ten years and was considered benign.

The two crew members said goodbye to their friend and started the walk back to the space docks. Once they were out of earshot, Scott turned to Carnahan. "Your assessment?"

Carnahan turned his head toward the café, then toward Scott. "The news reports seem accurate to me, sir. Sounds like the collaborative ministers focus more on their own butts than on whether Kyla Crist is implicated in anything."

"That's my sense too. I just wish I knew if that was a good thing or a bad thing."

* * *

"How easy will it be to see her?" McLeod watched as Raina Wolfe finished dressing for her planet-side assignment.

"That remains to be seen, Tucker." Wolfe checked her equipment a second time to be sure, then looked at her friend. "You heard the report from Carnahan and Scott. Crist is open about her living situation; she lives in a large home paid for by her government but doesn't have an active security force around her."

"That seems risky to me. How many government officials at her level don't have an active security force around them at all times?"

Wolfe shrugged. "I agree with you, but it's to our advantage that she's so open. That doesn't guarantee she'll let us into her home, however."

McLeod stood. "That's my concern, too. But I'm betting you and Chief Carnahan can handle it."

Wolfe shook her head, then smiled. "Just watch us."

* * *

McLeod and Wolfe walked to the bridge, collecting Carnahan along the way. McLeod turned to Carnahan, noting the enlisted man's confidence and manner. "You seem ready and able, chief."

"That's my job, sir." Carnahan dropped his voice to a whisper. "I've known people who didn't meet with Captain Wolfe's expectations; I don't want to be them."

"Chief, I am not that bad," Wolfe said, teasing.

"No, ma'am," said Carnahan, who looked again at McLeod and laughed.

McLeod smiled back before entering the bridge and taking his seat. "What's the status, Ava?"

"Ready, sir. There's nothing of note on the news reports or vids." She turned to face McLeod. "The collaborative has finished its work for the day and the ministers have gone home. There's nothing new on the housing project bombing in the western region, either."

"What's your plan for tonight, Raina?"

"It's 1800 hours now, Tucker. We should arrive at her home at 1900; we'll be there as long as it takes." Touching her waist pack, she added, "Communication should be constant unless we detect any tracking devices. In that case, we will turn off all communications." Wolfe turned to Driscoll. "You're sure we can avoid detection if our devices are inoperative, Ava?"

"That's what they tell me." Seeing Wolfe's eyes narrow, Driscoll added, "Yes, ma'am: Commander Shaw and I tested them against the known devices on Amaeus, and believe you will be shielded."

"Thank you, Ava." Wolfe gestured toward the bridge door. "Time to head out, chief." She and Carnahan advanced toward the door. Before they reached the door, Wolfe stopped and turned to McLeod.

"No worrying about us, Dad."

"No worries at all. And remember, I'm only older than you by three months."

McLeod rose and paced the bridge again, stopping at communications. "Have Scott and Ross meet me in my ready room, Ava. I want to track this carefully, so keep Captain Wolfe and Chief Carnahan in your sights the entire time."

"Aye, sir," said Driscoll, but before she could make the calls, McLeod stopped her.

"And Ava, I'd appreciate it if you would remain on post until they return; you may have your relief here as well, but I want continuity here."

"Aye, sir."

* * *

Wolfe and Carnahan hailed a public transport, and once they entered, tapped their payment card on the box and gave the address to the driver. He said nothing but pulled out immediately into traffic. Once they were driving, Wolfe turned to Carnahan. "That wasn't so hard, was it?"

"It wasn't. But that wasn't the hard part."

"Agreed." As she watched the hustle and bustle of after work traffic both on the roads and among the pedestrians and bicycles, Wolfe added, "This is a pleasant city. There's an openness that you can sense."

Carnahan nodded. "That's true. We observed that earlier when we were getting our jangulos."

"Mmm," Wolfe responded, though Carnahan could tell she wasn't listening anymore. They arrived at the coffee shop near Kyla Crist's home, exited the transport, and walked toward the coffee shop. Wolfe and Carnahan ordered drinks for them and for Kyla Crist, then began walking toward Crist's home.

The home itself was modest but of very high quality. Wolfe saw the com box and pressed the button. After ten seconds, a voice they recognized as Kyla Crist's came through the speaker.

"Yes?"

"Ms. Crist?"

"Yes. I wasn't expecting anyone."

"We understand, ma'am," Wolfe said. "But we're with ITC from the northern region and we weren't able to attend today's open session and conference." Wolfe changed her voice to a sheepish one, adding, "And to be honest, ma'am, we don't want to report to our boss that we don't have any direct information or quotes from at least one minister. You're our only hope."

Wolfe and Carnahan waited, then heard a sigh from the other end. "I've had a long and hard day, and I would be happy to—"

"That's wonderful!" Wolfe said. "And just to make it more pleasant, we have a warm cup of nu-cal for you. I'm sure this won't take long."

"I suppose that will be all right. Please load your credentials into the scanner."

"Yes, ma'am," Wolfe said. She took both her credentials and Carnahan's and placed them in the scanner. A minute later, the gate unlocked.

"I'll meet you at the first door."

Wolfe and Carnahan walked past the gate and heard the sharp snap of the lock behind them. As they approached the door, they saw Kyla Crist through the glass advancing toward the door. Crist smiled at them and opened the door.

A nice smile, Wolfe thought, but she could see the strain in Crist's eyes and face. "Ms. Crist, we are Pier Allen and Risa Murphy from ITC network. Thank for you making this exception. We promise not to take too much of your time."

Crist looked at the cups in Carnahan's hand. "That's all right: it comes with the job, and I don't always get a fresh cup when I meet with reporters, especially from this shop."

Carnahan laughed. "We hoped that would be to our advantage, ma'am."

"Come in."

Crist led the way through the anteroom into a large living space. Made to entertain groups and visitors, Wolfe guessed. Crist gestured at several seats, and once her guests were seated, she perched herself in an armchair. Carnahan passed her the cup of nu-cal. Crist smiled as she opened it and smelled the aroma. "I think it's at just the right temperature. This is a treat. Thank you."

"Our pleasure, ma'am," Wolfe said. She took out and turned on her pad before looking up again. "And to save your time, can we start?"

"Yes." Crist's eyes furrowed. "I've never seen you here before. I've spoken with other people from ITC: there's Berringer and Kappling, and—"

"And Saraming, I imagine," Carnahan offered.

"Right. Are you new?"

Wolfe shook her head and smiled. "Just to this beat, ma'am. We were formerly on the education and training beat, so this is new for us."

"Which is why we hoped we'd have the chance to speak with you and make a good impression," Carnahan added.

"I see. Sorry for the interruption; please go ahead with your questions."

"Good," Wolfe said. "Ms. Crist, first we want to know if you agree that it is the will of the people of Amaeus to join the Central Federation?"

"I don't know what you mean. You know the votes, perhaps even better than I do. Every region of our planet in favor, and the vote was decisive. As I recall, wasn't it around seventy-eight percent in the northern region?"

"Something like that," Carnahan agreed.

"Then what better measure of the will of the people could you want?"

"But your brother doesn't believe that," Wolfe said. Crist didn't flinch at the mention of her brother. *Too inured to the question.*

"My brother does not represent the will of the people," Crist began, "even in the central region. As I've said repeatedly, we will not be intimidated by those who oppose Federation membership for purely selfish reasons."

"That's rather strong, if you don't mind me saying," Carnahan said.

"We're in difficult times, Mr. Allen," Crist replied. "And it takes strong leadership and decision making."

"Yet you now find yourself on the firing line," Wolfe said. "Everyone is talking about the actions of the collaborative and your—how can I say it—tenuous status with them."

To this, Crist smiled. "Not as tenuous as you might think, Ms. Murphy. Whenever you put five politicians together you have conflicts, many of which have less to do with the issues than about the people themselves."

"Amen to that," Carnahan said.

"Ms. Crist," Wolfe began, "How far would you go to ensure that Amaeus achieves Federation membership?"

"What do you mean?"

"There are those who say that if you stepped down as prime minister of the southern region, the people might have greater confidence in the collaborative. Do you agree with that?"

"I don't. I think it would create instability within the collaborative and around the planet, and that would delay our work with the Federation."

"Do you believe the Federation is looking favorably on your application for membership?"

Crist sat up straighter in her chair. "I'm not clear on—"

"I mean, do you have indications that the Federation is likely to approve your application, or might they be having second thoughts?"

Crist thought for a moment. "I don't know. We're an excellent candidate: we have general economic and political stability, we're in a sector of space ripe for Federation expansion, and we share the goals for scientific and political cooperation the Federation stands for. Why wouldn't they look favorably upon us?"

"Don't you think Thorian Crist's activities in the central desert are an impediment to membership?"

"No. He is only one man and—"

"Yet your colleagues on the collaborative keep badgering you about that," Carnahan said. "Could they be acknowledging something you should as well: that the activities of Thorian Crist might lead to an unfavorable review by the Central Federation?"

"That is possible," Crist agreed. "But to say that would be to acknowledge that one man—whatever his family background—could control an entire planet's fate. I won't accept that." She saw that neither Wolfe nor Carnahan were taking notes and frowned. "Are you sure you're with ITC?"

Wolfe and Carnahan looked at each other, before Wolfe turned again to Crist. "Ms. Crist. We are very interested in Amaeus's membership in the Central Federation and want to help make that happen."

"So you're not with—"

"But we should tell you, minister, that your brother's actions are making the Federation nervous, and they will not approve your application until his activities, and those of any others like him that compromise the will of the people, are stopped."

Crist rose from her seat and put her cup on the table, frowning at it. With tight lips she said, "Just who *are* you?"

Wolfe closed her pad and looked up. "Who we are may not matter to you, and really isn't relevant, though we are committed to the Amaean goal of Federation membership. Your brother is an obstacle to that. We want to ensure that he doesn't make achieving your goal impossible. That's why we asked you earlier about the will of the people."

"I answered that," Crist snapped.

"You told us the official answer," Wolfe said, still seated. "We want your feelings about what the people of this planet want. Does it truly match the vote?"

"I do not—"

"Please, minister, it's an honest question, and the answer matters."

Crist fought with herself before sitting down again, looking at her nu-cal. "There's nothing in it but nu-cal," Carnahan said.

Crist picked up the cup and took another sip. "I don't know why I'm doing this." She was silent for a moment, savoring the taste of the nu-cal. "The debate about Federation membership was rich and robust, but there was a clear consensus even before the vote. My answer to your question is 'yes.' I believe the will of the people is to pursue Federation membership: our scientists are hungry for interplanetary exchange and are interested in developing new means of creating and harnessing energy to sustain the planet. And while we are in a sector of space with few adversaries, we also have few protections: Federation membership will give us access to a network for improved defense." She looked up again. "So yes: the people of Amaeus want to join the Federation, even with the many questions that remain unanswered."

"Thank you," Wolfe said. "We needed to hear that from you."

"So now what? Do you take that to someone—obviously not ITC— and report on it?"

"No," Wolfe said. "We partner with you to help reduce or eliminate the threat of Thorian Crist to the planet and to Federation membership."

"What does that mean?"

"It means we work with you as partners to help you realize your goal."

"And my brother?"

After a quick glance to Carnahan, Wolfe said, "As you think about your brother, would you want him removed—preferably without violence—so he can no longer wreak havoc on the planet? This is separate from his management and development of mineral and energy holdings."

Crist sat back in her chair and looked around her living room, studying every seam of the cushions. Wolfe and Carnahan waited patiently. "Yes. I would," Crist said after a painful few minutes. Then her mood changed and her lips tightened again. "And can you guarantee that you will not use violence against him?"

"That," Wolfe began, "will depend more on him than on us. Given his—"

Crist rose again and pointed toward the door. "Then you have to leave. To ask me to approve or look the other way when a family member is attacked or hurt is heartless." Crist stepped back from the table and looked Wolfe squarely in the eye. "Now!"

Wolfe and Carnahan rose from their seats and left the house.

Chapter Twelve

"Captain Wolfe and Chief Carnahan secure and back on *Raven*, sir," said Ava Driscoll.

"Excellent." McLeod rose from his seat and approached West. "Give me a rundown, Frankie. We need to be ready for our operation in the central desert."

"Aye, sir. I can run a review as soon as you're able."

McLeod checked the time. "Tell you what. Send me the file and I'll review it tonight. We want to take into account Captain Wolfe's report when she arrives." McLeod was cut off by the arrival of Wolfe and Carnahan on the bridge. "Speak of the devil." McLeod turned to his colleague. "We were getting worried about you."

Wolfe smiled and approached her chair, her face giving away her frustration. "Do you want the good news or the bad news?"

"You have good news?"

"Let me rephrase that: do you want the bad news or the worse news?"

"Ready room?"

Wolfe checked the time and nodded. "In thirty: bring the major players." She turned to exit the bridge. "I should have a good cup of tea and re-center myself by that time."

Wolfe turned without a backward glance, McLeod studying her. *That's not what I wanted to hear.*

* * *

Wolfe and Carnahan relayed what had happened at Kyla Crist's home, including their frustration with Crist's unwillingness to help them.

"I'm sure she wants the same things we want, Tucker," Wolfe began, "but she's committed even more to her brother's safety."

"I get that, Raina. But something has to give here. Is she so blind she can't see the damage he's doing?"

Carnahan shifted uneasily in his seat. "Chief?" McLeod asked.

"It's not than simple, sir," said Carnahan.

"Meaning?"

"It's the cultural difference, captain," Carnahan replied. "How a given people—"

McLeod raised his hand and frowned. "What Thorian Crist is doing isn't viewed so much as a crime as it is staking out his territory as an entrepreneur and protecting his business interests."

Carnahan stared at him McLeod, nodding his head. "Yes, sir. The terrorist label usually applies to his business dealings."

"Pardon my ignorance and impatience, both of you," McLeod said. "And I'm sure people other than Kyla Crist feel the same way. I mean, who could support violence against someone who hasn't officially committed a crime?"

"That's not uncommon, sir," Driscoll said. "You know how people in remote areas like the central desert of this planet often live by rules that others don't."

"Understood, chief," McLeod said. "What I'm having difficulty understanding is why Kyla Crist hasn't grown out of that."

"Does it matter?" Wolfe asked.

McLeod looked at her, then at the faces surrounding him in the ready room. "No."

"There's something else, sir," Driscoll said.

"What?"

"We just reviewed a news report that a growing number of people on the planet—except for the central desert—are doubting Kyla Crist's loyalty and integrity. That number has grown faster than you'd believe."

"Could that change have been created artificially?"

Driscoll frowned. "As in a planted story? I can't say sir, but I'll look for that."

"Good." McLeod caught Wolfe's eye and raised his head slightly.

Wolfe rose. "Our report will be transcribed by Chief Carnahan. Until then, continue to monitor what's happening on-planet, and review preparations for the operation in the central desert. Commander Shaw, please stay behind. Dismissed."

Carnahan, Ross, and Driscoll looked at each other, then rose and exited the ready room.

Shaw remained in his seat and turned to Wolfe. "Captain?"

"We're okay, Goody. But we needed to review certain items among the three of us before speaking with the rest of the team." Wolfe turned back to McLeod and waited.

"An honest assessment, Raina. Will we have support from Kyla Crist in this effort or do we need to go it alone?"

Shaw looked between both captains, frowning. He started to speak, but Wolfe beat him to it. "We do this all the time, Goody, so don't take it personally. Tucker and I have a silent way of communicating, and as next in the chain of command, you need to be in the loop." She turned again to McLeod. "It's worth one more try, Tucker, perhaps with a more explicit explanation about our role in helping Amaeus improve their application status."

"Risk level?"

"High, I should say. But I suspect she was blustering a bit when she told us to leave: she wants what we want. If we can convince her of our ability to end this conflict without undue damage or violence, we might tip her over the fence."

McLeod exhaled. "And that's what we needed you to know, Goody. A day or two from now, when the operation starts in the central desert, I'll be away from *Raven*, and Captain Wolfe may be occupied on the surface working with Kyla Crist. We need to build our contingency now in case anything goes wrong."

"I'm ready for that, sir."

"Good," McLeod replied. "In the meantime, I'll start developing our Plan B."

* * *

Thorian Crist studied the attack plan carefully. "You can make this happen quickly?"

Cordell nodded as he stood even more erect. "Of course, sir. Our forces can be ready in ten hours for most of our operations." Cordell changed his tone, adding, "But I don't believe the target to be a wise one."

"Why?"

"You forget, sir, that planetary forces are already looking at us for the last attack against the—"

"But we didn't attack the housing project!"

"We know that, sir, but they don't. And until they do, or until we figure out what's happened, we need to be on our guard."

Crist rose from his seat facing the wall, his shoulders rising and falling, getting control of himself. He turned again to Cordell, then resumed his seat. "Keeping us safe is your job, Cordell. As you plan this operation, find out what happened at the housing project. Our objective of autonomy depends on it."

"Yes, sir."

Crist waved his hand and Cordell left the room. Crist sat back in his chair, rubbing his temples.

* * *

Tyrus Landau smiled as he heard the report. His executive officer relished telling him of the successful attack on the housing project.

"It came off smoothly, sir," said Reed. "Our observations of Crist gave us the perfect ability to implicate him. The news reports from the planet are universally negative about him."

Landau frowned. "And his sister, the Planetary Collaborative minister?"

"Same with her, sir. There are even reports that she will be asked to step down by the other members of the collaborative."

"All the better. She's one of the strongest in favor of Federation membership. Perhaps discrediting her will stop this foolishness before it goes any further." Landau noticed a shift in Reed's shoulders. "You don't agree?"

"I don't, sir. All five members of the collaborative voted in favor of the application. Having Kyla Crist removed is unlikely to change that. Plus, the southern region had the highest approval for affiliating with the Federation. Who's to say that a new prime minister from the south won't have the same opinion?"

Landau had to admit the logic was sound. "No matter. We just need to whittle away at their support until it evaporates."

"Yes sir," Reed said, though he believed that work to be far more difficult than Landau imagined.

Chapter Thirteen

"This operation is complicated by having no support personnel on the ground," McLeod said, addressing *Raven's* senior staff. "And while Captain Wolfe and Sr. Altern Scott will return to Kyla Crist, we can't afford to remain in the central city during that time." He turned to Wolfe. "You'll be on your own, Raina."

"You sound like this is the first time. Kyla Crist seems reasonable to me, Tucker. We'll be fine."

"I have to agree, sir," Scott said. "Her reluctance to support violence against her brother is a natural reaction. She has to know we wouldn't use violence unless necessary."

"Don't be too sure, Altern," McLeod said. "People do illogical things where family relations are involved." McLeod turned to Ava Driscoll. "Chief, what other intelligence have you uncovered?"

Driscoll checked her pad. "Some members of the collaborative are ready to ask Kyla Crist to step down from her post. At least that's what several news agencies are saying. I wouldn't put it past the collaborative to have planted these stores to soften the blow for the southern region."

"I agree with that, captains," Carnahan said. "Zahara Ali has her fingers in every news agency; she can turn public opinion easily."

"A dangerous combination," said McLeod. "Raina, do you have what you need to attend the public session?"

"The credentials we had yesterday were convincing, Tucker. We should have no problem."

"Good. Once you're in the central city, we will make our second reconnaissance run at the Crist compound at 1400 hours." McLeod looked around the room. "Questions?" McLeod saw no objections. "Very well. Dismissed." McLeod locked eyes with Wolfe and stayed there. He saw her normal calm, professional demeanor tinged with only a hint of concern. McLeod then followed her out of the ready room; her to her quarters and him to the bridge.

* * *

"I do not intend to leave my post," Kyla Crist said. "And any recall action should be taken by the southern regional government or our house of delegates."

"You must be reasonable, Kyla," said Ali. "With your credibility compromised, we're all less effective in our work."

"Who is saying that my credibility is compromised?"

"Haven't you seen the news reports?" Anoki asked. "Polls show a growing unease with your leadership here on the collaborative."

"Not in the south." Crist smiled at Anoki. "And that's despite planted stories and innuendo."

"We're not getting anywhere here," Leyla Hill said. "Zahara, we must have decorum in this body, and we must also guard against removing members because we worry about public reaction."

Anoki raised his hand before Ali could speak. "Leyla, for someone as old as you are, you don't seem to know anything about politics. It is all about perception and—"

"You are a *child*!" said Hill. "I have outlasted people far better than you, Ian, so watch your tone!"

The rapping gavel threatened to split the wood on the table as Ali fought to regain control. "We will accomplish nothing if we don't work together!"

"I agree," Crist said. "And understand that I will engage in all of these discussions as prime minister of our southern government; don't count me out yet."

"Bravo," Hill said.

Ali shook her head, rapping the gavel again. "Let us take a break before we convene for the open session." With that, Ali rose and returned to her office.

* * *

McLeod stood by the port aft hatch as Wolfe and Scott walked down *Raven's* longest passageway toward him. Wolfe smiled when she approached, which lightened his mood. He glanced at his chron to check the time, asking, "How much time do you think you'll need?"

"That's hard to say. We could meet in either the office or in her home. I prefer meeting on her own territory, but she might be more comfortable speaking in her office. Trevor and I can handle ourselves in the public session. According to Ava, it's just an open forum and the only people speaking are those who have pre-registered. The rest of the people just sit and listen."

"That may give you additional insight into what makes her tick."

"I agree." Wolfe approached McLeod and punched him lightly on the arm, before laughing. "Now stand aside and let us do our jobs."

"Aye, ma'am." McLeod moved aside to let them pass and watched as the hatch closed. He smiled to himself, knowing he would never underestimate Raina Wolfe.

* * *

Wolfe and Scott left the public docking area, entering the Amaean sun. As she walked, Wolfe was reminded again of the difference in gravity between the academy and Amaeus. Once they hailed a transport, the ride to the Planetary Collaborative complex was far too short. Wolfe and Scott left the vehicle at the public access area to the side of the building and took out their credentials. Scott seemed confident, and while Wolfe didn't know him well, Araminta Ross had vouched for him. She looked up and caught his eye.

"Could be easy or difficult, Trevor. Are you ready?"

"Yes, ma'am. Just like any regular operation."

"Without the plasma cannon and communication devices."

"Well, there is that."

They fell in step behind three other citizens as they approached the security station. The security officer took their credentials, touched each to a blue box that glowed yellow after a few seconds, then lazily returned them.

"Do you know where you're going?"

"Yes," Wolfe replied. "Open gallery, right?"

"Yes."

"We have it. Thank you." Wolfe and Scott followed three other people to the public gallery, arriving early enough to sit in the lower gallery. At the front of the room stood a stage on which a long, curved table sat with five massive chairs behind it. She couldn't see the names in front of the chairs, but assumed the middle one was for the chair, Zahara Ali. In the short time they waited for the ministers to enter, at least fifty other people entered, closing off the lower gallery to any more observers. Just as Wolfe's mind began to wander, the ministers entered, wearing blue robes over their normal attire. The ministers lined up behind their seats and waited. Finally a small man entered and sat at a small table to the right and almost under the minister's table. He nodded his head to Ali. The gallery fell into silence, Ali raised her gavel, rapped on the table twice, and the ministers sat.

A minute later, Zahara Ali's clear voice came through the speakers. "Good afternoon, citizens, and thank you for taking this opportunity to participate in our government." Ali looked at the pad inclined in front of her. "As usual, we have a full agenda of speakers. We will call the speakers in the order in which they were reserved until we have exhausted each speaker's time, which should last no more than five minutes apiece. Our ministers may also speak, but this session is for our citizens to raise concerns and opinions and for us to listen." Ali nodded to the man in the smaller table, who cleared his throat.

"Citizen Bersand to speak on the topic of transportation in the northern region." Wolfe watched as a wizened older man walked to the elevated platform and stood.

"Thank you, ministers of the Planetary Collaborative. My community and I are concerned . . ." Wolfe listened to Citizen Bersand with only one ear, paying more attention to the citizens in the room and the ministers. She focused on the ministers' body language, stance, and what they said, if anything. It took until the seventh speaker for someone to mention Thorian Crist.

"Citizen Coolee to speak on the topic of violence in the western region." Citizen Coolee was a woman of Wolfe's age whose steps were more a march than a walk.

"Thank you, ministers," said Citizen Coolee. "My family and I live in the western region, and I first came to the central city to ask for tax relief for small businesses like ours. But I changed my topic after the violence at the Newtown housing project." Coolee stopped to catch her breath and to speak more carefully. "We have family members who were supposed to move into that project, and this has frightened us out of our minds." She gained momentum, speaking with her hands. "It was hard enough to see this violence and conflict in the central desert with its small population." Wolfe could hear annoyed murmurs within the crowd. "But in the western region where we're more densely populated, this is pure terrorism. I've already asked the western regional government what they're going to do, and I ask you too: what are you going to do about this violence, and about that horrible man?" Coolee didn't exit the platform after her statement as other speakers had. She stayed, daring the ministers to dismiss her. Ali looked at her colleagues, willing them to be silent. Less than ten seconds later, a microphone crackled to life.

"I agree with you, citizen," the man said. *Anoki*, thought Wolfe. "And we are committed to stopping Thorian Crist and putting him away forever. This violence cannot stand, and the collaborative is putting—"

"But what are you *doing?*" Citizen Coolee implored. "Everyone is committed, but no one is *doing* anything." Ali looked around the table again, hoping someone else would speak.

A microphone crackled and the weary voice of Kyla Crist came on. "Military and security forces are searching for survivors, which unfortunately have been few," Crist began, "and we are looking diligently for the specific people involved, and—"

"But we already know who's responsible! His hands are full of the blood of citizens who have died because of him." Citizen Coolee threw up her hands and left the chamber. Wolfe noticed Anoki sitting back in his chair smiling as he glanced at Crist's pained face.

Someone to watch.

Chapter Fourteen

Raven, in its clunky freighter form, achieved altitude and flew toward the central desert. McLeod reviewed his notes for the flyover and for the first stage of the operation at the Crist compound. He asked questions of his crew and gave answers to theirs as he focused on weighing several options in his mind.

"Estimated time to the central desert, Lily."

"Going the southern route, about fifteen minutes, sir."

"Very well. Make sure you give Commander Serrano what he needs."

"Aye, sir." Kono turned to him. "We have it worked out: two passes like last time at ninety-degree angles."

"Any communication to worry about, Ava?"

"No, sir. Aircraft fly over the central desert all the time, including over the Crist compound." Driscoll took her attention away from her console and turned to McLeod. "So long as we don't do this every day, we should be good."

"Good," McLeod said. "But just to be sure, let's shift to configuration two on the way."

"Science vessel?" Virgil Kelly asked.

McLeod shrugged. "That's probably the most common vessel around the central desert, wouldn't you say?"

"I agree," Kelly said.

"Good." McLeod turned to Driscoll. "All-com, Ava. Have all personnel move to core positions. Lt. Commander Kelly will shift to config two when ready."

"Aye."

"Good. Let's be ready, people."

* * *

"And that's why we want more attention paid to this issue by the collaborative," said Citizen Penay. Wolfe thought the man had a mature presence for someone so young. She saw Kyla Crist making notes as the man spoke, and as he exited the podium, she addressed him.

"Thank you, Citizen. We can only know of these issues when they are brought to our attention." The man walked toward his seat, and Crist swung her head and looked directly into the eyes of Raina Wolfe. Wolfe sat frozen as Crist examined her for a few seconds, then sat straight in her chair when the next speaker began. *A remarkable woman.*

* * *

McLeod had resumed an easy, slow pace around the small bridge. Max Serrano was looking at several indicators on his console when his eyebrows creased. McLeod wasn't the only one who noticed the sense of unease in the usually calm Serrano.

"You're making us nervous, Max."

"Sorry, sir, there's just—" Serrano looked to Kono. "Lily, can you do one more pass somewhere around this axis: 75 to 255?"

"Done."

McLeod stood behind Serrano, willing himself to be patient. "Something tells me you aren't happy about what you're seeing, Max."

"I don't know what anything means at the moment, sir. Minty?" he called, alerting Ross. "What was the exact time of the attack in the western region?"

"Hold on."

"It's either something that shouldn't be there, or it's something that should be there that isn't," McLeod said. "Which is it?"

"It was at 1500 hours, so about 26 hours ago," Ross said.

"That's what I thought," Serrano said. "And we're sure that Crist's forces stay either in this compound, or at other points mostly north or a little south, to protect their mineral interests?"

"That's what we've determined," McLeod said. He stood straighter and crossed his arms. "You gonna clue us in?"

Serrano set his lips. "There's no evidence of corsaa residue anywhere in this complex."

"At what levels?"

"At almost any level. You'd expect an elevated level because of the exhaust from most military vehicles. Crist uses a derivative of klocutin for his fuel, right?"

"Every military body on-planet does," Ross replied. "Private vehicles use less expensive fuels."

"Well, there hasn't been much movement from his complex for at least forty hours—maybe more. So the attack didn't come directly from this complex."

"Is that such a surprise?" Kono asked. "And can we get out of here now? I don't want to deal with anti-aircraft fire."

"We're good," Serrano replied.

"Tell me more, Max," McLeod said.

Serrano scratched his head as he examined his console. "No. Nothing, or at least not nearly enough." He looked up at Kono, then McLeod. "Could we trace the probable route from here to the bombing site?"

"I'm good with that," McLeod said. "Let's go, Lily." Turning to Ross and Serrano, he added, "So if they didn't get to the housing project from here, how did they do it?"

"A good question," Ross said.

"I'd rather have a good answer."

* * *

As the last speaker began in the open gallery, Wolfe nudged Scott. "The ministers' offices are that way," she said, pointing. "We want to be between Crist and her office."

"Right." They made their way to a hallway to the left of the chamber, surprised to see no security guards. "Guess they have a lot of trust on their planet."

"Hard to say," Wolfe said, distracted. "Maybe the security to get into the building is tight enough for them."

"What do you mean?"

Wolfe looked at the corner of the hallway and pointed. "There are those security cameras, every three to four meters, plus the full body scan as we entered the building. Maybe they figure that's enough."

Scott shrugged. "Maybe, ma'am. But I'd prefer more interior security than this."

"You and me both."

A noise behind Wolfe pulled their attention to the ministers filing out of the gallery and walking toward their offices. Kyla Crist exited with her colleagues, then turned to the right and saw Wolfe and Scott. She hesitated, then began walking toward them. "Have you something else to tell or ask me?" Her robe made her look all the more imposing.

"You may think so, minister," Wolfe said. "This is Mr. Scott, one of my colleagues, and we'd like to speak with you in your office."

After a moment, Crist said, "Very well." She glanced at the side door to the gallery, noticing that other members of the collaborative had gone to their offices. "My office is this way. But I can't promise you anything more than I did yesterday." Crist turned on her heel and led the way down the second hallway, then to an office in a side corridor. She led them past her assistant without introductions. Once inside, Wolfe took in the room with a glance: the casual seating area with couch, side table, and chairs, and the large desk in the corner with two chairs in front of it. Crist walked past the couch and planted herself behind her desk, saying nothing. Wolfe led Scott to the chairs and sat.

"I asked you a question the other day," Crist began. "I asked who you were, and I have doubts that you are who you say you are."

"Been researching ITC?"

"Not only that. But I confirmed that they don't assign new people to the Planetary Collaborative beat without prior introductions. Even if you are from ITC, they didn't send you to me."

"You've got us there," Wolfe said. "And while we can't tell you everything about our presence here, I can affirm again that we are interested in helping Amaeus join the Central Federation."

"Why does it matter to you? You're not Amaean. What's your interest?"

"Our interests are peace and cooperation around the galaxy, ma'am," Scott said. "Who isn't interested in that?"

"We are solely here to help Amaeus gain Federation membership," Wolfe repeated. "And understand, minister, that we have capabilities that are at your informal disposal."

"Why me?"

Wolfe smiled. "Because you are the only one who can help us understand Thorian Crist: what motivates him, what his weak points are, and how we might lower—or eliminate—his negative influence on this planet. We thought our task would be easier if we could work with you."

"I can't help you," Crist said, sitting back and rubbing her face, nervous.

"We have a job to do, minister." Wolfe softened her voice. "And we will try to accomplish these goals, which are Amaean self-determination and affiliation with the Central Federation. We know what being from a

Federation world is like: it's worth the effort, and the benefits last lifetimes. Do you really want Amaeus's application to be denied because you were unsure or hesitant?"

Crist leaned forward onto her desk. "How do I know you're not working for my brother, trying to infiltrate the collaborative? Do you have any idea of the pressure I'm under because of my last name?"

"We do. Which is why we'd like to help you."

"And I should trust you, why?"

Wolfe tipped her head. "What do you really believe, minister? Do you believe we would come to you twice offering our help if we were working for your brother? We are from Federation worlds and believe that both the Central Federation and the Star Alliance are good for the galaxy."

Crist was silent for a minute, then Wolfe saw her mood change. "I asked you another question last night. Do you remember it?"

"I do," Wolfe answered. "We came here without weapons and no intent to use force against you in any away. We hoped to enlist your support and work with you. If we can't do that, so be it. But we must continue our work."

"And to my question?"

"About violence against your brother?" Crist nodded. "Whether we can achieve our goals without violence will depend more on your brother than on us, minister. We will not initiate violence, but we must defend ourselves if necessary."

Crist looked at Wolfe and searched her eyes, then set her jaw. "That's what I thought."

A moment later, a man ten centimeters taller than Gordon Shaw entered the room from a door near the desk. His bald pate sat atop broad shoulders and a massive frame. He was a man of few words. "As head of security for the Planetary Collaborative, I must ask you to stand. You are in violation of section seventy-seven of the Amaean code, and therefore a danger to the government."

Wolfe and Scott stood, Wolfe still looking at Crist. "You're making a mistake, minister. But we will show you our good intentions by going peaceably." Wolfe waved Scott ahead of her and after a last glance at Crist, followed Scott out of the office, the security man right behind them.

* * *

McLeod sat at the ready room table surveying the faces of the people seated in front of him. Max Serrano's analysis of the corsaa emissions from the Crist compound to the housing area in the western district were conclusive.

"So, no possibility that they were transported from any of Crist's strongholds, Max?"

"None, captain. That doesn't mean Crist wasn't behind it, it just means that he didn't do it from his known locations."

"This makes no sense, captain," Shaw said. "We know Crist is big and incredibly well-connected, but all our reports are that he concentrates his efforts in the central region, particularly in the desert. Why this change now?"

"Wrong question, Commander," McLeod said, and he saw the chief engineer stiffen. "It's not why now, we know why now: the Federation application. What I can't figure out is how he pulled this off with no corsaa emissions, or if he attacked the housing complex from a new location . . . " he said, his voice trailing off. McLeod looked up, trying to read the answer.

"Sir, I—" Serrano began, but McLeod raised his hand. After an uncomfortable silence, McLeod lowered his eyes to the group. "Could this have been an aerial attack? Ava?"

"That's highly unlikely, sir. Nothing in the news reports implied any unusual aircraft sightings at the time of the attack, nor was there evidence of munitions that could come from aircraft or spacecraft."

"What about the possibility that those who set the bombs or mortars were from another force inserted into the area for this purpose?"

"Through a drop off?" Serrano asked.

"Or from other ground forces we don't know about?" Carnahan added.

Serrano sighed. "Anything is possible, but every factor we raise complicates the analysis."

McLeod stood. "Get started on it anyway. We know it will be tough. Because if Thorian Crist didn't attack that housing project, we have another player to deal with." McLeod sighed. "Let's get back to the central city and pick up Raina and Trevor. Maybe they'll have good news for us."

* * *

The holding facility for the Planetary Collaborative building was separate from the detention center for the central city. Wolfe noticed how mercifully cool it was as she walked with the head of security and Trevor Scott. She smiled twice at Scott to relieve his tension.

The security man walked them through a heavy door with an electronic lock, then opened a door to the left, motioning Wolfe and Scott inside. It seemed more like a studio apartment than a holding cell, except for the heavy double key and electronic lock on the door. The man stood in the room, waiting for Wolfe and Scott to sit. After they sat, Wolfe and Scott looked up.

"I am Mr. Blanks, head of security for the Planetary Collaborative of Amaeus, ensuring the security of the collaborative ministers and of this facility. You will be held here until Minister Crist tells me what to do with you." Mr. Blanks walked toward a smaller walled-off chamber, pointing. "This is the sanitary facility. You'll find a shower and items for personal care inside. Should you need anything, you may press the communication pad on the wall by the door." His manner was professional, yet cold. Wolfe wondered how often he hosted 'guests' in the holding facility.

"I don't suppose we could get cups of jangulo, could we?" Wolfe asked, hoping to connect with Blanks.

Mr. Blanks showed no irony when he replied. "Of course. Would you like it regular or some other way?"

"Regular. Two."

"They will be delivered to you. Understand that it may take a while."

Wolfe used her arms to indicate her surroundings. "Well, we're not going anywhere."

"Indeed."

* * *

McLeod returned to the bridge while waiting for Serrano's final analysis of what they detected at the Crist compound. Having to battle a second adversary attacking targets on the planet, or additional Crist strongholds, would complicate *Raven's* work considerably. *Not what I wanted for a first mission.* McLeod noticed his heightened excitement at the new challenge and shook his head. *No one should be like this: the job gets more difficult, and I get more energized. Good thing that didn't come up in my previous jobs.*

"Everything good, Lily?"

"Except for flying a science vessel with no chops, I'm fine, sir. We'll be back in the central city soon. How will Captain Wolfe contact us?"

"They'll make contact through the communication station ansible at the spaceport," Driscoll said. "I've been monitoring that station, but nothing's come up yet."

"Raina is very business-like, so I imagine they shouldn't be too long."

"Yes, sir." Driscoll continued monitoring news reports and stations on-planet, then sat up in her chair. She cocked her head to concentrate, then looked back at McLeod. "Possible complication, sir."

"I don't like surprises, Ava."

"No, sir." Driscoll listened again then started recording a combined radio and video report, then put her head in her hand. McLeod rose from his seat as others on the bridge focused on Driscoll. She finally looked up and saw McLeod standing over her. "It's big, sir. I recorded it. On screen?" McLeod nodded. Driscoll hit the playback and an attractive man in a news uniform appeared on the screen.

"—collaborative was breached today by two suspicious individuals believed to be working with Thorian Crist. They appeared at the office of Minister Kyla Crist and were taken into custody by security personnel for the planetary collaborative. Their faces will not be shown for security reasons, but they are described as a woman of 1.75 meters, with black hair and of average build, and a man of 1.9 meters, average build with beige hair, both with suspect security credentials. Persons with any information—"

"Freeze the playback," McLeod said. He walked toward the screen and looked at the figures of the two people in custody then pointed to the neck of the woman. "That's them. That's the tribal mark on the left side of Raina's neck."

"What does this mean, sir?" Driscoll asked.

"It means this mission just got even more complicated."

Chapter Fifteen

"—appeared at the office of Minister Kyla Crist and were taken into custody by security personnel for the planetary collaborative. Their faces will not be shown for security reasons, but they are described as a woman of 1.75 meters, with black hair and of average build, and a man of 1.9 meters, average build with beige hair, both with suspect security credentials. Persons with any information concerning these individuals are urged to contact authorities, as security personnel are concerned they may be connected to Thorian Crist and his recent activity."

Thorian Crist sat with his lieutenants watching the news report, confused and skeptical.

"I don't believe it," Ansara said.

"Don't believe what?" Crist asked. "That the planetary collaborative could be breached by someone? That's naive of you, Victor."

"No, sir. That they could connect any infiltrators to you and to us."

"Ha!" Crist replied. "You believe that? It's a collaborative plot to paint us in a bad light."

"And it's working!" Bokari moaned. "We've done nothing for three days, yet now the public thinks we attacked the housing project *and* placed spies in the collaborative." Bokari held his head in his hands. "This is not going the way it was supposed to go."

"Hold it in, Wen," Maddox said, her dark eyes flashing. "We're not going to abandon our mission now."

"But Wen is right," Crist said. "Twice we have been painted with someone else's brush, and I don't like it. What are we going to do about it?"

"We are ready for the operation against the storage facility, sir," Cordell said. "And the weapons systems and vehicles used will implicate the Armadon group."

"Might the attack on the housing complex and these people in the news report be part of a move by the collaborative to hurt our reputation?"

"I wouldn't put it past them sir," Ansara said. "Zahara Ali is a nasty woman."

"But we don't want to take her out, sir," Cordell offered. "Her popularity in this region is based on longevity and backroom deals; she actually has more support in the west and north than here."

"That's not a surprise," Crist said. "We've made it tough for her here, and I don't apologize for that."

"We need to know more about the people in custody," Maddox said. "Who they are, where they came from, and what they're doing here."

"That's more in your line than anyone else's, Cordell," Crist said. "Can you handle that along with the operation against the energy storage facility?"

"Yes, sir. I only need thirty people for the attack: that leaves others for intelligence gathering."

"Then do it: we need to investigate quickly to minimize the damage." Cordell pointed to the door. Crist nodded, and Cordell rose and turned toward the door. "And find out how that housing project was destroyed."

"On it, sir."

After Cordell left, Crist again addressed his team. "Who could they be? What organization has the resources to place spies into the collaborative?"

"None of the youth groups would ever do that, sir," Bokari said. "Plus, they didn't appear to be young."

"I agree," Maddox said. "The news reports always mention youth when they want to target or smear those groups."

"Who else opposes Federation membership?" Menzel asked. "Maybe another group wants to scuttle the Federation application and lay the blame at our feet."

"A good question, Walker," Crist said. "But not one I have the answer to." Crist looked to his right and noticed that Ansara was looking away, distracted. "Victor, you're not paying attention. This is extremely important. We cannot allow other people to direct this opposition."

"Understood, sir."

Cordell reentered the room and strode to his seat.

"On track?"

"Yes, sir," Cordell said. "We can move in twelve hours. We have only to assemble and move the equipment to the strike team."

Crist looked at the faces of his lieutenants, seeing resolve and anger on the faces of Cordell and Maddox, and indecision on Bokari's and Wenzel's. "Since this is not a democracy, I will not ask for your opinions." He turned to Menzel. "Walker, you focus on the money and financial reports so we are as clean as possible. The rest of you, minus Cordell, return here in four hours so we can discuss the operation against the Berrett tullarium holdings; they need to be ours within the week."

"Yes, sir," said his group, almost in unison.

As they rose, Crist said, "Hold a moment, Victor." Ansara resumed his seat as his colleagues left the room, then turned his attention back to Crist. "This work is getting complicated, Victor, and I am seeing cracks in our armor."

"Wen has the pulse and trust of the younger people on-planet, particularly those who are frustrated about the lack of jobs. He is pivotal for our cause."

"He is," said Crist. "And he doesn't have the strength to oppose me. The person I'm worried about is Walker. We can't afford leaks regarding our financials. He knows too much, and his only investment is in the day-to-day accounting and money laundering; he doesn't understand what we're fighting for."

"What should we do with him?"

"Nothing as yet. But you need to be thinking about that possibility."

"Yes, sir."

Crist rubbed his eyes. "Very well." He looked up. "I will see you in four hours."

* * *

"I will take suggestions, people," McLeod said. He spoke to a group including Shaw, Ross, West, Carnahan, and Driscoll. "But don't take too long: I'm not a fan of Amaean justice, and our people need to be out of there."

"Agreed, sir," Shaw said. "But there are parameters we need to look at, and—"

"Which is not what either you or I do on a regular basis, Goody." McLeod turned to the covert operations personnel in the ready room. "I'm waiting."

Ross and Carnahan traded glances before Ross spoke. "Our plan is a simple extraction, sir. We've analyzed the security arrangements of the planetary collaborative. They're in the central facility in the basement."

"Did you use their ID chips?"

Carnahan nodded.

"And activated without Central Federation or Star Alliance authorization, I imagine?"

"*Raven* is authorized to activate them at any time."

"I know that, Minty," McLeod said. "But the authoritarian aspect of that gives me chills. What do we know about this detention facility?"

"That's where we need more time, sir," Carnahan said. "We need someone on the ground to enter and tie into the building's central control protocols. That will help us with the electronic locks, scanners, and personnel movements."

"Who's going to do that?"

"I am," said Ava Driscoll. "You'll need Commander Ross and Chief Carnahan for the primary extraction mission, and it wouldn't do to have their faces connected to a breach should something go wrong. I can get in, hook into their system, and be out of the building in ten minutes, barring any unforeseen problems."

McLeod looked at Carnahan, Ross and Driscoll. "You're all confident with this decision?"

"Yes sir," Ross replied. McLeod leaned back briefly, then brought his chair back up straight. "How many people for the extraction?"

"The smaller the better in this case," Carnahan said. "Our preference is the two of us, Commander Ross and me. We've trained and worked together enough to pull it off."

"Two is adequate?"

"For flying under the radar, sir, yes. We may encounter overwhelming force, but security isn't Amaeus's strong suit."

"They don't seem to think the same as many of us do about security and redundant systems, or at least that's not what our intelligence says," Ross added.

McLeod smiled. "Let's hope that our intelligence is accurate." He paused, looking once again at Ross, whom he had known for years. "Very well. We will go with this plan with one change; I will replace Chief Carnahan in the operation."

Ross and Carnahan looked at each other, then looked down briefly.

"And don't tell me Minty, that you didn't expect this."

"Expect sir, yes. But that doesn't mean I like it."

"Understood, but we need someone with Chief Carnahan's experience on *Raven* to develop contingency plans if necessary. If you're both on-planet, we lose that expertise." McLeod turned to Shaw. "While you'll be in command, Goody, please understand Chief Carnahan's central role here."

"I do, sir." Shaw leaned on the conference table. "But it doesn't make me happy, either."

"Noted," McLeod said, then rose. "And I get it. We shouldn't have both commanding officers away from the ship at the same time. But this time we need to improvise. I have full confidence in your leadership, both with the ship itself and our personnel, Goody. I couldn't leave her in better hands."

"Thank you." Shaw suppressed a smile.

"We have two priorities here, people," McLeod continued. "The first is the extraction; the second is stepping up the mission and timetable for getting to Thorian Crist. Given the instability of the situation, this may blow up sooner than we expect. I want the final plan for getting to Crist ready before Minty and I head to the collaborative. Dismissed." His personnel began leaving the ready room, with West remaining.

As McLeod turned to leave the ready room, Francine touched his arm.

"Frankie?"

"She can bounce back from anything, you know."

"Minty? I should hope so."

"You would never have that look on your face about Minty, sir, as much as you like her. And for what it's worth, I think you should go to get them out. We have to be confident operating when both of you are off the ship: there's no time like the present."

McLeod smiled. "I'm glad we brought you onto *Raven*."

Chapter Sixteen

Scott opened his eyes to see Wolfe sitting cross-legged on the floor of the holding room. He shook himself and looked on his wrist for the time. "Did I oversleep?"

"I don't know when you normally get up, Trevor. I have an internal clock and seldom get up after 0500."

"It's only 0430."

"I felt rested." Wolfe rose and stretched her arms above her head. "Any thoughts on how we get out of here?"

"Not yet, ma'am. May I assume we should eat and drink if they offer us something?"

"Well, the jangulo was as good as you said it was."

"That it was."

"Let's just play this by ear."

"Let's hope my ears work as well as they need to."

* * *

Carnahan and Driscoll stood across from the planetary collaborative building studying the entrance.

"You're sure these devices in our mouths and ear canals won't be detected?" Carnahan asked.

"As sure as I can be. They're partly organic and it's unlikely a sensor looking for metal will detect them. Plus the signal is weak and only carries for seventy-five meters—barely enough for you to hear me." She turned to her fellow chief. "I'll be fine, so long as I can get in and get out."

"Then have at it." Driscoll nodded and crossed the avenue to the building entrance, finding a place in line. She presented her identification credentials to a bored guard who glanced at them then handed them back once his scanner light went yellow. Driscoll breathed in and out to calm herself and entered the building, immediately looking to corners and walls for security system access ports. She saw a port ten meters to her right and another twenty meters to the left by the open gallery. Too open, but she noted the pattern. Driscoll saw signs for sanitary facilities and strode toward them as though she needed to use them.

"I've found the ports," Driscoll said. "They're in open areas for easy access and I'm sure I can configure our detector to fit in them. Acknowledge." Driscoll soon heard Carnahan's brusque voice through her ear canal and cursed herself for putting in no volume control.

"Understood. Be careful."

"Story of my life." Driscoll continued walking to the facilities, noticing another port only three meters away from the women's door. She slowed her pace hoping to arrive at the port alone. Driscoll stopped at the port and plugged in her detector, praying there wouldn't be an alarm.

Driscoll leaned over as if she was having difficulty walking and watched the detector fly through potential access codes before the light turned green and began downloading data. The process took less than a minute.

"Do you need assistance?"

Driscoll turned to see a young woman in official attire. She smiled as she turned and block the port. "Not at all. Something I ate didn't agree with me. I'm heading to the facility, but just needed to catch my breath."

"I'm happy to help you," the young woman said, "and—"

"No bother." Driscoll smiled. "I'm trying to regain my dignity." She leaned toward the young woman. "This is my first time in the collaborative, and I don't want my husband to think I couldn't handle myself, if you know what I mean."

The young woman nodded, though her eyebrows knitted in confusion. "All right. But if you need assistance, our security personnel are trained to help people with basic health needs."

"You're very kind," Driscoll said. "I'll be all right. Thank you."

"Pleasure." The young woman continued down the hallway, shaking her head. Driscoll tracked her until she went out of sight, then heard a low volume beep in her ear canal. Looking back at the detector, two green lights told her the download was finished. Driscoll pulled out the device and entered the sanitary facility. She waited for two minutes, then exited the facility, turning to her right to exit the side door. She waved to the guard and smiled and was twenty meters away from the building before she spoke.

"Where is that coffee shop? I want some of that jangulo everyone's talking about."

* * *

Wolfe and Scott heard several noises in the hallway before the electronic locks clicked open and Kyla Crist entered, accompanied by Mr. Blanks. Mr. Blanks was carrying a tray with food and drink.

"We don't want you to starve while you're in here," Crist said, trying to lighten the moment.

Wolfe returned a neutral gaze, while Scott crossed his arms on his chest. "We appreciate that. And the jangulo was quite good last night, Mr. Blanks. Thank you." Blanks set the tray on a small coffee table in the room, then stood back.

"You may as well sit down," Wolfe said. "We can't do anything to you, after all." Crist answered by sitting on a chair by the coffee table, while Mr. Blanks faded toward the door. Three cups sat on the tray. "You're joining us?"

"Just for tea," Crist answered. "I didn't sleep well last night and need to wake up."

Wolfe reached over and took the large pot and poured a cup for Crist. "That's interesting. We slept well."

"Well, you don't have the same concerns weighing on you that I do."

"You needn't go through those alone, minister," Wolfe said. "And you should have brought a cup for Mr. Blanks."

"I don't think Mr. Blanks ever eat or drinks; I believe he survives from breathing alone."

"Never while on the job, ma'am," Blanks said. Wolfe saw his mouth edge into a slight smile. *A sense of humor.*

Crist took a sip of her drink while Wolfe poured for her and Scott. Scott was wary as they waited. Finally, Crist looked up. "You've said over and over that you are interested in Amaeus joining the Federation. May I ask why?"

Wolfe hesitated. "Minister, we've told you we are from two member-worlds within the Central Federation. And we've further told you that membership in the Federation is an opportunity and one that pays dividends for its members." She glanced at Scott. "And knowing the Federation as I do, I know that what Amaeus has to offer is attractive, except for a sense that the planet is not as united in its desire for Federation membership as you might believe. The Federation doesn't affiliate with worlds where there is not significant, even overwhelming, interest in membership."

"And no significant opposition, I imagine."

"Exactly."

Crist put down her cup. "But my brother isn't in the opposition. There is an active opposition to Federation membership, but it's tiny, and many in the opposition tell me that their votes against affiliation had more to do with a single issue—taxes—and that they really do want the protection and collaboration that Federation membership offers."

"Just showing their strength through the vote?" Scott asked.

"Exactly!" Crist exclaimed. "They're no threat to the planet or our ability to continue as potential members of the Federation."

Wolfe sat back. "But your brother is."

"My brother—"

"And public opinion in the central desert region is shifting slowly; perhaps out of fear, or out of a genuine sense that joining the Federation would hurt them," Wolfe continued. "Nothing has happened on Amaeus to make you *more* attractive to the Federation in months."

Crist stood. "Who are you to lecture me about my planet and public opinion? Maybe instead of working for my brother you're spies from some other force or planet!"

"Do you believe we're working for your brother?" Wolfe asked.

"The news reports suggested you might be."

"That's not what I asked."

Crist shot a glance at Mr. Blanks, whose face was—blank. "I wouldn't say so. No. But that doesn't mean I can trust you."

"The fact that we're interested in helping Amaeus join the Central Federation doesn't change your mind?" Scott asked, his tone testy.

"Frankly, no. What's in it for you?"

"Does there have to be something in it for us?" Wolfe asked. "My colleague is right: our only interest is seeing Amaeus be successful in its application to join the Central Federation."

"No one is that altruistic."

Wolfe picked up her cup. "I'm beginning to see that." Wolfe took a sip from her cup then replaced it on the table. "This is very good." Wolfe looked again at Crist. "Minister, we've gotten in to see you twice with no difficulty. If we meant you or the planet harm, don't you think we could have done it and gotten clean away?"

"I can't answer that."

"I can. We came to you hoping you would help us approach Thorian Crist so we could stop him from hurting Amaeus's application to the Central Federation. The attack on the housing project is his first outside the central region, and these attacks may escalate. If you don't want them to continue, you have only to ask how we might help you."

"I am responsible for the safety and security of my region and this planet! Yet you give me cryptic pledges of help, saying you're only interested in us joining the Federation. I can keep you in here as long as I wish: you don't have many rights here as aliens." Crist's breathing was heavy as she exhausted herself.

Wolfe smiled. "Well, that's something the Federation wouldn't be happy about, but no matter. What does matter is we can't help you if we're locked in here—your choice."

Crist was deflated. "This is all confusing and unsettling. I need to think."

"We understand," Wolfe said, after glancing at Scott. "But trust your instincts. If we meant you harm, we could have done so days ago. Mr. Blanks can tell you that."

"I have to go," said Crist, distracted. "I need to decide what to do." She turned and walked toward the door as Mr. Blanks reset the electronic locks.

"Don't take too long, minister," Wolfe said to the retreating figure. "Time is of the essence."

* * *

"There's good news and bad news." Driscoll was presenting data from her search into the collaborative's security arrangements.

"Break it down for us, Ava," McLeod said.

Driscoll put a schematic on the screen in the ready room. "You can see the access route here, and the location of the holding area," she changed the photo to the lower level, "is in the basement, right here."

Carnahan got up from his seat and approached the screen, followed by McLeod. "I don't see the hard part, Ava. This seems straight forward: we hack into their security system to gain access, then head to the basement. What am I missing?"

"There's only one means of egress from the basement, for one," Driscoll replied. "But the biggest issue is I can't disable the security system remotely: I have to do it from inside the building." She turned to McLeod and Ross. "Or one of you will have to."

"Is it that hard to do?" Ross asked.

"No, ma'am, but I'm not sure it will work, plus you won't be able to enter the building with weapons because of their security scanners."

"So we'd be going in without weapons?" Ross asked. "That means we wouldn't have any greater ability to defend ourselves than Captain Wolfe and Sr. Altern Scott have."

"That's it," Driscoll said. "I haven't figure out the alternative yet."

"But you need to, Ava," McLeod said. "I don't go anywhere without at least one alternative." He turned to Shaw. "What are *Raven's* capabilities to handle this remotely, Goody? Can we take out some of their security capabilities from an aerial intrusion, then send the team in?"

"What do you mean?"

"Remote ability to jam signals long enough for us to gain access or to put a bug into their system—anything that can make gaining access quicker and allow us to enter with weapons."

"We have some ability to do that, sir, but we'd have to be close enough to do it, and that could compromise stealth."

"How about an independent drone?"

Shaw searched the table. "We could use one, but I don't know how much capability we could equip an "indro" with, or if it would be sufficient." He looked up at McLeod. "Let me think about it."

"Do it quickly. And the rest of you need to determine the best plans once we're inside. I don't want Captain Wolfe or Sr. Altern Scott in there any longer than necessary."

Chapter Seventeen

The mood inside the *Lance* was light. Few ships from the loose confederation of worlds that comprised the Shan Confederacy had the opportunity to bring new worlds into alignment with the Shan's goals. Landau sat in his conference room looking over the final plans for the latest attack on Amaeus. The victory already tasted sweet.

"How close to the central city will this be?"

"About four kilometers, sir," Bahira Massi replied. "Close enough to frighten them and close enough to rock even the collaborative building itself."

"I am only interested in scaring the Planetary Collaborative, Bahira. If they panic, it will infect the entire planet and may compromise our efforts. If we play this right, the battle can be won even before it begins." Landau noticed the face of Cleve Rubinco, *Lance's* communications officer. "Problem, Cleve?"

"No, sir. I should report to you, though, that the latest news reports say that two people are in custody for being in league with Thorian Crist. That may complicate things."

"Why?" Reed asked. "That just confirms the theory that Thorian Crist is behind everything."

"Not exactly, sir," Massi said. "If these people are working for Crist, they may convince the authorities that Crist didn't attack the housing project."

Landau sat back in his chair, thinking. *Is that possible? Could our plans have been commandeered by two new players?* "I should think that's unlikely," he said finally. "With our new target, there should be little doubt that Crist is behind it, regardless of who is in custody."

"You seem sure of that, sir," Reed said.

"That's the difference between you and me, Jolon." Landau smiled. "I know exactly what I'm saying and what's happening around me. Something for you to think about."

"Yes, sir."

"Back to the task at hand," Landau continued. "Describe the target and how we'll strike."

Massi showed a point on the screen in the map of the central city. "The energy storage facility is located underground here. It's heavily guarded and shielded, but there are weaknesses that we can exploit."

"How easily?" Reed asked.

"With little difficulty, sir," Massi replied. "The point will be to move onto the facility with overwhelming force. We can lob two missiles from a remote location ten kilometers away from the target. While that will give their people time to retaliate, that's not what they're geared up to do: they are best prepared for a frontal attack at one of the entrances."

Landau frowned. "How many entrances, Bahira?"

"Six. They have double redundancy walls and plenty of security. But one thing Crist and his general are masters at is knowing how to distract and misdirect. We're following his lead, so we'll do the same."

Massi moved a light over the southeast entrance, marking a circle around the door. "We can lob the missile toward a specific door at a predetermined time. By doing that, we'll draw people away from other entrances and be able to breach another door." She looked up at Landau. "We're prepared to breach any of the remaining doors, sir. We only need one."

"What weapons will you use?"

"The same ones we used at the housing project: grenades and penetrating mortars. They're easy to transport and to set. The projectiles will sink into the floor, then damage the storage pods: that's what leads to the big explosion. We can be as close as fifty meters away and be safe."

Reed sat up. "Wait a minute, Bahira. What's our casualty exposure?"

"Less than ten percent: it's a very safe operation."

Landau noticed Reed's brow and laughed. "You haven't gone soft on us, have you, Jolon? That's an acceptable risk."

"It is, sir. I'm just thinking about those two prisoners in the central city. I still consider them to be wildcards."

Landau waved his hand impatiently. "There is nothing to worry about, Jolon, that's the one thing we have under control." Landau sat back and addressed his weapons officer. "Bahira, how do you propose we get the strike teams to the surface? We have to be careful of air security, particularly around the central city."

"Tal?" Massi asked, speaking to the helmsman. Tal Vereen was a lanky man who didn't waste time on words. "Two pods, one east of the city and the other at the edge of the central desert. They move in from those directions on mark of the commander."

"Were we to leave in—" Landau checked the time, "three hours, how long until the diversionary strike?"

"Six more hours, sir," Massi said. "That gives time for each of the teams at the secondary doors to be in position. That's plenty of time."

"Can you assemble in three hours?"

"I can do it in two and a half."

* * *

"Given the challenges of this situation, Minty, I'm surprised you're back so quickly," McLeod said.

Ross smiled. "Yes, sir. There weren't any alternatives, so Commander Shaw adopted your suggestion."

"The indro?"

"Yes," Carnahan said. "Commander Shaw's confident it can work. The indro just needed minor adjustments so it can stick close to the buildings to avoid surveillance cameras. He even sent one out about an hour ago, with positive results."

"And?"

Shaw smiled. "The indro behaved perfectly, sir. And we've learned enough about the surveillance cameras to duplicate its success now."

"Commander Shaw also configured it to transmit the proper sequence of codes and frequencies to jam the security system from outside the building—at least long enough for us to gain entry and plug into the ports," Ross added. "It was amazing."

"Let's hope it stays that way. Will this allow us to bring in weapons and tools past the checkpoint?"

"We believe so, sir," Carnahan answered after receiving a nod from Ross. "You'll have several plug-ins in case one is discovered. Once that happens—if it does, you'll implement Plan B. There's a temporary shelter in this basement level storage room, right here." Carnahan pointed to the screen behind McLeod. "We can't find out what's in it based on these schematics, but I believe it can be a temporary refuge until you can gain entry to the cells."

McLeod stopped for a moment, then rose and approached the screen. For a minute, he traced his finger along corridors, looking at size and distance. Finally, he turned to Ross. "So head in one of these doors toward the rear, then down this corridor to the stairs, then to the holding area?"

"That's it."

"And is this the storage room?"

"Yes, sir," Ross said. "Far enough away that our breach isn't obvious, yet close enough to give you an escape."

McLeod nodded. "This is a good plan, people. And you're confident, given the stakes and the challenges of the operation?"

"Yes, sir. Chief Carnahan and I have worked all the angles. Whatever could be planned has been planned."

McLeod smiled. "Is there an alternative plan of action?"

He smiled. "Of course, sir." Ross pointed to the screen. "We can work ourselves to the basement through this secondary door here. It's not as neat, but it still allows us to access the basement through this side shaft."

McLeod followed Ross's logic. "Understood. Everything beyond this alternative plan is seat of the pants, then?"

"That's it," Ross said.

McLeod stood and brushed his suit glancing at Gordon. "Your ship, Goody."

"Aye, sir."

* * *

Vereen looked up from the helm. "In position for the drop, sir. Both pods can be dropped now, with estimated touch down in twenty minutes."

"Steady as she goes, Tal." Reed turned to Landau. "Has Massi done anything like this before?"

Landau shook his body as if he had a chill. "She's done this too many times to even think about, Jolon. That woman scares me sometimes with her clinical approach to death."

"But nothing to worry about?"

"Nothing. Once they touch down, it's only a matter of time. The only hard part will be the extraction, but we have plenty of time for that." Landau turned to Rubinco. "Drop the pods at will."

"Aye, sir."

* * *

"Indro launched, sir," Shaw said. "And working well so far."

"Very well," McLeod said, his voice tinny over the speaker. "Commander Ross and I have exited and are moving toward the central city now."

"Any problem with the weapons?"

"None. Their size and configuration make them easy to hide." He looked back at *Raven*, calculating the distance. "We'll be out of range soon, Goody, at least with the organic earpieces. If we need anything else, we know how to find you."

"Yes, sir. And good luck."

* * *

"Strike teams close to their locations, sir," Rubinco said. "They should be able to commence in fifteen minutes."

Landau smiled. "Excellent. Has Massi reported?"

"Yes, sir."

"Tell her to move at will, Cleve. We needn't string this out any longer than necessary."

"Aye, sir."

"Feeling confident, captain?" Reed asked.

"Of course! Aren't you?"

Reed smiled. "I am, sir. I'm just aware that things can still go wrong." He frowned. "How long until our strike teams can meet at the rendezvous point?"

Landau looked to Vereen. "What do you recall about that, Tal?"

Vereen checked his console before turning around. "Taking into account travel time and terrain, approximately twelve hours once they start walking, so perhaps up to fifteen."

"Good," Landau said. "Make sure we're in the prescribed position before that time." Instead of answering, Vereen only nodded his head.

* * *

"Strike teams report," came the crisp voice of Bahira Massi. Her team coordinating the initial mortar strike against the energy storage facility had been in place for twenty minutes, and she was pacing in her normal impatient manner.

"Team one in position," came a voice.

"Team two in position," came the second.

"Team three location," the voice hesitated. "Half a kilometer from strike position."

"Acknowledged," Massi said. "Team four?"

"Also half a kilometer out, ma'am," came the final strike team leader's voice. "We can be in position and ready to move in ten minutes."

Massi checked the time and looked at her team, all of whom were ready. "Strike team three," Massi began, "Is ten minutes sufficient for you as well?"

"Yes, ma'am. We're making easy progress."

"Very well. Initial attack will be in twelve minutes at 1920 hours; strike teams move to the doors after the mortar attack and enter the facility two minutes later on your own marks. Acknowledge."

The voices of the four strike team leaders acknowledged her commands and Massi settled back to wait, smiling. *I do love this too much.*

* * *

Only a block away from the planetary collaborative building, McLeod and Ross walked confidently around the central city streets. They could still communicate with *Raven* through their link with the indro, but there was a half second delay because of the relay.

"Progress on the indro and security, Goody?" McLeod's tone was even.

"It shouldn't take more than five or ten minutes, sir. Location is on Liston Street?"

"Yes, less than a block away from our objective." McLeod gestured to Ross, pointing to the street that led to the side entrance. Ross nodded and they changed direction.

"We're shifting to the side street now, Goody."

"Aye, sir." McLeod and Ross continued down Liston, sensing the indro as they went. No one paid them any attention during the rush hour pedestrian traffic. As they examined the side door to the collaborative, they heard Gordon Shaw's voice.

"Indro in place. Stand by."

McLeod and Ross shifted closer to the building and took out their credentials and security badges for the collaborative. They approached the side door and waited until they heard a series of clicks in their earpieces.

"System down and access granted," Shaw said. "Time for the show."

"Acknowledged. McLeod out." He inclined his head toward the door, and McLeod and Ross opened the door, McLeod in the lead.

* * *

At 1920 hours, Raina Wolfe heard the click of the electronic locks on her room in the holding area of the planetary collaborative and watched Kyla Crist walk in.

"Good evening, minister," Wolfe said, smiling at the younger woman. "To be honest, you don't look any better than you did this morning." Scott moved from his chair and invited Crist to sit.

Crist rubbed her eyes. "I'm not feeling very well. Today was a difficult one for the planetary collaborative, trying to pick up the pieces from the recent attack at the housing project." Crist looked up. "That took place in our western region."

"Is there any doubt that Thorian Crist was responsible?" Scott asked.

Crist sighed. "None. Or at least very little. It has all of Thorian's trademarks, though I don't believe him responsible."

"Why?" Wolfe asked.

Crist moved her hands, trying to speak. "Because Thorian has adopted some kind of pact with the desert. He views himself as the anointed protector of the desert and much of the central region. He is very self-directed and motivated by profit, but he doesn't care much for people or interests outside of his region." She looked up. "That's one reason he opposes Zahara so fiercely: she's the one who first proposed applying for Central Federation membership. Thorian felt betrayed since they had worked on a few projects and initiatives together. He sees her as the ultimate traitor."

"And you don't think he would conduct an attack outside of the central region?" Scott asked. "Pardon me, but that seems a bit naive, minister."

Wolfe wasn't happy with Scott's tone, but agreed with his sentiment. She turned to Crist. "My colleague has a point, minister. Who knows how desperate he might get if he felt he was losing ground in his effort to scuttle your Federation application."

Crist deflated in her chair. "Maybe I just don't want to believe he might have attacked that project, but perhaps that is naive, as you say. But I can't give up hope."

"Hope can be your comfort, minister," Wolfe said. "But it can't be ours."

* * *

Once inside the planetary collaborative building, McLeod and Ross assembled their weapons, leaving the cases by the side entrance, then attaching the small weapons and flash grenades to their clothing. They turned and walked toward the right toward the secondary stairs to the basement. They passed small groups of personnel within the collaborative without acknowledgment on either side. McLeod realized the collaborative couldn't have weapons detectors within the building because their security people would set them off constantly. *All the better.*

Once at the bottom the stairs, McLeod followed Ross's finger as she pointed to the only door with a secondary lock on top. Nodding, McLeod walked toward the door, his hand closed around his first plug-in. He pressed the small box into the port and waited for the signal that the code had been breached. Twenty seconds later, the two green lights on the plug-in made him smile. Ross held up her hand, motioning to McLeod to follow her lead, and opened the door to the holding area hallway. Neither of them could hear anything through the heavy doors except the low hum of the air conditioning system. Ross took out her first plug-in and approached the port at the first door. A scant few seconds later, they heard the soft click of the door, braced themselves, and slid the heavy door to one side, where they saw the startled face of Kyla Crist having tea with Raina Wolfe and Trevor Scott.

"Well, you could have waited for us, Raina." McLeod was smiling.

"Sorry. No coffee, just tea," Wolfe said as she rose.

McLeod bowed to Kyla Crist. "Minister. It's good to make your acquaintance." He returned his gaze to Wolfe, asking, "Are you ready?"

"Yes and no."

McLeod said nothing, just inclined his head while searching Wolfe's eyes. "We're having trouble convincing the minister of our good intentions, Tucker."

"Which is why we're here to rescue you."

"Who *are* you people?" Crist asked, regaining her confidence. "And how did you get past our security arrangements? I'm going to—"

McLeod raised his hand and moved forward. Crist stopped talking, giving in to fear. "We're not here to harm you, minister: quite the contrary. We are trying to reduce or eliminate the threat of your brother's influence on this planet, and help Amaeus gain admittance to the Central Federation, but you don't seem inclined to help us."

"Because she won't guarantee my brother's safety! What kind of person do you think I am?"

"We think you are a person who is troubled and torn about your responsibilities to your family and to your planet," Wolfe offered. "And we appreciate that. But my associates and I don't have the luxury of waiting for you."

Crist's voice was almost a whisper. "Are you going to kill me?"

McLeod and Wolfe shared a quick glance before McLeod said, "Of course not, minister. We are here to help promote peace, but—"

"With weapons and a means to evade our security systems! That is not promoting peace!"

McLeod stood over her again. "And you could just as easily have let my friends go. We're not leaving them behind. Make of that what you will."

"This is getting us nowhere," Wolfe said. "Minister, if we haven't convinced you of our intentions, we'll just do things our own way."

"But we can't countenance violence on our planet by outsiders! How would it look if I'm seen helping aliens interfere in our government's affairs?"

McLeod was suddenly weary. "Minister, did you even ask my colleagues how they hoped to reduce your brother's influence in Amaean politics? And do you really believe we shouldn't defend ourselves against someone if they attacked us? The attack on the housing project—outside of the central desert, I might add—should convince you that your brother is out to cause dissension and conflict in Amaean politics and on the planet. He needs to be stopped—or at least contained."

As McLeod finished speaking, Wolfe approached Crist again. "Minister, our objectives are your objectives. And achieving those objectives are not only our aims, but they are our orders."

"Are you some kind of—"

"That's all I can say, minister. And it may have been too much."

Crist sat down shaking her head from side to side. "This is too much for me to deal with right now."

Wolfe sat next to her and touched her arm. "You can handle it, minister. You are the youngest minister on the planetary collaborative: you must have a talent for this sort of thing."

Despite herself, Crist smiled. "I suppose I do." Looking up, she added, "But what do I do now?"

"What our team does now is leave this building to continue our mission," McLeod replied. "We don't expect you to—"

But McLeod's voice was muffled by a huge concussion that rocked the foundation of the planetary collaborative and threw the five of them to the floor.

Chapter Eighteen

News of the attack against the energy storage facility reached the Crist Enterprises compound mere minutes after the attack. Thorian Crist sat in his office watching the news reports and seething.

"What is going *on* here?" he screamed as his inner circle joined him. "We are losing control of the situation, and that is unacceptable!"

Crist's lieutenants looked around the table at each other, no one daring to speak first. Crist rose and walked from behind his desk to the conference table, looking into each face. "We are at a crisis; someone is threatening our victory, and this is all you can do? You're pathetic." Still, his lieutenants were silent.

Victor Ansara was the first to speak. "Again, sir, I wonder what the harm is? Hear me out. So far, no one has connected this attack with us, so it may not harm our public position." Gaining momentum, Ansara was more animated. "If this results in more unease among the people, and less confidence in the collaborative, that plays into our hands."

"That's what I thought, too," Bokari began, "but—"

"So you want some other force to be in control on Amaeus when the collaborative is defeated? Have you people lost your minds?" Crist struggled to control himself. "The only way to ensure the future we want is to create it ourselves. Now, are you with me on this or not?" Bokari's and Menzel's eyes widened for a second before they regained their calm.

"I'm waiting."

"We're with you, sir," Maddox said, a grim set to her face. "But we are trying to build the right future for the planet. And the problem—"

"Someone is taking our future away from us, Cole, and—"

"—any reason to believe Thorian Crist might be behind this attack on the facility, Rando? As we understand it, the authorities are still looking through the rubble and confirming the casualties. There is always the possibility that Crist has stepped up his attacks, and the investigators will look to see if the method of attack and the explosives used implicate him."

"What's your best guess, Rando?"

"To be honest, Ben, the only entity launching these kinds of attacks in the last few months has been Crist or people connected with him. I can't say anything else."

"Thank you, Rando. And that is the status of the investigation. We will bring you updates as they become available through ITC news."

Ansara rose and turned off the vid screen. He turned back to Crist, his hands in surrender. "Sir, before we go any further, we need to conduct our own investigation. We should—"

"Victor, I respect your judgments and your dedication," Crist began, "but those decisions are mine to make."

"Of course, sir." Ansara backed away, resuming his seat. "This was just a suggestion."

Crist resumed his pacing. "We have not come this far just to come this far. We are committed to autonomy and freedom for Amaeus, but that means we need to control how that is implemented. The collaborative has abandoned Amaean autonomy to join the Central Federation." He faced his team again. "And if someone else is controlling these attacks rather than us, can't you see that we are no better off?"

After a few seconds, Maddox said, "I see that, sir. We will be at someone else's mercy if we don't find out what is going on, and—"

"And control what happens and how it happens," Crist added. "That's why this second attack is particularly unacceptable. It is our job to make sure that Amaeus maintains its autonomy. That is our job, and anyone who opposes us is the enemy: the planetary collaborative is the enemy, and whoever is conducting these attacks is the enemy, and I will not stand for it." Crist saw approving nods and agreement around the table.

"And now that we are in agreement, what do we do about it?"

* * *

Jolon Reed saw the smile on Tyrus Landau's face. Landau was content as he consulted with his bridge personnel after the attack on the energy storage facility.

Landau returned to his seat and turned to Reed. "Are you still not happy, Jolon? I would think you would revel in this."

Reed smiled. "I am, sir. Everything is going well, plus the latest news reports have suggested that Crist attacked the facility, which is what we wanted."

"But?"

"No buts, sir. I'm always a little nervous when so many of our security and strike personnel are off the ship."

Landau sat back in his command chair. "Well, that makes sense at least." He turned to Vereen. "Hours until we can rendezvous with the strike team?"

"We're right on schedule, sir," Vereen said. "Another twelve hours should do it." Vereen smiled. "We just need to be patient."

"I get it, Tal, and I will try not to ask you again."

Vereen chuckled. "I've known you too long, sir."

Reed sat for a minute, then turned again to Landau. "Given that we are on schedule and we have successfully implicated Crist, sir, my suggestion is that we hold for a few days to see what happens."

Landau was already nodding. "I agree, Jolon." He looked up. "Just give me the chance to gloat a little."

"I understand sir," Reed said, who still thought there were things his commanding officer wasn't telling him.

* * *

"What was that?" asked Kyla Crist, disentangling herself from McLeod. The light had flickered in the holding area, then returned, and she was trying to reorient herself.

Wolfe, Ross, and Scott were already on their feet, looking into corners of the room and checking the hallway outside the holding cell for security personnel.

"No way of knowing, minister," Wolfe replied. "It's possible it was a direct attack on the planetary collaborative building." Wolfe looked around the room, assessing whether the building was on emergency or regular power. "But given the concussion, I think a direct attack would have caused much more damage."

Ross nodded her head. "I agree, ma'am. But I also don't want to wait around for somebody to try again."

"Agreed," McLeod said. "We need to exit now." McLeod turned to Wolfe and Scott, reaching into his jacket and producing two small devices, handing each of them one. "Minty has your earpieces."

Wolfe took her stun weapon and smiled, noticing its light weight. "More engineering by Frankie?"

"She thought you'd like it." McLeod moved toward the door. He looked at Crist. "We are leaving now, minister. Last opportunity for us to work together."

Crist looked at Wolfe, still disoriented. "I don't know what to do."

"We understand, minister," Wolfe said. "But we know exactly what we have to do."

Wolfe turned to follow McLeod when Crist stopped her. "Wait. Maybe we should go to my office and speak. I mean, the only reason you're in custody is because I put you there: I can remove you from custody if I want."

McLeod frowned but said, "The clock is ticking, Raina—your call."

Wolfe searched Crist's eyes, then turned to McLeod. "We go to the office."

McLeod stood aside at the door. "Lead the way, minister."

* * *

The Planetary Collaborative employees were confused and frightened, and while security personnel urged calm, most staff members were talking in the hallways, getting no work done at all. Many were surprised to see Kyla Crist leading people they hadn't seen before. Crist smiled as she greeted them and urged calm, trying to allay their fears. McLeod, Raina, and the other *Raven* personnel did the same, smiling as they walked down the hallways. They climbed one set of stairs and entered a large hallway off of which were several office doors. Crist opened her office door and led the way in.

Her administrative assistant rose as she entered. "Minister," the young woman began, "we were worried about you and the blast. Do you know what's going on?"

"I don't. Have you heard from Minister Ali?"

"No, ma'am. I spoke with her admin just before you arrived. Minister Ali left the building for another appointment right after your last open meeting."

Crist followed the eyes of her administrative assistant to the people standing behind her.

"Oh. These are some—" she hesitated, "constituents and reporters I was going to talk to. We'll be in my office."

"Yes, ma'am. Shall I bring refreshments for you?"

"No. Just find out what's going on, please." Without waiting for an answer, Crist opened her office door and ushered McLeod, Wolfe, Ross, and Scott inside. She sat behind her desk, and eyed them, a stern look on her face. "I need to know more about you and what you're doing on this planet."

"That, minister, is a long story," McLeod said, "and we don't have time for it right now. But we've told you repeatedly of our support for Amaeus's application to join the Federation."

"So you've said. And how do I know you weren't behind that explosion?"

"Again, minister—" Wolfe began, but she stopped when Mr. Blanks entered the office.

"Minister." Blanks stopped when he saw Wolfe and Scott. He returned his attention to Crist. "I came here to see how you were doing and tell you what we know about the blast." Blanks stood stiffly, surveying the faces of the others.

"Thank you, Mr. Blanks."

Crist waved Mr. Blanks toward a chair, but instead, he walked to stand at the side of Crist's desk, eyeing the outsiders"With these people here, minister, I—"

Crist shrugged. "You may speak, Mr. Blanks. It will likely make little difference at this point."

Blanks squared his shoulders. "The blast was an attack on the energy storage facility in the eastern region."

"The facility that holds the tullarium reserves?"

Blanks nodded. "Yes, ma'am. There was at first a blast on the main entrance which brought more of the security personnel there to contain it. The full breach came through the second and third entrances."

Crist blinked. "How was it done, I mean, was it an attack from the air?"

"No. They used penetrating mortars." Blanks noticed Crist's frown. "They are placed into the ground and then shoot projectiles into the ground which later explode."

"I don't understand."

"This method ensures that the explosives penetrate deeper into the ground, bringing much greater destruction than a normal bomb would do. Someone wanted those energy stores destroyed and unavailable for use by anyone or anything else." Blanks stopped and pressed his lips together. "And while these weapons aren't uncommon, an attack on the tullarium stores suggests that someone wants to keep us from accessing them."

"Which are primarily used for weapons, I take it?"

"That's one major use, yes." Blanks turned his head toward the *Raven* crew, then faced Crist again. "And if you don't mind my saying so, ma'am, is it wise for the prisoners to be out of the holding area during a time such as this? They may have coordinated this attack."

"I don't think they would be here if that were the case, Mr. Blanks. Would you position yourself so close to a blast area if you had planned it?"

Mr. Blanks only shrugged his shoulders in response and continued looking at and assessing the *Raven* personnel.

"I think not," Crist offered. Then she sat back in her chair. "And I think we should find out more about this attack before we make any more assumptions."

"I understand, minister," said Mr. Blanks. "But we must get you and the other ministers out of the building in case there is an attack planned for the collaborative."

"We can't run in fear from attacks, Mr. Blanks. How can we encourage confidence in the populace if we run whenever something like this happens?"

McLeod cleared his throat. "This gentleman is correct, minister. Regardless of how much you want to show confidence for the people, you can't do that if you're dead."

Mr. Blanks stared at McLeod, saying nothing. He finally turned his gaze once again to Crist. "We have a car waiting for you. It will leave at the rear entrance as soon as you arrive." He pointed to the prisoners with his hand. "And I must insist again that the prisoners be returned to custody, either here or somewhere else."

"Thank you, Mr. Blanks, but I take full responsibility." She rose and Mr. Blanks bowed and walked toward the door. The room was silent until he closed the door behind him.

"We can continue this conversation at your personal residence, minister," McLeod offered. "Unless you have determined you don't want to speak with us anymore. If so, we're wasting time, and if this latest attack is any sign, we need to act quickly in the central desert."

"Are you suggesting that my brother was behind this attack as well?" Crist was incredulous. "You are just like the rest of the collaborative and half the news people, accusing him of everything that goes wrong on Amaeus. I should have—"

"With all due respect, minister," Scott said, "even this conversation should take place in another location, don't you think?"

Crist regained her self-control and nodded.

"Good," McLeod said. "Now if you will lead the way toward the rear entrance, we'll get out of here."

Crist led the group toward the rear staircase, which McLeod knew led to the rear entrance of the collaborative. None of them noticed Mr. Blanks, who came out of an adjoining office and watched them walk down the hallway. He took out a small comm device, beginning a call as they disappeared from sight.

"Yes," said Mr. Blanks. "She is leaving the building now." Blanks nodded his head several times, adding "correct," and "yes, sir." He ended with "I'll make it happen." Resetting the device, Mr. Blanks began a more complicated series of calls.

As the group exited the doors, they saw three transport vehicles waiting for them. Crist began walking toward the closest one when McLeod stopped her. "Not that one, minister. Come with us." McLeod led the group down the street toward the main entrance, hailing a transport on his own.

At first resistant, Crist asked, "Why all of this? Our transport has been arranged!"

"Please just follow us, minister," Wolfe said. "We know how these things go." She looked again at Crist. "Please." Crist relented, then followed Wolfe to the waiting vehicle. Wolfe gave the driver their destination.

"That's not—" Crist said, but a look from Wolfe silenced her. She sat among the four strangers, not knowing if she was making a grave error, but she stayed silent. The group arrived at the destination, and Crist noticed McLeod used an Amaean X card to pay the fare. The group exited the transport and began walking toward Crist's home two blocks away.

At the last turn before heading to her home, McLeod, who had been in the lead, changed direction, indicating with his head something near

Crist's home. Wolfe, Ross, and Scott followed his lead and continued walking, the minister between them.

"They may not have seen her," Ross said.

"Who is—"

"Shh," Wolfe said as she picked up the pace. McLeod soon hailed another transport and the group entered that vehicle when they heard a loud voice.

"Minister Kyla Crist, we are authorized by the Planetary Collaborative to take you into custody for—"

Crist was shocked at the man's words, but was then blinded by a bright light engulfing the security forces near her home. McLeod urged the transport driver to move at the touch of metal to his neck, giving him the spaceport as their destination. He then turned to Crist. "We can talk about this later, but we saw the security personnel even before they addressed you: we couldn't take the chance they wouldn't listen to reason." Then McLeod held up his hand, again asking for Crist's silence. He touched his ear and began speaking.

"Goody, prepare an additional berth for a guest. We experienced a little friction and pushback from the collaborative. More details when we arrive. McLeod out."

They arrived at the spaceport a difficult ten minutes later, and McLeod led the group through the main building, then to the annex where *Raven* was docked in its freighter form. Ushering Crist into the ship, McLeod smiled. "Welcome to our humble abode, minister." Crist walked into the entry way of *Raven* and frowned, noticing the inside of the ship didn't match the scarred exterior.

"I don't understand," Crist began, both weary and compliant. Then she stood straighter and balled her hands into fists. "I have been kind and understanding with all of you, which has gotten me into even more trouble and allowed you to lead me away, and—"

"Later, minister," McLeod said. He touched a button on the console of the entrance. "Goody, we need to head up: there's likely to be some commotion on the surface around *Raven,* and we can't take the chance of being noticed."

"Yes, sir."

"Minister," Wolfe offered. "We need to take our seats. Let me help you." She led the way up a ladder and onto the bridge. Kyla Crist trudged behind Wolfe, noticing all the people in odd, unmatching dress, who nevertheless acted like a military unit.

What have I gotten myself into? she thought to herself.

* * *

"Again, how can we keep the collaborative unsteady and vulnerable?" Thorian Crist said, rising from the table and flexing his hands into fists. "We must develop a plan, and *now.*" He turned to Bokari. "Now, tell me what is happening in the planetary collaborative: Victor, Wen."

Bokari shuddered. "Yes, sir. Their expulsion of your sister has created a rift among the ministers. There are two—Leyla Hill and Takoda Marten—who are urging caution, while—"

"While Zahara Ali and Ian Anoki still insist on a strong response?"

"That's our belief, sir. We'll continue whittling away at Ali's support in the central region to force the vote."

"But will it be enough? And if not, how else will we—" Crist grew agitated again, looking at the walls as his team spoke.

The usually timid Wen Bokari took Crist's silence as an invitation to continue. "You talk about getting the support of the people, sir," Bokari continued. "But if all we do is attack targets, we develop fear within the people, not their support."

Crist raised his hand to stop Bokari. "I agree with you, Wen. Before we talk about other initiatives, we need to understand what is going on with these attacks." He rose. "And so far, none of you know what the hell is going on."

"But if—" Bokari began, but Maddox held him back with a shake of her head. Bokari looked back up at Crist.

Crist gave Bokari a cold stare. "Someone, or some organization, is attacking targets in our name, and while they are hurting the collaborative's support among the people, they can't be trusted to be in line with our objectives. Therefore, they are a threat, do you agree?" Crist turned again to Bokari. "And only once we regain the initiative in this effort can we entertain the community activities and organizing that Wen is proposing. Fair enough, Wen?"

"Yes, sir."

Crist looked at Cordell. "Elvin, please take care of the previous mission I gave you. We can't afford to be left out of this one."

Cordell rose. "Yes, sir. I will report once we have additional information."

"Good," Crist said. "Now, where was I?"

"If our current efforts are not enough—on the vote, I believe you meant," Ansara said.

"Yes. We should plan the next part of the operation in case the vote does not go our way." Crist sat down again and pondered. "And once we have the vote, what then? I have no interest in governing, just in maintaining our financial independence." He shook himself. "No matter—there are plenty of people who will want to rule once the current ministers are discredited, including my lovely sister."

Crist's lieutenants looked at each other and said nothing.

Chapter Nineteen

McLeod and Wolfe slid into their seats on the bridge as Ross and Scott brought Kyla Crist behind them. McLeod inclined his head toward a seat near his and directed Ross to her usual station. "Have a seat here, minister. The fun is just starting."

"We have the latest news reports, captains," Driscoll said. "Shall I put them onto the screen?"

"Given what it's likely to show, yes." Wolfe turned to Crist. "This won't make you happy, minister, but these actions were in place long before we arrived." Crist nodded her head, already fearing what would come.

"The explosion is being blamed on Thorian Crist, owner of the largest tullarium holdings on the planet. Authorities believe he is sabotaging the tullarium storage facility to force up the price. And in another report from the planetary collaborative, Acting Chair Minister Ian Anoki issued a recorded statement with two other ministers of the Planetary Collaborative which we will play for you now.

'It pains us to report that Minister Kyla Crist was last seen in the company of several prisoners who escaped from the detention center in the planetary collaborative. While we do not know what happened with this group or Minister Crist, we must issue a censure of our colleague and a directive that she be brought in for questioning. Citizens with any information about Minister Kyla Crist are urged to contact local police authorities. And while we have no information that links Minister Crist to the recent attack on the energy storage facility in the eastern region, we urge caution when making contact with Minister Crist.'

"Our news service will continue to update you on the status of the search for Minister Kyla Crist and for the cause and details of the attack on the energy—"

"Turn it off, Ava," McLeod said. "As Raina said, minister, this was moving even before our arrival, and—"

"But your presence has made things *worse* instead of better. Now I am disgraced and connected even more closely to my brother." She looked up at McLeod, looking far older than her thirty-eight years. "And I have you to thank for it, whoever you are."

Wolfe and McLeod shared a glance, after which McLeod nodded.

"Everything we've told you is true" Wolfe said. "Except that we are a joint team from the Central Federation and the Star Alliance, and—"

"The Star Alliance?" Crist asked. "But why? We have no connection of any kind with the Star Alliance!"

"True. But the Central Federation and the Star Alliance work together to promote peace across the galaxy. We also cooperate when planets whose applications for membership in either organization are promising, but have issues that need to be resolved before they can be approved."

"Then they send in a bunch of troublemakers like you?"

Wolfe smiled. "None of us provoked or conducted attacks on the housing project or the energy storage facility, minister. And whether your brother or another person directed those attacks, we are here to help eliminate that threat from Amaeus."

"But why? What's in it for you?"

McLeod rose and stared at Crist. "We've said this one too many times, but we do it because it matters to us. And if you don't understand that, I can't explain it any better." McLeod turned and approached Driscoll. "Ava, please monitor communications from the collaborative and from the Crist compound. We need to know what's going on there."

"Aye, sir. The collaborative may be a problem, though: they've put new signal jammers in place. I can get around them, but it will take time. The Crist compound won't be a problem."

"Any reason for us to change our configuration?"

Driscoll shook her head. "No, sir. There's nothing in the news reports about our presence at the spaceport: no one's looking for us." Driscoll looked at her commanding officer. "We can always shift to another configuration when we return."

"Good point." McLeod resumed his seat. He looked again at Crist, and his face softened. "Minister, we did our own reconnaissance at the housing project, and found no evidence that your brother's forces moved from his compound in the hours before the attack."

"What?"

"I said we couldn't find evidence that anyone from the Crist compound moved to the housing project to conduct the attack."

"But that means nothing. Thorian has holdings all over the central desert."

"We checked all of them," Wolfe said. "We know he could have moved his forces long before the attack, so this evidence doesn't mean much."

"But it tells us that another force may be trying to build resistance or fear among the people," McLeod offered. "And whether that has anything to do with the Federation application is unknown."

Crist sat back in her seat, looking around at the faces and backs of the *Raven* crew. "Why is this so complicated?"

"Because it is," McLeod said. "And it won't do for us to complain about it. If we believe we can't help Amaeus succeed in its bid for Federation membership, we'll report that to our superiors."

"Our original objective was to prevent Thorian Crist from hurting Amaeus's chances for Federation membership," Wolfe said. "But as you said, now it's even more complicated, and we're not leaving until we have answers."

"You want answers," said Crist. "*I* want answers. I want to know where Zahara Ali was during the attack, I want to know about the storage facility, how Ian Anoki found out we were leaving the building and—"

"The security person—Mr. Blanks," Wolfe said. "He told Anoki."

"But he's the one who arranged our transport, and—"

McLeod sighed. "He was going to arrest you then, or at least when you got to your home."

"But he's always—"

"He was doing his job, minister," Wolfe said. "Like him or not, he was just doing his job, so let's not dwell on Mr. Blanks or his motives."

Crist's eyes fell to her lap. "Will I ever go home? There is still so much to do."

Wolfe placed her hand on Crist's shoulder. "And that's why we're here to help you."

* * *

Thorian Crist watched the news reports in shock. He knew his sister well and had never considered her his ally. The news reports were mistaken. He turned to see his lieutenants sitting at the table, waiting for him.

"And what do we have here?" Crist asked. "Can someone please explain to me how this attack was made in our name and how my sister was implicated?"

"She is not our friend, sir," said Ansara. "She has pushed as hard as anyone for Federation membership."

"And she's supported raising taxes, just like the rest of the collaborative," said Crist. "But to suggest that she is allied with us or involved in an attack against the collaborative is folly."

"This makes no sense to me," Bokari said.

"I think it's that Ali woman," Cordell said as he entered the room and sat down. "She's been outspoken in opposition to business expansion and self determination for this planet. She could be attacking her own facilities to implicate us and your sister."

"Hah!" Crist's voice was a sneer. "I've known Ali for a long time, and I wouldn't put it past her." He raised his finger. "And how convenient it was that Zahara Ali was away from the collaborative building during the attack?"

"The attack wasn't directed against the collaborative, sir," Maddox said. "They just got hit from the concussion, or whatever it's called."

"Concussion," Cordell confirmed.

"Perhaps, Cole. But that doesn't eliminate her from the equation." Crist sat back and smiled. "Maybe what we ought to do is to bring about more dissension *within* the collaborative."

"What do you mean?" Ansara asked.

"Kyla Crist is on the outs now, since she was practically named as a co-conspirator along with us. What if we conducted another attack and implicated Zahara Ali for that one?"

Bokari's eyes widened. "How? She's done nothing against the collaborative."

"Neither has my sister and look what happened to her. Besides, it needn't be an actual attack. We can just distribute news reports reminding people that Ali wasn't in the building at the time of the attack, or that she was seen on several occasions having private conversations with my sister."

"Collaborative members do that all the time," Bokari replied. "What's different about Ali and your sister doing it?"

Ansara smiled as he raised his hand to Bokari. "It's the appearance of something that matters, Wen. If people are told something is shaky or suspect, they begin to believe it." He turned to Crist. "We can do that through our staff, sir." Ansara glanced at Cordell and smiled. "It will be child's play."

* * *

"You believe we ought to stop for now, Jolon?" asked Landau.

Reed looked at his commanding officer, confident in his conclusions. "I do, sir. We need to analyze the fallout from the attacks. I agree that so far our actions have hurt the collaborative and their goals."

"Explain your best understanding of the situation on-planet."

"Yes, sir." Reed checked his notes. "The news reports have connected the attack on the energy storage facility to Thorian Crist. The unexpected bonus is they've also implicated Kyla Crist, so she's on the run with several other people, too."

"That's what worries me," said Landau. Seeing the confusion on Reed's face, he added, "because we don't know who those people are. They could be terrorists themselves, or people connected to a group protesting against the government."

"What difference does it make, as long as it gets Kyla Crist out of the way?"

Landau brushed Reed's comment aside. "I don't like loose ends or things I can't explain. And until we have more information, I'm not lowering our alert." Landau smiled. "But I understand your concerns about our security and strike personnel being off the ship, and I agree we should hold fast for a day or so."

"Thank you, sir," said Reed, who turned to Rubinco. "Cleve, what is the status of communications to and from the planet?"

"I'm being careful, sir. I'm only using short bursts of signals to avoid detection."

"Well done, Cleve," Landau said. "And now, Jolon, we have to decide what to do after those two days, should we need to continue our operation."

"Should we conduct another attack implicating Crist?"

"No. We don't want him eliminated just yet. If Crist was out of the picture, the people might believe the threat is over, and that won't suit our purposes." Landau sat back in his chair, thinking. "What if there was a way we could push the collaborative to attack the Crist compound—an attack that wouldn't go as planned? Now *that* would be worth seeing!"

Chapter Twenty

The bridge of the *Raven* was humming, and Kyla Crist watched the people and consoles with wonder. As she sat to the side of the command chairs, she looked up and saw Raina Wolfe, who squatted on the deck next to her.

"I'm sure this is a shock, minister, but we are here on a mission to help Amaeus, and to prevent the terrorism you've been seeing from your brother, or any other sources, on-planet."

"How do you know my brother was responsible for these latest attacks?"

"The evidence is strong in that direction, though I concede that we don't have proof: we still need to investigate. In the meantime, we want to prevent Thorian Crist from waging any more attacks."

Crist looked around the bridge, knowing she couldn't prevent action by the *Raven* crew. "Are you going to his compound now?"

"Not yet. We have to decide how to get in and out of the compound so we minimize the danger to ourselves and to him." Wolfe smiled again.

"Despite what you may think, we are committed to peaceful action. And if we can pull this off the way we hope, there need be no violence against your brother or anyone else."

Crist looked away again. "I believe you will try, and I'm grateful for that."

Wolfe started to speak but was interrupted by Driscoll. "Captains? I'm getting unusual communications from the Crist compound."

"What's the nature of the communications?" McLeod asked.

"Scrambled and unknown, sir. But they are broadcasting on an odd band—at least for Amaeus." Driscoll frowned as her fingers danced across the console.

"Chief?" asked Kono. "Anything I need to know before we get there?"

"No, ma'am. I'm just trying to identify—damn."

Wolfe got up and approached the communications console. "What is it, Ava?"

"The signal, ma'am. I looked at the band they're using, and it's one I've seen before."

"What are you not telling me, Ava?"

Driscoll turned to face Wolfe and McLeod. "It's a band the Shan Confederacy uses."

* * *

McLeod convened the meeting in the ready room fifteen minutes later. Ross, Scott, and Carnahan sat at the head of the table with Wolfe discussing how to enter the Crist compound. Before them were schematics and maps of the compound and the locations that Driscoll thought the signals had come from.

"Now that we're all here," McLeod began, "what can you tell us about the signals, Ava, and where they came from?"

Driscoll rose from her seat and approached the screen. "My detectors aren't too accurate at this, but as best we could determine before, the communications array is in this area of the spider. That doesn't mean that's where the signals came from, however, since this signal I detected was very low power. It was on an isolated band, so it didn't need to be very strong."

"Is that a Shan characteristic?" Wolfe asked.

"No, ma'am. But in an area of space where no one else uses those bands, they have free rein."

"Smart," Carnahan said.

"It is," McLeod agreed. "And we'll discuss the possibility of Shan involvement or presence at a different meeting." He turned to the others. "I'm tempted to take out the entire communications array to prevent these communications from complicating matters."

"A total communications blackout?" Wolfe asked.

McLeod shrugged. "It may give us the greatest cover, though it clearly compromises the covert nature of our mission. Are you concerned it would put them on the alert too early?"

"That's one possibility. But with the right timing, it could work." Wolfe turned again to Driscoll. "Ava, how close do we need to be to check those signals again, to get a better sense of location?"

"Close, ma'am. From our current location, I'm only accurate to within one hundred meters. We need to be within ten kilometers—maybe closer—to get a more accurate fix."

"Best guess, Lily," McLeod said. "If we're trying to avoid weapons or detection, how close is too close to that compound?"

"We can get within ten kilometers, sir, but we can't stay long." Kono turned to Driscoll. "How much time do you need, chief?"

"Three to four minutes."

"Then that's the plan," Wolfe said. "Now let's look at possible access routes to enter the facility and find Crist."

Ross shifted the screen. "We've been looking at that for the last hour and have identified two routes that should work for us." Ross walked to the screen and pointed at the western arm of the spider, showing two access ports on the southern side of the arm. "These are normal doors, with what we believe is minimal security. We could—"

"Wait a minute," McLeod said. "Before you continue, where are Crist's personal quarters?"

Ross changed the picture to a close-up of the northern arm. "We believe they're around here, sir. We can't be sure of that, and he may not even be there when we arrive. There's a lot of ground to cover."

"Is that also his office location?" Wolfe asked.

"No," Ross said. "His office and conference room are at the edge of the inner circle toward the northern arm. We can breach the compound through the northern arm, but it's also the most heavily defended area of the compound."

"Understood," McLeod said, "though we should consider it one of the options. What other route are you considering?"

Ross shifted the picture again, showing detail on the southern part of the western arm. "This is the area nearest the communications array. While it isn't as heavily defended, if we want to take out or compromise their communications, that's the way we ought to go."

McLeod stood and began to pace as Wolfe approached the screen. "Show me your best sense of the security arrangements, Minty," Wolfe asked.

Ross turned to the screen, then stopped, looking back at McLeod.

"Don't worry about Captain McLeod; he's listening just fine."

"Yes, ma'am." Ross pointed toward the western arm. "The primary access doors have minimal security; alarms and sensors but few guards." Ross looked up. "Remember, ma'am, this is in the middle of the central desert. They can see attacking forces as they approach the complex, so they don't need a huge standing security force, just cameras and alert personnel."

"We'll get back to the personnel in a minute. How is security in the northern arm different?"

"We checked that out too, ma'am," Scott said. "In fact, Chief Carnahan found some of the original building plans."

"How did you do that?"

Carnahan shrugged. "Crist submitted them for an award. He may have changed some of the details over the last five years, but I doubt the basic design has changed."

Wolfe smiled. "Good." She traced her finger along the western arm, then turned to Ross. "Change to the northern arm, Minty." The picture changed and Wolfe traced her finger along those edges. "What about radiation, signals, or control rooms?"

"It adds nothing to the equation, ma'am. The controls and radiation from weapons and other devices are concentrated in the northern area of the hub and in the northern arm where you would expect them to be."

Wolfe glanced at McLeod, who had stopped his pacing and approached the screen. "Are these the only two access routes you recommend, Minty?" he asked.

"Yes, sir."

"And your preference?"

"That's where it gets complicated, sir. Chief Carnahan and I think heading into the western arm is best, while Commander Shaw and Sr. Altern Scott propose the northern arm. We're presenting both to you with no specific recommendation."

"Not a majority rule, then?" Wolfe asked.

"Too important for that, ma'am," Ross agreed.

Wolfe smiled in agreement, then turned to McLeod. "Tucker, what's your preference?"

McLeod looked at the picture of the northern arm, then changed the screen to the western arm. Finally, he changed back to the northern arm, and pointed to the screen. "Northern arm," he said. "It's more direct and gives us access to both of Crist's primary areas."

Wolfe smiled. "Well, that's not going to work. I would have said the western arm, so we can put the communications array out of commission first. We're also not that far away from the northern arm, so if we entered at the top of the arm we could make our way to the northern right after taking out the array."

The door chime rang, and as the door opened, Kyla Crist entered, accompanied by Crystal Gunderson. "She asked to join you, sir, ma'am."

"Thanks, Gunny, and welcome, minister," McLeod said. He pointed to his empty chair. "We've saved you a seat."

Crist sat down, her face focused on the screen at the front of room. "That's my brother's complex."

"It is," Wolfe said.

"You're going in, aren't you?"

McLeod approached her. "As Captain Wolfe told you, we have a job to do: that's where your brother is and that's where we can reach him."

Pressing her lips together, Crist said, "I guess I understand that." She looked at the screen again. "How will you do it?"

"Whatever you learn here will have to be kept to yourself."

"But he's my brother! You can't expect—"

"Minister," McLeod began. "We will accord you the respect due a high-ranking member of the planetary government, but we will not compromise our mission. I hope you understand that."

As McLeod approached the screen again, Crist called out. "They called you both captains. Is this a military mission? Are you invading Amaeus and implicating me in the process?"

"No," Wolfe said. "We are in the last stages of a delicate operation. If we are to do this with minimal risk to your brother, you need to cooperate—or at least not impede us."

Crist sat back. "And I guess I don't have to like it, do I?"

Wolfe smiled and returned to McLeod and the *Raven* crew. "Have you decided anything yet?"

"No," said McLeod as he inclined his head toward Crist. "Why don't we discuss positives and negatives of each access route and make a final decision?"

Ross began the discussion, pointing out the advantages of taking out the communications array so Crist was isolated. She also didn't want to enter the complex where they could be captured easily. Scott countered that the northern arm brought them closer to Crist's usual locations, so the mission could be quicker. He suggested that a single person head to the communications array when they breached the northern arm, but Carnahan said that the delay in getting to the communications array would be a risk. McLeod and Wolfe asked questions of both sides and asked for questions from all the personnel in the room. McLeod's last question broke the impasse.

"Chief Driscoll, can you rig a communications-jamming device we can carry on the pod that could suppress signals in and out of the Crist compound? Even if it's not one hundred percent effective, it would buy us time to get to the compound and neutralize his communications array."

"I'd say so, sir. But it would require *Raven* to be much closer to the compound when the pod was dropped."

"How close?" Wolfe asked.

"No more than ten kilometers, preferably closer."

Wolfe turned to McLeod. "Lily can handle the flying."

McLeod nodded. "She certainly can." He looked at the faces of the surrounding crew, assessing their agreement. Satisfied, he turned to Wolfe.

"I already agree, Tucker," said Wolfe. "This should work."

"Good, but before we settle on this solution, will *Raven* be impacted by the jamming, or can it be shielded from it?"

Gordon Shaw, who had been silent for much of the discussion smiled. "*Raven* can be shielded from anything, sir."

McLeod returned the smile and shook his head. "You continue to amaze me, Goody." McLeod looked up. "Then let's make the final arrangements." He turned to Carnahan, Ross, and Scott. "Work with Commander West for weapons and defensive equipment and contact Captain Wolfe and me when ready."

"Aye, sir."

As the group began to deliberate, McLeod took Wolfe aside. "What are our plans for Crist?"

"Kyla?"

"Yes."

"She stays with us. There's too much risk of a security breach if we return her to the surface, in addition to the danger to her."

"I agree. On both counts." He leaned closer, adding, "But you're responsible for her. The last thing I want to worry about is the sister of a terrorist throwing off our game."

"Still don't trust her?"

"Do you?"

"Enough."

"Well, let's hope your trust isn't misplaced."

Chapter Twenty-One

After returning to the bridge, McLeod stood next to Ava Driscoll. "Give me some good news, Ava."

"I have good news and bad news."

"I'm getting tired of hearing that," Kono sighed.

"So am I," McLeod said. "What do you have, Ava?"

Driscoll pressed a button on her console. "I was right about the signal, sir: it is from the Shan."

McLeod exhaled. "What did you receive and how did you figure that out?"

"It wasn't as hard as all that, sir. I intercepted messages going to and from the compound to the Shan ship, which has since moved out of range."

"Any sense of the vessel ID or anything about it? And what was the substance of the messages?"

"They were cryptic, sir. But they were communicating about an upcoming attack, without specifying what it was or where it would be."

"That's interesting," McLeod mused. "Thorian Crist and the Shan: that's a nasty combination."

Virgil Kelly broke in. "You've tangled with them before I take it?"

"The Shan?" McLeod frowned. "Frequently, and I don't want a repeat experience."

"I've never encountered them," Kelly said. "In fact, I don't even understand how they can be so against organization or collaboration when the Shan Confederacy is its own kind of super organization."

McLeod smiled. "If you can figure that out, Virgil, you'll be ahead of me." He turned to Driscoll. "Continue to monitor those messages, Ava. Delay or scramble them if you can to give us time to analyze what's going on. They may not know we're on to them."

"Yes, sir."

McLeod approached his seat then turned again to Driscoll. "Another thing Ava: did the signals emanate from the communications array?"

"No, sir. I meant to tell you that. The signals came from an area between the communications array and the hub, right near the northern arm, close to Thorian Crist's inner circle."

"Which means Crist doesn't want his lieutenants to know what's going on," McLeod said. "That's interesting."

"What's interesting?" Wolfe asked as she entered the bridge.

McLeod gestured toward Wolfe's seat, urging her to sit. "Ava intercepted a communication between a Shan vessel and the Crist compound."

"We knew that before."

"No. This time Ava's confirmed it's from a Shan vessel."

"Do we know the vessel, its configuration, or—"

Wolfe stopped as McLeod was shaking his head. "Not yet, Raina. But the communication is coming from Crist's stronghold and not the primary communications array."

"Damn. I hadn't intended to tangle with the Shan *and* Thorian Crist."

"You and me both."

Wolfe stood again. "We need to tell Minister Crist about this."

"Will it make a difference to her?"

"Hard to say. I doubt she knows how much the Shan opposes Federation or Alliance expansion, or what they may try to do on Amaeus. But if she knows about the Shan, I want to know why she hasn't told us that."

McLeod rose. "So do I." Turning to Kono, McLeod added, "Stay the course, Lily."

"Aye."

* * *

"I know little about the Shan," said Crist. "I mean, I've heard of them, but don't have any details." She looked up. "And you say my brother is cooperating with them? Why?"

Wolfe sat in a chair near Crist. "This is complicated, minister, so please just let me speak." Wolfe took a deep breath and smiled. "The story of the Shan can't be told in a straight line. The upshot of it is there

173

are many worlds in the galaxy which welcome working with the Central Federation or the Star Alliance. They see us as positive forces for good in the galaxy and believe the collaboration we promote helps maintain the peace among the planets and star systems. But there are other worlds who say that the existence of any super organization, like either the Federation or the Alliance, by definition removes the sovereignty of allied worlds."

"That's not what they do," Crist said. "The Federation and the Alliance are voluntary organizations, and—"

"And worlds can affiliate or disaffiliate as they wish," McLeod replied. "And while disaffiliation has happened on only a few occasions, worlds are always free to leave either organization, you're correct."

"But that isn't good enough for the Shan," Wolfe continued. "They prefer bilateral negotiations between worlds instead of having larger collaborative organizations that promote uniform or nearly uniform agreements."

"Given how many planets there are, doing everything bilaterally would be cumbersome," said Crist.

"It is." Wolfe shook her head. "But that's what the Shan prefers. They go to great lengths to discourage worlds from affiliating. And to be honest, the Shan as a loose confederation has several very wealthy worlds among its affiliates, and seem most interested in financial gain over peace."

"And among their affiliates are several unstable worlds and those with completely wrecked economies," McLeod offered. "Plus, the Shan has engaged both Federation and Alliance ships in battles over planets seeking to affiliate with one of our organizations."

"What they prefer, however, is to tighten their grip on a planet so they have little choice but to negotiate deals with their member planets, rather than affiliate with either the Alliance or the Federation," Wolfe continued. "They don't like to engage us in battle since we're better trained, better disciplined, and we know how to work together, a talent they've never mastered."

Crist put her head in her hands. For a moment Wolfe thought she was sad, but Crist then looked up, a grim set to her face. "If the Shan is communicating with my brother, then it's possible they're trying to prevent us from joining the Federation. That would mean that either or both parties could have committed the attacks on the housing project or the energy storage facility." Crist stood. "This is much bigger than anyone thought it was. The collaborative needs to know about this."

Wolfe rose and raised her hands. "I agree with your intent, minister. But do you think it's wise to return to the collaborative, given that they've issued a warrant to bring you into custody?"

"I have to. It's my duty as a member of the collaborative."

"The same collaborative that's abandoned and criminalized you?" McLeod asked. "Consider that before you walk head-first into danger."

"I have thought about it, and I need to go." Crist's eyes narrowed. "Unless you're prepared to keep me a prisoner here on your ship." Wolfe and McLeod were silent for a moment.

"Minister," Wolfe began, "I understand your sentiment and sympathize with you, but understand that we cannot have this mission compromised. Any information you give the collaborative about this ship would change everything for the worse."

Crist rocked on her feet for a few seconds, before nodding. "I understand, and I won't do that to you. But I have to go back." She looked first to McLeod, then again to Wolfe. "This is my planet. It may be your mission, but it's my *home*. If the Shan are trying to control Amaean politics, or our sovereignty, the collaborative has to be told."

"And the danger?" McLeod prompted.

"I'm prepared to deal with that." Crist stood her ground, flexing her hands into small fists. She was annoyed until McLeod smiled and offered his hand. She shook it, surprised.

"You are as impressive as Raina said you were." McLeod turned to Wolfe. "But we still have to keep you as safe as we can."

"I agree," Wolfe said. "And since we're such good friends now, I'm going with you."

"You're in more danger from security forces than I am."

Wolfe smiled. "Let me worry about that."

* * *

Gordon Shaw tried not to frown at his superior. "I'm obligated to raise an objection, ma'am. Returning to the central city with Minister Crist in tow is a risk you should not be taking."

"Noted, Goody," Wolfe answered. "But we have little choice: we can't keep her as a prisoner, and to have her go alone is not my way." She smiled at Shaw. "And you knew that answer even before you raised the objection."

"I did, ma'am. But if Captain McLeod doesn't point these things out to you, someone should."

"Tucker didn't bother. In fact, my accompanying Minister Crist was his idea."

"Hmmph," said Shaw, with a dismissive wave of his hand. "Star Alliance officers—"

"Have been our allies since before either of us was born, Goody. And you know how good they are. Enough of this nonsense: take *Raven* to the city and then to the compound to get the extraction going. You'll be in command then."

"Aye, ma'am."

* * *

"Nearing spaceport, sir," said Kono. "Touchdown in twelve."

"Final clearance, Ava?"

"Yes, sir. And no indication of issues or problems on the ground."

McLeod looked up at Wolfe. "Good. Let's hope it stays that way." McLeod examined his friend's silhouette. "Light armor?"

Wolfe nodded. "Yes. Just enough to withstand lighter attacks, even some blunt force. I don't intend to get into anything with people, and it's unlikely they'll take a second look at my clothing, so I should be okay."

"Let's hope they believe Crist—or at least listen to her, rather than put you both in prison."

"No assurance of that either way."

"Which of course makes me nervous."

"You and me both, Tucker. And I'll remind you of that later." Wolfe shook herself. "The extraction plan looks good, Tucker, and Goody will make smart decisions about the Shan if something breaks while you're in the compound."

"I agree." McLeod leaned forward. "I assume Commander Shaw raised objections to you going with Crist?"

"He did." Wolfe frowned. "You knew?"

"Suspected. He has a great deal of respect for you."

"He just worries about me."

"He does. Make sure he has nothing to worry about."

"On it," Wolfe said as she turned toward the hatch leading away from the bridge.

"On the ground, captains," said Kono.

McLeod nodded toward Driscoll, who hit the all-com button. "All decks, all crew. Prepare for a very short docking."

Chapter Twenty-Two

Kyla Crist looked carefully at Wolfe, awed by the older woman's confidence. "What is your plan now?"

"That's up to you, minister, this is your party."

Crist turned to examine the spaceport before turning back to Wolfe. "We should get to the collaborative as soon as we can." It was only then that Crist noticed a small bag Wolfe was carrying. "What is that?"

"This is what we need to convince the collaborative that something other than energy production is going on at your brother's compound." Wolfe pointed to the exterior doors of the spaceport and began walking. She looked over her shoulder. "How much do you and the other collaborative members know about the Shan Confederacy?"

"Very little, I expect. I know little myself, other than what you've told me."

"And that's why I have this with us." Wolfe opened the exterior doors and searched the street. "We need to find a transport." Wolfe hailed a passing transport and gave the driver an address near the collaborative. Crist noticed the location and turned to speak, but Wolfe shook her head, looking forward at the driver and at the passing pedestrians. They arrived ten minutes later, and Wolfe led Crist around the block to the rear of the collaborative building.

"Why are we here?"

Wolfe held up two small plug-in devices. "We have two alternatives: we can go in the front door and hope to avoid arrest, or we can get in a side or rear door and just show up at the gallery or at Zahara Ali's office—your choice."

"I'd like to surprise Zahara and see what she's made of," Crist said, her eyes dancing.

Wolfe smiled. "I knew I liked you."

* * *

On the bridge of Central Federation Vessel *Pathfinder*, Su-Captain Lena Gattiger was bored. The regular patrol for *Pathfinder* took it into several sectors of the Alpha quadrant, often to worlds where she had personal contacts and connections. This sector of the Delphini star system had few habitable planets and none were part of the Federation. *Pathfinder* was on its way to other Federation worlds and had been asked to sweep through the area around Amaeus, since it was an active applicant to the Federation.

They couldn't find another ship to do this? she thought. As she surveyed the faces of her operations and tactical officers, Gattiger saw the same boredom she was feeling. Five more days to next liberty, she thought, then she noticed a change in the posture of her weapons officer, Tara Worth.

"Problem, Tara?"

"I'm not sure, ma'am. But I'm detecting some odd radiation in the space around here that shouldn't be here."

"How do you know that?"

"Because the radiation suggests a ship with an antimatter pion drive, and that's not what any of the ships in this sector use."

"Couldn't the radiation be from a transport or other vessel visiting the planet?" asked Drayden Jarvis, executive officer of *Pathfinder*.

"Doubtful, sir," said Worth. She turned to face Jarvis. "Plus, the amount of radiation suggests a much larger vessel, not a regular transport."

"Which suggests weapons?" Gattiger asked.

"Yes, ma'am," Worth said. "Including phase weapons, so this is not a nice little party going on."

Gattiger looked at Jarvis. "Something may be going on around here that we don't want," she said. "We need to conduct a larger sweep to identify the source of this radiation and find this ship."

Worth nodded. "Aye, ma'am."

Gattiger rose from her command chair and approach the communications console.

"Beckett," Gattiger began, speaking to her communications officer, "begin a broader sweep. Look for any suspect communications or transmissions from the surface."

"There's something else you ought to know, ma'am," Worth added.

Gattiger turned and noticed Worth's face. "What is that?"

"Hard to say, but I thought you'd like to know."

"What?"

"These radiation patterns? They're a classic for ships of Shan Confederacy manufacture."

Gattiger exhaled. "Now that's *just* what we need."

* * *

Wolfe and Crist entered the collaborative through the side access door, and Crist led the way up the rear staircase toward the ministers' offices.

"At this time of day, most of the ministers will be in their offices."

"Are you ready to see your colleagues?"

"No." She sighed. "But I have no choice." She continued down the hallway, then stopped by a closed door. Crist opened the outer door of the collaborative's chair, Zahara Ali, and approached the desk of Ali's assistant, whose mouth opened in shock.

"Good day, Ms. Lua," Crist said, a broad smile on her face. "I hope I'm not too early for my appointment."

"Minister Crist!" Lua cried. "I didn't you know you had an appointment, umm—" the young woman tried to compose herself. "Minister Ali is busy at the moment, and—"

"I'm sure she will see me and my friend, Ms. Lua. You needn't announce us," Crist added, as she opened the door. Crist knew that Lua would contact Ali, and she wanted to surprise her colleague. She opened the inner door to Ali's office and called out.

"Zahara! And Mr. Blanks! So good to see you both in the same place!"

Ali's eyes widened, and she turned to Mr. Blanks, whose face showed no emotion at all. He searched Crist and Wolfe's faces but gave no reaction to their advance. Wolfe opened her hands to show she had no active weapons in them and walked in behind Crist.

Finally, Ali found her voice. "This is a surprise, Kyla. I wasn't expecting you."

"No matter," Crist said as she stood by Ali's desk. "I'm here now so we can talk." She glanced at Mr. Blanks, then back at Ali. "And since I've come in here on my own, I don't think we have need for the warrant, do we?"

Ali was unconvinced. "Well, the warrant is—"

"The warrant was to bring me into custody to speak with me: it was not for my arrest." Crist resisted the urge to sit in the chair in front of Ali's desk. "I'm here now. What did you want to ask me?"

Ali glanced at Mr. Blanks, who neither moved nor spoke. "I suppose you could stay here now, Kyla." Ali looked at Wolfe. "But as for your friend, we don't know her intentions or why she broke out of the holding area." Ali gained momentum. "In fact, we don't know why you helped them break out."

"She didn't," Wolfe said.

"What?"

"Minister Ali did not break us out of the facility," Wolfe repeated. "She was visiting Mr. Scott and me in the holding area when my associates entered the building to free us right around the time of the explosion."

"And I told Mr. Blanks that since I had brought these people into custody on my say so alone, that I could also free them on my word,"

Crist said. "We left with his instruction that we take one of the transports from behind the building." She turned to face Ali and spoke more deliberately. "I did not expect it would lead to an *ambush*. Near my *home*."

Ali blanched, avoiding Crist's eyes. "Well, you have to understand, Kyla. With the evidence Ian saw—"

"There is no evidence I've done anything to challenge the collaborative nor any treasonable act."

"You were in the company—"

"Of people who have said from the beginning that they were interested only in our application to the Central Federation. There is no reason to expect that they would do anything to compromise our application."

"And nothing to suggest that they wouldn't."

Crist turned to Wolfe and held out her hand. "On that point, you're wrong, Zahara." Crist looked at Mr. Blanks and raised her palm in surrender. "Just evidence, Mr. Blanks. Something you'd like to see, given your background."

"What is it?" Ali asked. "What evidence can you have?"

Wolfe walked forward. "It's evidence of communications from Thorian Crist's compound to another ship somewhere near or in orbit around Amaeus."

"What ship?"

Wolfe walked forward again and opened her bag. "A ship we believe is connected with the Shan Confederacy."

"The Shan?"

"Yes, minister," Wolfe said. "And we think it very interesting that the Shan would be here now without contacting the collaborative."

"But why would they contact us?"

"Is it because they want to keep us from affiliating with the Federation?" Mr. Blanks asked.

"Something like that," Wolfe agreed. "My guess is they want to help Thorian Crist create the conditions where you decide joining the Federation isn't worth it, and then choose a voluntary affiliation with the Shan."

"But how would that benefit us?"

"I doubt it would, minister. But that's not the way the Shan see it; the same may be true for Thorian Crist."

"I still don't understand," Ali said.

"The Shan prefer to keep planets from affiliating with larger organizations like the Central Federation or the Star Alliance," Wolfe offered. "They prefer bilateral agreements that, in their minds, preserve sovereignty and free enterprise." She paused. "Their rhetoric matches the way Thorian Crist feels about Amaeus joining the Federation. Thorian Crist and the Shan are a match made in heaven."

"You seem to know an awful lot about Thorian Crist," said Ali, who rose from her seat. "How do I know you aren't working for him?" She turned again the Kyla. "How do I know you're not both working for him?" Ali began to sneer. "That would certainly be evidence of treason."

"Call the ministers, Zahara. We need to discuss this in chambers."

"You don't have the right to call us into session."

"But I have the right to ask and petition our colleagues, Zahara." Crist stood over Ali. "And I'm doing that right now."

Ali glanced first at Mr. Blanks, then again at Crist. "And you think I'll allow this?" Turning again to Mr. Blanks, Ali said, "Perhaps another few days in the holding area will change your mind." Mr. Blanks said nothing and made no move toward Crist or Wolfe. Ali frowned, then noticed that Crist was smiling.

"Loyalty to procedure is one of Mr. Blank's virtues, Zahara. While he may be loyal to you as chair of the collaborative, he is more loyal to our values and procedures. My request is valid and Mr. Blanks knows it."

Ali hesitated, look back and forth among Mr. Blanks, Crist, and Wolfe. Finally, she said, "Fine," as she pressed a button. "You'll have your day in court."

Chapter Twenty-Three

Gattiger moved quickly among her bridge crew's consoles, listening to the ideas bouncing between them. Executive officer Drayden Jarvis conferred with Tara Worth. He hoped the weapons officer had suggestions on how to handle a Shan ship with little dispatch, but his glances to Gattiger told the ship's captain little.

"I'm waiting for some good news here, Beckett," Gattiger said.

"Depends on what you mean by good, ma'am. But the more I look at these signals, the more I'm convinced there is a Shan vessel in this area."

"That is not good news," Jarvis said.

"No. And I don't want to tangle with a hostile right now." Gattiger turned to Worth. "You mentioned the radiation, Tara: what can you tell us about the vessel it came from?"

"Not much, ma'am. In terms of tonnage, it could go from as little as thirty to more than one hundred and twenty gara-tons, I'd guess, so not particularly helpful there."

"For Shan vessels of that general size range, what weapons would they have?" Gattiger asked.

"The normal, ma'am: pulse weapons, plasma cannon, and phase weapons if they're so inclined."

"They usually are," Jarvis said.

Gattiger only nodded and returned to her seat, but stood in front of it. "We need to find that Shan vessel, people. And once we find it, we need to get between it and the planet in case we're needed." Gattiger turned to communications.

"Sound the alert, Beckett."

* * *

"And you expect us to jump just because you returned to the collaborative of your own accord?" Ian Anoki was furious at Crist and continued to stare at her, even when someone else was speaking.

"You're not helping, Ian," Ali said. "We're here to speak about several items; Kyla's status with the collaborative is just the first."

"I thought that was clear," said Anoki. "When there is a warrant for your arrest—"

"Not arrest," Crist said, with surprising calm. "To be taken into custody for questioning." She looked up at the impassive face of Mr. Blanks. "And since I've come in voluntarily, there's no need to activate the warrant."

"You're grasping at straws, Kyla," Anoki replied. "And you won't get away with it."

Ali rapped her gavel to bring attention back to her. "That's only one item we have to discuss, and we can delay that for the moment. The other has to do with the possibility that a Shan Confederacy ship is in the area."

"Why would they be there?" Leyla Hill asked. "This is very confusing."

"It is," Ali agreed. "Though it may not be as confusing as you think." She turned to Crist. "Kyla has brought us information about both radiation and communication signals coming from Thorian Crist's compound. It's evidence they've been communicating with a Shan vessel."

"And you trust this intelligence?" Anoki asked. "This is the height of naivete, Zahara: I thought you were smarter than that."

The angry stare went this time from Ali to Anoki, who sat back in his chair. "I am no more naive than you are," Ali said, searching the eyes of the other ministers. "We can reject this information if we wish. However, we needed to bring it to your attention."

"Show us the evidence," said Takoda Marten. "We need to see it. If we think it's valid, we can take action."

"But what action can—" Hill began, but Ali rapped the gavel again.

"We can bring that in now, Leyla." Ali turned to Mr. Blanks, who left the room and returned with Raina Wolfe.

Anoki shot up from his chair. "*Her?* The conspirator who escaped from the holding area?" Anoki shouted. "*She's* your evidence?" He shook his head. "Then we can end this charade right now."

Wolfe continued walking to the table, standing by Mr. Blanks. "Neither Minister Crist, Minister Ali, nor Mr. Blanks seem to think so, minister. You can ignore what I show you, but that would be extremely unwise."

"Who *are* you?" Anoki asked.

"A friend, Minister Anoki. And before you object to that, I'll show you the evidence we collected." Wolfe gave the small module to Mr. Blanks, who plugged it into a console near the conference table.

As the system was booting, Anoki broke the silence again. "And how did you obtain this evidence? We don't know you and have no—"

"No reason to trust me," Wolfe said. "I get it, minister. All you have to do is verify it yourselves."

"How could we do that?" Marten asked.

"You just need to know where to look and how to look. It's not complicated with the right equipment."

"You don't have any equipment on you that I can see," Anoki said.

Wolfe looked at Anoki, smiled, and turned her attention back to Mr. Blanks. The picture of the Crist compound came on the screen and Wolfe walked toward it. "This is Thorian Crist's compound in the central desert of Amaeus," she began. "I'm sure you've seen this many times." She used a pointer to show the western arm. "Crist's primary communications array is in this area, and—"

"So you *did* know more about your brother's compound," Anoki snapped at Kyla Crist. "That *alone* is treason!"

Crist jumped for a moment, then leaned back on the conference table, pointing at the screen. "This information came from her and her group, not from me."

"Can we just listen to what this woman has to say?" Marten asked. "If there is real danger to our planet here, we're wasting time."

"You are," Wolfe answered. She turned back to the screen. "This is the primary communications array, and were you to listen to transmissions only from that array, nothing would be amiss." Wolfe trained the pointer on the junction of the northern arm with the central hub of the compound. "But here, which is near where Thorian Crist meets with his people and his personal area—the northern arm—that's where several signals have been traded between this compound and a ship we believe is of Shan manufacture."

"But you're not sure?" Hill asked.

"Not one hundred percent at the time we returned to the collaborative," Wolfe replied. "It's likely been confirmed by now. You see—"

"How can you know about the ship without seeing it?"

Wolfe turned back to the table. "Does anyone here have a military background?" Mr. Blanks raised his hand, but Wolfe saw that no member of the collaborative raised theirs. "That's what I thought. But this isn't too hard to understand, even without military background. Military forces in the galaxy use a variety of communications frequencies. There are certain bands your news reports or entertainment transmissions use, for example, and different ones for your security forces." Wolfe looked around the table and saw understanding. "Well, there are also specific bands commonly used by the Central Federation and by the Star Alliance, and those used by other organizations, the Shan Confederacy being the largest of those informal bodies."

"Bigger than what other forces?" asked Marten.

Wolfe hesitated. *We don't have time for a civics lesson.* "The Molandrans, for example, but they're a smaller force and are more localized. The Shan has members and affiliates throughout the galaxy, so their communications frequencies are better known."

Wolfe changed the picture on the screen to a graph. "This graph shows the range of frequencies that should be common on this planet, and as you can see," Wolfe pointed to a gap in the graph, "almost everything on Amaeus is within this range." She pointed to a series of lines far higher than the other lines. "These transmissions are in a range that your security forces don't monitor." Wolfe glanced at Mr. Blanks, who didn't react. *How does he live like that?*

"The Shan uses this range because it is so distant from other common frequencies. In addition, because nobody else uses them, the Shan can transmit at very low power, making intercepting their transmissions even harder."

"I think I understand that," Hill said. "But how did you find it?"

"My people make it a practice to monitor these transmissions." Wolfe raised her hand. "And before you ask me again about my people, let me finish."

"We also found significant radiation, the kind that comes from pion drive engines, which we know the Shan use. Finally, we determined that there was almost no movement of personnel or equipment from the Crist compound for about forty hours before the attacks on the housing project and on the energy storage facility. That means that while Thorian Crist may be responsible for the attacks, he didn't move any personnel from the central desert to do it."

"How is that relevant?" Anoki asked. "He could have had forces already in place well before the attacks."

"He could have," Wolfe agreed. "However, that doesn't fit the patterns of his previous attacks. Those have been against industrial targets: against his competitors in the tullarium and klocutin markets. The attack on the housing project was out of character."

"That doesn't mean that he hasn't done some horrible things on this planet, whoever you are," Anoki countered. "And do you have a name?"

Wolfe smiled. "Your first statement is correct, minister. And as for my name, Mr. Blanks has my credentials."

"I still don't know what to make of all of this," Anoki said. "I don't trust anyone associated with Kyla, and I don't trust her, either."

Ali saw confusion on the faces of her colleagues. "I am inclined to agree with Ian. This information is interesting, and perhaps we ought to confirm it, so—"

"You should," Wolfe said. "That's exactly what you should do. And if I were you, I wouldn't delay that process while you debate over whom to trust. I've fought against the Shan before: you have no idea what you're up against."

* * *

Jarvis remembered his superior's boredom only an hour ago and marveled at how calm and focused she was now. "What is our responsibility here, ma'am?"

"You already know that, Drayden. We're to confirm what we've discovered so far and intervene as necessary." She turned to Jarvis. "And once we're ready to take direct action, we communicate with the planetary collaborative, the governing body on Amaeus."

"A body that doesn't even know we're here."

"Correct."

"And the first thing we tell them is that they have a Shan Confederacy ship in orbit around their planet?"

"Also correct."

Jarvis shook his head. "Hell of a way to start a relationship."

Chapter Twenty-Four

McLeod worked quickly in his quarters, selecting light armor and close weapons for the extraction. The door chime startled him as he opened to door to see Mark Carnahan and Gordon Shaw.

"Gentlemen," McLeod said. "Come in." He moved aside to allow Shaw and Carnahan entry, then stood by waiting.

"Do you have something to tell me?"

"Yes, sir," Shaw said. He glanced at Carnahan, then added, "We've lost contact with Captain Wolfe."

"Which means?"

"That either she surrendered her earpiece or lost it," Carnahan said. "Commander Shaw and I believe she surrendered it or turned it off."

"Can she do that?"

Shaw laughed. "You should know, sir, that Captain Wolfe can do just about anything she wants."

"Understood. And I agree." He exhaled. "Implications for the extraction?

"None, sir," Shaw said. "It doesn't change our objective or our plans."

"What about the Shan: have you gotten anything else on them in the last," he consulted his chron, "twenty minutes?"

"No, sir," Carnahan said. "It's hard to imagine a Shan vessel we couldn't take on if necessary. But it would be better if we weren't doing it alone."

"Agreed. Goody, you have the ability and authority to engage as necessary: don't shy away because neither Raina nor I can be here: command means command."

"Understood, captain."

McLeod smiled again. "Also feel free to shift configuration to the starfighter. Lily loves playing with that one."

"We all do, sir," Shaw agreed. "But I hope we won't need to."

* * *

"And just how can we verify your information?" Anoki asked. "I believe you're working for Thorian Crist and his co-conspirators." Anoki focused his attention on Kyla Crist, making it clear who he viewed as one of Thorian's co-conspirators.

"I'm sure your security forces can probe the same areas of space that we did and find residual evidence of the radiation," Wolfe replied. "They can also monitor these same frequencies," Wolfe pointed again to the screen, "and find out what we found out." Seeing no movement among the ministers, she added, "I'm sure Mr. Blanks can do that."

Zahara Ali looked at Mr. Blanks, who nodded, but did not move. "How easily can you conduct this operation, Mr. Blanks?"

"It shouldn't be difficult, ma'am. I can direct that to happen if you wish."

"We wish," Marten said. "I'm tired of not knowing."

Hill nodded. "I agree. It is—"

"But I don't," said Anoki. "To waste time on unsubstantiated claims from an alien invader and a co-conspirator of a terrorist is idiotic."

"That's why we need to verify it!" Hill screamed. "Are you against even seeing if it's true?" Hill rose for the first time, a difficult task for someone of her health. "Are you so set against Kyla to risk danger to our planet to satisfy your ego?"

Anoki rose. "How dare you! To imply that—"

"Enough!" Ali said, rapping her gavel on the table. "We cannot afford to fight amongst ourselves over this." Anoki regained his composure and sat. "And while I agree with Ian that this is a waste of time, we have no choice." Ali turned to Wolfe. "What else can you tell us about the Shan?"

"I should think I've given you enough, minister. The Shan dislike the Central Federation and the Star Alliance, and *encourage* worlds to develop bilateral agreements with the planets they care about rather than working with our organizations. They see the Alliance and the Federation as oligarchies that stifle private enterprise and economic development and threaten the sovereignty of planets."

"Have you ever seen them use violence against worlds that didn't see things their way?" Marten asked.

"Minister, they have starships for a reason."

"I've heard enough," said Hill. "We need to look into this now."

"Agreed," said Ali, then she hesitated. "But, and I hesitate to say this," Ali pointed to Wolfe, "but I don't trust you to be with us alone."

"I'll go with Mr. Blanks, minister." Mr. Blanks gave Ali an almost imperceptible nod.

"Very well," Ali said. "Mr. Blanks, please take her with you and get to the bottom of this."

* * *

"I'd like more information on this Shan vessel before we engage," Gattiger said. "Any new info on her, Tara?"

"None, ma'am."

"That's not what I want to hear, Tara. We need more information as we move into an intercept position."

"When do we contact the collaborative?" Jarvis asked, hovering over the communications console.

"When we're in position. The last thing I want to do is to shock them before we have to."

* * *

"Where are you going?" asked Mr. Blanks, as Wolfe turned to the right after leaving the chamber room.

"Toward your operations area. Isn't it this way?"

"It is. You're quite familiar with our security arrangements. Perhaps being alone with you puts me at risk, too."

Wolfe closed the distance and lowered her voice. "Mr. Blanks, as much as I enjoy hand to hand combat with a worthy opponent, this danger is real: let's not engage in this dance right now."

Blanks nodded his head and began walking again toward operations.

* * *

"Status update?" McLeod asked, returning to the bridge.

"In position in ten minutes, sir," said Kono. "Lt. Commander Kelly is ready to send out the indro to make a final check."

"Good. Once the indro is launched, call the team to the ready room. We can track progress from there."

"Aye."

Just then, they heard the bridge door slide into its pocket, revealing Francine West. "Final equipment checked and prepared, sir." West smiled. "You have a nice little bag of goodies."

"Thank you, Frankie," McLeod said. "I enjoy all the toys you provide us."

* * *

"We can't take on a large attack from a hostile vessel," Hill said. "What do we do if we're attacked?"

"If you believe a Shan vessel is here," Anoki began, "you're a bigger fool than I thought you were." Anoki scoffed as he rose and walked around the room. "This is a delay tactic by Kyla and her brother so they can launch another attack."

Crist sat, shaking her head. "You are the only fool here, Ian," she said, thinking to herself that perhaps Ali was a fool as well. "I'm here with all of you, and I don't intend to have an attack launched against me if I can help it. Are you so blinded by ambition that—" Anoki turned, ready to spring but stopping and moving back instead.

"We will not allow you to dictate what this collaborative does, especially with a cloud over your head."

"A cloud that you've put there, Ian," Crist said. "You more than anyone else."

"What are you saying, Kyla?" Ali asked. "Do you have evidence of something that Ian has done?"

"Evidence? No. But these constant attacks on me—with no basis in fact—calls into question: what does he have against me, and what is motivating that hatred?"

"I'd like to know that, too," Marten said. "What is the source of this vendetta?"

Anoki regained his seat. "I won't dignify that with a response. The only one with a warrant over her head is Kyla, not me."

* * *

Mr. Blanks and Wolfe stood over a communications technician, making her nervous. Wolfe could sense Mr. Blank's breathing getting heavier, as though his level of overall tension was rising.

"Anything?" Mr. Blanks asked.

"There was a transmission there, sir," the technician said. "I've never monitored that area of the band before, so I can't say what it is." She turned to Mr. Blanks. "But it wasn't a direct communication that I could understand; it may be scrambled."

Blanks shook his head. "There may not be any direct transmissions now, but please continue monitoring those bands: something may come up on them and I want to know."

"Yes, sir."

"There is a rise in radiation, sir," came the voice of an operations officer to Wolfe's left. Mr. Blanks and Wolfe walked over to the console.

"What can you tell me about it?"

"That's hard to say, Mr. Blanks. There are elevated levels of chromaa emissions in a few specific areas of space."

"What areas?"

"Well, here, at five point four clicks away."

"What could it mean?"

"Lots of things," the technician said, "but nothing conclusive."

"Could it be a starship?"

The technician frowned. "It could be, sir. But it wouldn't be one of ours. We don't use anti-matter pion drives, and that's what this radiation residue means. The amounts are faint now, so if something was there, it's gone now."

Mr. Blanks looked first to Wolfe, then back to the technician. "Continue to monitor and inform me of any significant changes." Blanks stood straighter, addressing the five people in the room. "I want to know of anything unusual you detect. Focus on the areas near the collaborative—well—the entire central city, and the space above it, and over the central desert."

"The central desert? Why there?"

Mr. Blanks shook his head. "Use your imagination, *boy*," he said, as he led Wolfe from the room to return to the ministers.

* * *

"And you're sure about this?" Jarvis asked. "We don't want to contact their central government and find we've made an error."

"No error, sir," Worth replied. "There's nothing we're sure of other than the fact that the Shan Confederacy uses this combination of minerals in its drives and causes these emissions." Worth pointed to her console. "And I believe them to be in this location." She turned to Jarvis. "Whether we head there now to intercept is a command decision. But I'd stake my reputation that we are looking at a vessel of at least one hundred gara-tons with the usual complement of phase, plasma, and pulse weapons."

"But no idea of how much of each?"

"That I don't have, commander."

"You've done a lot, Tara," Gattiger said. "Thank you." Turning to Julie Beckett, she said, "Time to make a call."

Chapter Twenty-Five

"Indro launched, sir," Kelly said. "We should have additional data in less than an hour."

"Thank you, Virgil," McLeod said, who then turned to the second command chair. "What we still don't know, Goody, is the location of the Shan vessel."

"True." Shaw could sense that something else was on McLeod's mind. "Is there something else I should know?"

"Yes. You need to take *Raven* and find out more about the Shan vessel."

"Right, but if you're with the extraction team—"

"You need to do it anyway. I don't relish walking into danger with little to no backup. But we need to protect the planet from a Shan attack." McLeod leaned toward Shaw and spoke more quietly. "Take as much time as you need, but gather more intelligence and see what our options are with that vessel."

Shaw's jaw tightened. "We can do that, sir. But if you don't mind me saying so, I don't like it very much."

McLeod smiled. "Noted. And to be honest, neither do I." He sat straighter in his seat. "But with limited choices, we do the best we can. You also need to return to the central city to ensure that Captain Wolfe is okay."

Shaw nodded, almost in resignation. "Yes, sir."

"You're got a lot of work to do, but I have confidence in you and in this crew."

"Thank you, sir."

* * *

"What does this presence mean?" Landau asked. He faced Rubinco with a scowl on his face.

"What we're reading is the presence of a hauer-drive capable ship, sir. It's not strong now, but—"

"I asked what it meant, Cleve, not what you detected. Now, do you have that information or not?"

"Yes, sir." Rubinco cleared his throat. "What we've detected suggests a Central Federation ship has been in this area within the last four hours."

"While we were over the central desert?" Reed asked.

"Yes, sir. I can't tell you the size of the vessel, because I don't know when it was here—"

"But you know when we left this area," Reed replied. "What was it now, about six hours ago?"

"Yes, sir."

"Then assume the longest time away and calculate a projected size."

"On it, sir."

Reed looked to Landau, wondering what was going on. "If it is a Central Federation vessel, sir, what do you want to do?"

Landau shook his head. "I don't want to engage them if we don't have to, particularly if it's a large ship. We can defend ourselves, but our work depends more on stealth than on firepower."

"Would it be so difficult encountering a Federation vessel, captain? We're not in a state of war with them."

"That's not the whole story, Jolon. The way the Federation works, once a planet has applied for membership, that planet is under their active protection. In fact—" Landau paused, confusing Reed.

"What else, sir?"

"It just occurred to me, Jolon. Amaeus might be under the protection of both the Federation *and* the Alliance under their cooperation agreement."

"You think there's an Alliance vessel here too?"

"I doubt it. I was just pondering the state of affairs here." Landau turned to Reed and smiled. "But don't worry about that, Jolon. If we need to retrench here to avoid the Federation, we can always return later to complete our work."

Reed smiled in response, but his heart wasn't in it.

* * *

"Status of hail, Ms. Beckett?" asked Lena Gattiger. Beckett held up a finger before responding to her CO.

"The collaborative will be online in a moment, ma'am. I've contacted their central communications center and they're connecting us."

"Audio and visual?"

"That's what I asked for, though we only have a small field of vision in either direction."

"Understood," Gattiger smiled. "I'll get ready for my closeup." Gattiger waited and saw a chuckling Drayden Jarvis.

"Couldn't help it, ma'am."

"No matter, I'll just—"

"On screen, ma'am," said Beckett, who pointed to a view of a meeting chamber in the planetary collaborative, showing Zahara Ali, Ian Anoki, and Leyla Hill, but no one else. Gattiger stood and straightened her uniform.

"Good day, ministers of the Planetary Collaborative. I am Su-Captain Lena Gattiger, Commanding Officer of the Central Federation starship *Pathfinder*."

"The Central Federation?" Anoki laughed. "And here we were worried about the Shan Confederacy. We should—"

"You *should* be worried," Gattiger said. "That's why we're contacting you. We have direct evidence of a Shan Confederacy starship in orbit around your planet, and we need to intercept it."

"There *is* a Shan vessel nearby?" Ali asked. "We thought that was a ruse presented by, um, well, by someone on-planet."

"It is no ruse," Gattiger replied. "Have I the honor of addressing Minister Ali, head of the Planetary Collaborative?" As Gattiger spoke, Wolfe searched her mind. She recalled *Pathfinder* as a Banti-class vessel with average defensive and offensive capabilities. Wolfe believed it was up to the task of a head-to-head battle with most Shan vessels. What she couldn't remember was if anyone aboard *Pathfinder* knew her personally. Wolfe knew of Gattiger by reputation and recalled that she was skilled but as new to command as she was.

"Yes, I am Minister Ali of the collaborative. And your name again?"

"Su-Captain Lena Gattiger, Commanding Officer of the Central Federation starship *Pathfinder*. And before you ask, minister, we were in your sector on the way to another location, but once we realized a Shan vessel was nearby we had the responsibility to stop and offer our assistance."

"What assistance can you provide?" Marten asked. "We are only an applicant planet to the Federation. We—"

"And you are under the direct protection of the Federation should you so choose." Gattiger smiled. "No planet affiliated with the Federation is left out in the cold."

"And you have definite proof of this vessel?" Anoki asked. "As my colleague said," Anoki said, looking to a location outside of the field of vision of the video link, "we need to be sure that there is a Shan vessel around our planet before we take action."

"Understood, minister. What information do you need? We can transmit what we've found: what will be missing is an analysis of what the data means."

"Please send us what you have, captain," Ali replied. "We are somewhat taken aback by this whole development."

Gattiger nodded to Beckett, who began gathering the files. "Minister, *Pathfinder* is at your disposal and here to coordinate with your security forces. Going up against the Shan can be a very nasty business."

"And if we choose not to accept your help?" Anoki asked. "We are still a planet with its own sovereignty."

"You are," Gattiger replied. "And we recognize that now *and* if your application for Central Federation membership is approved." Gattiger returned to her chair. "You're Minister Ian Anoki, correct?"

"Yes, I am."

"Minister Anoki, have you ever gone into battle against a force like the Shan Confederacy?"

"No, and I don't appreciate—"

"There is no accusation in my question, minister. Except that I have engaged in battle with the Shan, and while we prevailed, it was not something I would ever do again unprepared. You haven't asked for my help, but I'll give you all a piece of advice: our offer is one you should not refuse."

* * *

"Analysis complete, sir," said Virgil Kelly.

McLeod remained in his command chair as other members of the extraction team gathered on the bridge. "Report, Virgil."

"It's as we expected, sir. There is good cover on the easternmost arm and on the western and northern arms near the hub. But we've found something else, sir."

"Go on."

"Now that we've gotten close into the compound, we can confirm that there has been no movement in any direction, including the underground areas that lead toward the west, and no one has moved from the compound for at least four days."

"That's still no evidence Thorian Crist didn't conduct the attack," Shaw said. "And more than that, if we believe the Shan are in league with Crist, what's stopping them from conducting the attack?"

"That's what I was leading toward, sir," Kelly answered. "Our analysis suggests that the attacks were not launched from the central desert, and we detected only the last parts of the transmissions. Specialist Driscoll can play it for you." Kelly nodded to Driscoll, who pressed a button.

The transmission was crackly and hard to understand. "Here it is, sir." " . . . operation . . . third phase . . . Crist reaction." With that, the broadcast fell silent.

"Why would Crist be transmitting something and talking about his own reaction?" Kelly asked.

McLeod scratched his head. "A good question. It could refer to Kyla Crist's reaction, but I'm not inclined to believe that." He sat back. "So what we're confronting now is the possibility that perhaps it's not Thorian Crist directing these operations, either from his compound or with the Shan?"

"Is that a good or a bad thing?" Shaw asked.

"That *is* the question."

Chapter Twenty-Six

Jarvis glanced at Gattiger, imploring her to pause the transmission. Gattiger nodded and turned again to the screen. "If you will pardon us, ministers, I need to confer with my staff."

"Of course," Ali said.

Beckett muted the transmission as Jarvis and Gattiger left the camera's field of vision. "You have a concern or suggestion, Drayden?"

"Not exactly, ma'am. I just want to be clear about how far we'll push this. I know that the Federation offers protection for every planet, but we can't force them to accept our help."

"That's true." Gattiger gestured with her hand toward the screen. "I'm trying to let these people know that they shouldn't mess with the Shan alone: they are a force to reckoned with. And for a planet like Amaeus, that to my knowledge has encountered few full-scale attacks by well-equipped forces, taking on the Shan could be devastating."

"I know, ma'am. I just needed to hear it from you."

"No, you're right," she said. "It's an important question." She paused. "And regardless of what they decide, we'll remain in this sector longer than we had planned. We can continue to gather intelligence about the Shan vessel to prepare for an attack if one is necessary."

"I agree." Jarvis grinned. "We can always say we're sticking around to get better acquainted with them."

"You always were the diplomat, Drayden."

* * *

"In position, sir," Lily Kono said. "If you call in the middle of nowhere 'in position.'"

"Thank you, Lily," said McLeod with a smile. "It works for us now, I suppose." McLeod turned to Shaw, noticing stress on the older man's face. "It's not a problem, Goody. Raina will be okay and so will we. We may need more firepower as we complete the extraction, and if we're lucky, the pod will be all we need for that defense."

"Understood, and while we can't communicate with Captain Wolfe, we have a plan for the central city as well."

"Which is?"

"We will return there with one of our covert personnel to see what's happening with Captain Wolfe. We'll return here immediately afterwards to aid the extraction team."

McLeod nodded. "Carry on as you see fit, commander. I'll have my own problems to handle."

Shaw laughed. "I doubt that, sir."

McLeod turned again to communications. "Ava, continue to monitor the relevant frequencies. We don't want any surprises from the Shan."

"Yes, sir."

McLeod rose. "Then it's time for a little ground action." He smiled at Ross, Carnahan, West, and Kelly. "Time to hit it, people. Our pod is waiting."

* * *

"You must understand our position, captain," Ali implored. "We are not accustomed to dealing with either the Central Federation or the Shan Confederacy in Amaean space. This situation is unfamiliar to us."

"Understood." Gattiger resisted the urge to rub her throbbing temples. "And the ultimate decision about what you do and how you do it must be yours: the Central Federation does not impose defense on applicant or affiliate worlds without their consent, though defense is one reason worlds choose to affiliate with the Federation in the first place."

Ali looked uneasy. "You also have to understand, captain, that we must justify allowing the Federation to take action in our space to our populace, and—"

"Are you referring to the populace that voted overwhelmingly to affiliate with the Federation?"

"We are still the governing body of this planet, captain," Anoki said. "And we must make the final decisions about how we defend ourselves."

"Yes. You do." Gattiger sat back in her command chair. "What is your decision?"

Ali and Anoki shared glances, and Gattiger could see Ali look to other corners of the room out of her vision. Finally, Ali spoke. "We have decided to use our own security and defense forces first. That is how—"

"With all due respect, minister," Gattiger replied, "your defense forces are ill-prepared for this operation without backup."

"Which you can provide when the time comes, *if* it comes," Anoki added. "If we cannot at least try to defend ourselves against enemies, what does that say about the planetary collaborative and our forces?"

Never ask a question you don't want the answer to, minister.

After a brief silence, Ali addressed Gattiger again. "A moment, captain." Ali muted her part of the conversation. "I suppose we should listen to what you have to say," Ali said to Wolfe, who had been trying to get her attention.

Wolfe took a deep breath, glancing first at Mr. Blanks before answering. "The captain is correct, minister: unless your forces have encountered a stealthy and capable attack force like the Shan before, they will be significantly outclassed. How high will your losses be when you finally call in the Federation?"

"And what will be the public reaction be if we don't put forth the effort first?" Marten asked. "That would suggest that the collaborative can't do its ultimate job of defending the planet."

Politics, thought Wolfe, who tried to find a delicate way of answering Marten and placating Anoki, a man she liked less and less the more he spoke. "Minister, I can only say that the people will be even angrier if you suffer losses because the collaborative didn't use all the forces at its disposal."

Anoki began to rise in anger, but stopped when he saw Ali pick up her gavel. Ali looked to Mr. Blanks. "Mr. Blanks, you've listened to everything said here. Have you a recommendation?"

Mr. Blanks couldn't suppress a quick glance at Wolfe before answering. "I have no authority here, ma'am. If you and the other ministers prefer that we engage with the enemy before calling in the Central Federation, we will do so. I'm confident in our people, though I also acknowledge the challenge they face."

"And if we direct you to take action?" Hill asked.

"We take action," Mr. Blanks said, as he held up his finger. "But first, we have to verify or continue to verify what we've been told: that's in process. Second, we use that information to mobilize the proper forces to take this on."

"How much time will you need for that?" Anoki asked.

"And how quickly can we call in the Central Federation if we fail?" Crist asked.

"The answer to both questions is quickly." Mr. Blanks turned to Anoki. "We can mobilize our forces in less than an hour once we have the information we need, which includes location and any data we discover about the Shan vessel. The decision of when to call in the Federation is more in your hands as the collaborative than in mine." He pointed toward the screen. "The captain and her ship are ready to help us now."

Ali looked in the eyes of her fellow ministers and took a risk. "Kyla, you brought this to our attention. What is your opinion?"

Crist girded herself. "From what I hear, not calling in the Federation now is unwise, though I understand your position as well, Zahara. What I—"

"Why are we even asking her for an opinion?" asked Anoki. "We've already determined—"

"Enough!" Ali said. "Ian, I am still chair of the collaborative and there is no need for this kind of discourse." Ali turned again to Crist. "Go ahead, Kyla."

"As I was saying, I suggest we give Mr. Blanks a time table for when we need to decide to call in the Federation, say, six hours. If we are losing the engagement, or it looks as though we are at that time, we should ask the Federation for help."

"If I may, minister?" asked Mr. Blanks. "I support Minister Crist's approach. Our security forces should have a sunset before you call in the Federation, and six hours seems proper to me."

Hill nodded her head. "That may be the smartest thing we've heard all day here. I'm in favor."

"So am I," Marten agreed.

Ali looked at Ian. "What do you say, Ian? You've heard the proposal, do you support it?"

"We still use our forces first?"

"Yes. Always under our initiative."

Anoki stole a glance at Crist before speaking. "I can support it."

"Good," Ali said. "Let's continue our discussion with Captain Gattiger."

* * *

McLeod stood at the pod's hatch as it opened, revealing the central desert. He looked over this shoulder and smiled at his team, focusing on Ross. "Minty, activate the jamming device." He approached Ross. "Will this do anything to our communications?"

Ross looked up. "It's quite powerful, captain, so you may lose some clarity with yours." She tapped her headphone. "But I can detect anything: not to worry."

"Never."

Ross pressed a series of buttons, and the team could hear a brief screech in their headphones, then silence. "Hope that didn't hurt."

In answer, McLeod pointed at the small grove of trees that lay two kilometers away and one kilometer away from the Crist compound. "Let's go. Once we're at those trees, we can assess and implement the next phase of the plan." He looked at Carnahan. "This may be the last time I say this to you, chief, but I'd like you at point."

"Yes, sir." Carnahan approached his commanding officer. "I've been there before."

"That's why you're there now, chief." McLeod, Carnahan, Ross, and Kelly hustled from the hatch and ran toward the trees. Once there, they turned away and hit the hot sand as *Raven* continued its climb.

* * *

"I understand, minister," Gattiger said, trying to smile. "Though I believe you're making a grave mistake."

216

"Do you blame us for trying to maintain our own sovereignty?" Anoki asked.

"That's your purview, minister, not mine. *Pathfinder* will—"

"Wait, captain," Ali said. "We don't mean for you to go or leave Amaean space. What we, I mean, what the collaborative has decided is that we need to engage with the Shan first, but we may still ask for your help if the work appears to be beyond our abilities."

"Explain this arrangement to me again, minister."

"It's simple, captain," Marten said. "It is our responsibility to use our own security and defense forces first. They are, after all, under our command and direction. If, as you say the Shan prove too much for us, we would then ask for your help."

"We assume that offer is still available to us," Hill added.

This is either a dream or a nightmare. Gattiger briefly locked eyes with Jarvis, who was shaking his head. "The offer stands, ministers." Gattiger forced a smile. "Let's hope that you are correct and I am not. Call us if you need us." Gattiger looked at Beckett. "*Pathfinder* out."

Once the connection was broken, Jarvis vaulted from his chair. "What are they thinking?"

"That's the question of the hour," Gattiger replied. "But as far as I'm concerned, this is a disaster waiting to happen."

Chapter Twenty-Seven

As *Raven* lifted completely out of view, McLeod turned to his team. "Check earpieces and communications. We don't want anyone to get lost." The extraction team members checked their communications gear and frequencies, then turned again to McLeod and Carnahan.

"Remember our objective, people. Once inside, Chief Carnahan and Commander Ross will take out the communications array, while the rest of us head to the central hub and the northern arm to wait for them, understood?" Heads nodded among the team, and McLeod turned to Carnahan. "Lead the way, chief." The team began the trek to the Crist compound.

* * *

Mr. Blanks turned to leave the chamber when Wolfe stopped him. "I should go with you, Mr. Blanks."

Mr. Blanks looked first at Wolfe and then to Zahara Ali, who said nothing. "Very well." Mr. Blanks turned to leave the room again and did not slow his pace as they walked down the hallway toward the operations center.

As they neared the door, Wolfe stopped him. "Are you as confident as you appear to be?"

Mr. Blanks's face was impassive. "I don't know what you mean."

"I mean you seem confident about your planetary security and defense forces, yet I doubt you've taken on an enemy like the Shan any more than your people have, is that right?"

"Correct. But I prefer to say I am going into this with cautious optimism."

Wolfe studied his face for movement. "This could end badly for your people."

For the first time, Wolfe saw Mr. Blanks's face soften. "I understand that, and I hope to minimize the damage as much as I can."

"How?"

"By keeping to a strict and short timetable for our part of the operation, then hope that your Federation allies will still help us if and when it's necessary."

Wolfe frowned. "First, I'm sure they will, and second, why do you call them 'my Federation allies?'"

Mr. Blanks shrugged. "It doesn't matter, I suppose, but your commitment to helping Amaeus join the Federation has to come from somewhere. I assumed it came from your having a Federation connection."

"Oh, you did, did you?"

"Yes." Mr. Blanks smiled. "But that shouldn't concern you. I know when I have an asset with me."

"Which means?"

"It means I expect you to help me keep more of my people alive until we can call in *Pathfinder.*" Mr. Blanks turned toward Wolfe and searched her face. "Will you do that for me?"

"Just show me the way, Mr. Blanks."

* * *

"I would be more confident if our security forces were onboard before we take on this Federation vessel, sir," Reed said. Before Landau could answer, Reed turned to Celia Kane, *Lance* operations officer. "Status of the strike team, Celia."

Kane checked her records. "Our planned rendezvous is in nine hours, sir. We can shift to an alternate position near the central desert and then come back to pick them up in the original pods if you prefer."

"We could," Landau pressed himself into the conversation. "But it is better to send a shuttle to that location and allow them to control their own departure. That also keeps us in a better position."

"Yes, sir," Kane said as she turned to her console. "And that also offers them much more protection. Shall I send the shuttle now?"

"Jolon? Do you agree?"

"I do." Reed turned again to Kane. "Would this bring the team back onboard earlier, Celia?"

"Hard to say, sir. But it won't make it any longer."

"Agreed," Landau said. "Deploy the shuttle, Celia."

"Yes, sir."

Landau turned again to Reed. "About this Federation vessel: do we have a fix on its location?"

"Not yet, sir. For a long time it was located above the central city, but it has since moved away. Do you think they were looking for us?"

"It's likely. If we can detect their presence, they can detect ours." Landau turned again to Kane. "Celia, use whatever means you have to find out about that Federation ship. Her beacon may be cloaked, but try to get through that."

Reed frowned. "What's our objective, sir?"

Landau shrugged. "The only objective now is to gather more intelligence. If we learn more about the vessel, such as its configuration, class, or crew size, we can be better prepared to handle it."

"Might we stand down?" Reed asked. "I don't mean to suggest that we are incapable of—"

"That's a valid question, Jolon. Our job is to do what we can to maintain Amaeus's independence and our access to it. If we believe that mission is compromised, we may retreat." He looked at Reed and smiled. "But I'm not ready to do that yet."

Reed returned the smile. "Are you ready for a fight?"

"If they want one."

* * *

The *Raven* extraction team reached the trees near the compound. "*Raven* is out of range, people," McLeod said.

"I'm getting some very odd signals in my earpiece," Ross said, who had a broader range of frequencies at her command than anyone else on the team. "There's some kind of interference with the signals."

"In *and* out?" Kelly asked.

"Far as I can tell. And since *Raven* isn't doing that, and our jamming device isn't doing it, do you think the Shan vessel is?"

"I'd like to know that soon," McLeod said. "I'd prefer to have the element of surprise on our side."

"We don't have time to confirm that now, sir," Carnahan offered.

"You're right, chief, we don't. So let's get in and out of this compound as quickly as we can."

* * *

Wolfe suppressed her reaction as she stood with Mr. Blanks to consult with twelve of his prime defense force pilots. To a person, they were young and inexperienced, and Wolfe thought she detected more than the usual arrogance from fighter pilots. *If only they had experience to back up their swagger.* She listened to Mr. Blanks's detailed explanation of the mission ahead of them and hoped they would ask searching questions: they didn't.

Mr. Blanks glanced at her several times during the briefing, and noticed several of his pilots looking at Wolfe, wondering who she was and what she was doing there. When she could stand it no longer, Wolfe cleared her throat. She looked at Mr. Blanks who sat back and waited. Wolfe stood and faced the pilots.

"Taking on the Shan Confederacy is a challenging job, people," she began. "It's imperative that—"

"Who is this woman, sir?" one pilot asked. "Are we taking orders from her?" The murmur continued among more of the pilots assembled.

Mr. Blanks raised his hand and the murmuring stopped. Instead of speaking, Mr. Blanks turned again to Wolfe, who continued. "No orders, just suggestions from someone who has taken on the Shan more than once, sometimes with unsatisfactory results. You don't want to go in there unprepared."

The pilots were silent until one raised his hand. "Mr. Blanks, we don't know this woman or anything about her. Can we trust her?"

"I trust her to know what she's talking about," Mr. Blanks said. "I suggest you listen to her." Mr. Blanks turned again to Wolfe.

"The Shan Confederacy uses stealth for its attacks more than direct action," Wolfe continued. "They are unlikely to launch fighters and engage with you. Instead, they will say that they have every right to be in Amaean space—which is accurate—and they will permit you to approach them for inspection or conference. Once several of you are within their perimeter, they may use either plasma cannon or phase weapons to take out half of you."

"That's insane!" cried one pilot. "I mean, the radiation, and—"

"Beside the fact that the Shan have just about the best hulls to withstand radiation and fallout from phase weapons, they are also ruthless. And so long as they believe they can attack with impunity, they will do so." Wolfe faced Blanks and mouthed the word "Federation," to which Mr. Blanks nodded.

"There is anther wrinkle here that is to your advantage. The Central Federation vessel *Pathfinder* is in Amaean space, and has offered to help as needed, and while—"

"Why do we need them?" one pilot said. "Defending Amaeus is *our* job. Don't they have any confidence in us?"

Mr. Blanks stood to join Wolfe. "The planetary collaborative has every confidence in you as a force, so much so that they have given us a window during which we can engage with the Shan vessel to contain it and direct it away from Amaean space. We will only call in the Federation ship if we need backup."

"How long do you have to make that decision?"

"You afraid of a little Shan ship, Percy?" said one pilot, taunting his colleague, the red squadron leader.

You should *be afraid*, thought Wolfe, who said nothing.

"We have until I say we need to call in the Federation ship," Mr. Blanks said. "And I will use my best judgement on that." Mr. Blanks stopped speaking and returned to his impassive face. No one spoke or asked another question. "The information on the Shan vessel will be available on your in-flight computers. I want us in formation within the hour. Squad leaders, take command of your squadrons."

* * *

Gordon Shaw was troubled as he sat in the command chair. Torn between his obligation to the extraction team and to Wolfe in the central city, he considered deploying a small scout ship to either party but dismissed the idea. *The more we deploy, the more likely our mission is compromised*, he kept telling himself, but it didn't make him more comfortable. He turned to Kono.

"Time to central city, Lily?"

"Just under an hour, sir." Kono sensed Shaw's mood, and added, "Anything you need, sir?"

Shaw smiled. "Not now, Lily, but thank you."

Shaw stood to pace the cabin, a habit of McLeod's that he disliked, when Serrano interrupted him.

"Sir."

"Yes, Max."

"I've been monitoring something here, and I'm now sure of something that I wasn't before."

"Which is?"

"Which is that there's another Federation vessel in Amaean space."

Shaw frowned as several faces on the bridge shifted to Serrano. "What's its beacon?"

"It's partially cloaked, sir," Serrano began, "but I suspect something in the Banti class."

"Interesting," Shaw said. "A Banti class vessel in Amaean space: who would have thought it?"

"Maybe that will make our job easier, sir," Driscoll said.

Shaw smiled. "Now *that* would be a good thing."

Chapter Twenty-Eight

Elvin Cordell returned to Thorian Crist's private area without his customary arrogance.

"You have news for me, Elvin? What is it?"

Cordell hesitated before walking the last few meters to Crist. "We have identified interference with normal communications at the compound, sir."

"What does that mean?"

"It means either an outside force is sending signals jamming our transmissions or that there is an internal problem with them."

"So fix it," Crist said, with a wave of his hand. "Why are you bothering me with these problems?"

"Because we've also determined that there are two larger vessels in the surrounding space. We didn't know that before."

"How did you discover this?"

"Purely by accident. We used a temporary surge in the signal boost for our sensors when we were trying to figure out what was wrong with our transmissions."

"You don't do that all the time?"

"We can't. Surges can damage the components so we can only do it in short bursts with lots of time in-between."

Crist looked down at the table as he thought. "Tell me again what you found, and why we should worry about it?"

"Worry may be the wrong word, sir. But this jamming—if it is jamming—is very sophisticated. I'm surprised the Planetary Collaborative has that capability."

"Who else could it be?"

Cordell took a deep breath before answering. "Well, it's possible the collaborative has called in the Central Federation because of the recent attacks."

"But they're not even part of the Federation yet. Is that possible?"

"I don't know. But how else could our signals be jammed so easily?"

Crist frowned. "That's your job to find out, Elvin."

"Yes, sir."

Crist rose and walked around the room to spur his thinking. "This is a complication, and I don't like complications. Having the Federation here now alters our plans."

"No, sir. This needn't be our priority."

"What do you recommend?"

Cordell shook his head. "Without the ability to communicate the way we wish to, it will be hard to find out what's happening out there."

"Which means the priority has to be our communications."

"Exactly. It's more important than our investigation of the other attacks."

"I agree. Make it happen, Elvin."

"Yes, sir."

As Cordell left the room, Crist added, "And no need to tell anyone else about this, Elvin: they will know when they need to know."

"Yes, sir," Cordell agreed. "Just between you and me."

* * *

Wolfe shook her head as she and Mr. Blanks left the Amaean defense forces.

"This could be a suicide mission."

"Not necessarily." Mr. Blanks slowed his pace as he walked. "They are capable pilots who make very good decisions on the fly."

"But they've never taken on an enemy like this before."

"Which by your own admission uses stealth rather than direct attacks," Blanks countered. "Who's to say our awareness of them doesn't prompt them to retreat?"

Wolfe raised her hands. "You are correct. That would be typical Shan behavior." Wolfe lowered her head as she walked. "I just don't want to see too many of your pilots die testing the Shan's resolve."

"On that we agree." Mr. Blanks he continued down the hallway. They soon reentered the collaborative chamber to the sound of elevated voices.

"—lack of leadership on your part, Zahara," Anoki was saying. "We either need to embrace the Federation or not. Choosing to look the other way isn't enough."

Wolfe saw Ali's fingers drumming on the table. The chair was agitated. Ali looked around the table before responding.

"The plan to use our forces first came from all of us, and as I recall, you weren't the vanguard of that, Ian. That plan preserves our sovereignty and demonstrates our resolve to defend our planet on our own when we can. If that's not leadership and decision making, I don't know what is."

"Perhaps that is our problem," Kyla Crist said. "We've been so busy trying to demonstrate leadership and look like leaders we forgot how to do it, how to lead." She shook her head with a small smile. "That's on all of us."

But what will you do with that feeling? thought Wolfe, who noticed Mr. Blanks waiting in the doorway, holding our his arm to stop her from entering the room. He glanced at Wolfe and then back at the collaborative. It was Marten who first noticed them.

"Mr. Blanks. What is the status? Are our forces ready?"

Mr. Blanks strode forward with confidence. "I believe so, Minister Marten. They know what we are facing and they will engage this enemy to the best of their ability."

"Will we need to call in the Federation vessel?" Hill asked. Noticing the faces of her fellow ministers, she added, "What? This is important. This woman," she pointed to Wolfe, "has said we are ill-prepared to take on the Shan. I want to hear from Mr. Blanks—now that he has spoken with our forces—what he thinks."

The room was silent as Hill finished speaking until Ali spoke. "Mr. Blanks, what say you?"

"Minister, they are prepared for this stage of the operation. But having the Central Federation ready to help us is wise on your parts."

"Are you expecting causalities?" Hill asked. "Surely, something as—"

"Casualties are always a possibility. No force is invincible, and that includes the Central Federation. We must be prepared for the possibility of causalities any time we engage with an enemy."

Civilians, Wolfe thought. *We work for their benefit, but they'll never understand what it means to go to war.*

"What do you think?" Hill asked of Wolfe, whose mind had been wandering.

"About what?"

"About the possibility of casualties. You said before that we were not prepared for this kind of enemy. Do you still think so?"

Wolfe paused. "Minister, I can't evaluate your defense forces in less than an hour." She glanced at Mr. Blanks, then back at Hill. "Mr. Blanks laid out the mission and the short-term objective, and I gave them additional information to help them take on the Shan if necessary. Only Mr. Blanks can assess the readiness of your forces."

"So you just avoid the entire question?" Anoki complained. "After all your complaining before about how tough the Shan are, you still can't give us a straight answer, can you?"

Wolfe smiled as she faced Anoki. "Minister, taking on the Shan is a nasty and very difficult task. If your forces are as good as you say they are, why does my opinion matter?" Wolfe smiled again and turned her attention back to Ali, noticing a proud smile on the face of Kyla Crist.

That was for you, girlfriend.

* * *

The extraction team from *Raven* crested the last hill to the Crist compound. "We need to step to our left, sir," Carnahan noted, "then make the first breach on the northern wall of that arm."

McLeod nodded to Carnahan and signaled the rest of the team. "Communications still jammed, Minty?"

"Nothing should be coming in or out of the complex, sir."

"Just the way we want it. Continue on, chief."

Carnahan checked his earpieces for sound, then led the way toward the northern wall as McLeod took his flank. He turned back to McLeod with a question in his eyes. McLeod's nod brought one of Carnahan's own and he turned to breach the wall.

* * *

"Shuttle deployed, sir," Celia Kane said. "We included a brief communication to the attack team. The shuttle beacon will give them the complete communication once they're in range of the shuttle."

"Thank you, Celia," Landau said. "Inform me when they contact the shuttle."

"Aye, sir."

"Jolon. A word, if you will."

Reed saw Landau's face and joined his commander near his chair. "Yes, sir?"

"I believe we should shift our position to put distance between us and the Federation vessel."

"We have every right to be here, sir, and—"

"And you know that the Federation may view our presence as a provocation." Landau raised his hand. "I am not proposing abandoning the mission, just a strategic retreat."

"What will that accomplish?"

"It will reduce tensions until the Federation vessel leaves; assuming it will, that is."

"Perhaps." Reed frowned. "Why do you think the Federation is here, anyway?"

"I don't know, but this is only a temporary move on our part."

"Understood." Reed gestured toward Kane. "What about the strike team?"

"The communication to the team includes instructions to contact us once they're in the shuttle. Getting them back on *Lance* shouldn't be difficult, given all the small craft traffic around Amaeus."

"They'll rejoin us and then we'll move back into position around the planet?"

"That's the plan, Jolon. My hope is the Federation vessel will be out of Amaean space by then."

Reed nodded, appreciating the simplicity. "Sounds like a plan."

* * *

"Through the wall, sir," Carnahan said. He removed the scrambler box and returned it to his pocket. "The scrambler has saved the codes. That should make it easier inside the compound."

"We can only hope." McLeod turned to Ross. "Your turn, Minty."

"Is this still important given the status of their communications array?" Kelly asked.

"I think so, Virgil," Ross replied. "Communication can be jammed and then un-jammed. It's unlikely, but they may find a way to work around our jamming device: we can't take that chance."

"Understood." Ross and Carnahan moved toward the communications array in the western arm.

As they left, McLeod turned again to Kelly. "We can't be sure of resistance in the other arm, Virgil. Let's just hope that the armor Frankie gave us will withstand a little skirmish."

Kelly's eyebrows creased. "Will the pod be enough to get us out of here?"

"Commander Shaw has a few things occupying his time in the central city. The pod should be enough, unless they deploy anti-aircraft."

"Isn't that a gamble, sir?"

McLeod smirked as he shook his head. "Why does everybody try to spoil my fun?"

Chapter Twenty-Nine

Wolfe sat with Mr. Blanks as he reviewed his defense forces before deploying them in their search for the Shan vessel. She watched with unease as the pilots, confident to the point of haughtiness, spoke with each other and to Mr. Blanks. As the pilots and other support personnel left the briefing to begin the operation, Wolfe tapped Mr. Blanks on the shoulder. "Where's our observation post?"

"Still nervous about the outcome?"

"That's not relevant. You're aware of my concerns; I just want to know where we'll be sitting during the operation."

Mr. Blanks inclined his head toward a separate room. "Over there. Our primary control modules have two locations: one in the central control facility, and the other here in the collaborative. We'll be in this one."

"What's your background, Mr. Blanks? Are you former military, perhaps military police?"

Mr. Blanks chuckled. "That's not important, but all I've done for the last twenty years is protect Amaeus from enemies both on the planet and from outside sources. Now that I'm older, I let others take care of the more challenging work." Mr. Blanks opened the door to the control room, a massive area with consoles, controls, and lights that was almost too overwhelming for Wolfe to take in.

She turned to Mr. Blanks. "Were you ever a fighter pilot—or someone with enough experience to direct them yourself?"

"No, but the people in this control room will advise me. I remain here and evaluate the data they give me and either accept or reject their recommendations."

"And are you as famous as your name implies?"

Mr. Blanks frowned. "Why do you say that?"

"Anyone who can go by the name of Mr. Blanks is probably someone everyone knows and fears."

Mr. Blanks turned away, suppressing a smile. "You *are* a wise one."

* * *

Victor Ansara was the last to enter the conference room. He walked to his customary place, looking distracted.

"Problem, Victor?" Crist asked.

"Problem?" Ansara repeated. "No, no problem at all." He shook himself and smiled at Crist. "Sorry, sir. There is just a lot going on."

"True." Crist turned his attention to the entire group. "And one of those things we have to contend with is a problem with our communications."

"What do you mean?" Bokari asked. "With the array itself?"

"No," Cordell replied. "We are having difficulty receiving signals and normal communications and we suspect, by extension, problems getting information out."

Maddox scowled. "But how is that possible? Ours is one of the most sophisticated systems on the planet."

"That's correct." Cordell shrugged. "But any system can be penetrated with the right personnel or equipment."

"So that's it." Ansara's voice was a whisper.

"What was that, Victor?" Crist asked.

"Nothing, sir. Just that this will make our operations more difficult."

"That's not the half of it," Crist replied as he nodded to Cordell.

"We've also determined that a Central Federation ship may be in Amaean space."

"What?" Ansara stood. "How did they get here—and why?"

"Calm yourself, Victor. It won't do to overreact." Crist turned again to Cordell and nodded.

"We must content ourselves with the possibility that the collaborative has called in the Federation to help them because of the recent attacks."

"But we didn't launch the attacks!" Bokari cried. "We planned one of them, but—"

"Does that matter, Wen?" Crist asked. "The point is, if the Federation *is* here, they will take their information from the collaborative and not from us. We have to develop contingency plans."

* * *

"Did you get that transmission?" Sean Latimer asked his commander, Bahira Massi.

"I did." Massi frowned. "I only wish they'd given us more details." She turned to Gwen Tilley. "Are you receiving interference as well?"

"Yes, ma'am." They both turned to other members of the attack team and noticed their confusion as they tapped their earpieces. Massi turn on her local communicator. "Alright, people. What I heard on that last transmission is that *Lance* is sending one of the larger shuttles for us. We—"

"Why?" asked a foot soldier. "That wasn't the plan."

"I don't know," Massi replied. "That's what *Lance* told us, and if that bothers you, the person to ask is Captain Landau, not me."

"Yes, ma'am."

Massi turned again to Tilley. "Do you have the coordinates for the rendezvous point?"

"I do, ma'am. I'll determine the route and our estimated time of arrival in a moment."

"Don't take too much time. We don't know what prompted this change in plan, or if either we or the ship are in danger."

"Yes, ma'am." Massi had hoped for another engagement on land before their release. *This is such a high,* she thought, as she sat down to wait.

* * *

"Ross, Carnahan, report," McLeod said as he tapped his foot in the hallway. Before his team responded, he heard a muffled report like small arms fire. He and Kelly both sprinted toward the communications array. Right before they entered the door, Carnahan and Ross exited, coughing as they approached McLeod and Kelly.

"Couldn't be helped, sir." Ross said through her coughing. "We had to make sure they wouldn't develop a work-around to our jamming until we were gone, and couldn't rig some way to ensure that. We couldn't risk it."

"Which was *my* decision to make, Minty." McLeod bristled. "So much for a surprise entrance. Virgil, let's head to the northern arm to salvage this operation." McLeod began walking with Kelly as Ross and Carnahan followed. He got control of himself, slowed and waved Ross forward.

"Sir?"

"Forgive my outburst, Minty. Our next challenge is opening the doors to Crist's private area. We want this next phase to be quick and painless."

"Another thing you ought to know before we enter."

"Make it quick."

"I just intercepted the last part of a transmission, which said something like 'on your own.'"

McLeod frowned. "But you said the array wasn't functioning."

"It isn't. This transmission didn't come from the array." McLeod opened his mouth, but Ross cut him off. "And it also didn't come from anywhere Crist usually hangs out."

"You mean the northern arm or that part of the central hub?"

"Correct. It came from another part entirely in the eastern arm."

McLeod shook himself. "Are you recommending we stick to the original plan, or that we head to the eastern arm?"

"The alternative, sir," Carnahan said, breaking into the conversation, "is to complete the extraction, and while two of us escort Crist out of the compound, the other two investigate the transmission source in the eastern arm."

"Divide us up again?" McLeod asked. "We don't have many of us as it is."

"We understand that, sir," Carnahan continued, "But Commander Ross and I discussed it as we left the array. This is our best chance to learn more about Crist's connection to the Shan."

McLeod thought for ten seconds before nodding his head. "Understood. But even though time is of the essence, we should investigate the transmissions first, then go as a team to get Crist out of here."

"But why—" Ross began.

"Because we don't want to remove Crist and have some lieutenant of his take over with no change in direction or strength. Removing Crist is only the first step in bringing down his organization. We need to know how extensive this work is, particularly among his inner circle."

"Bring down all of them?" Kelly asked. "Is that even possible?"

"We won't know until we try. And now is as good a time as any to try."

* * *

The concussion from the western arm startled Crist and his lieutenants, who all rose to investigate. Cordell put out his arm. "No. You should stay here." He turned to Crist. "Especially you, sir."

Crist leaned forward to move but stopped. "You're right, Elvin." Turning to the table, he added, "Everyone, please sit." He turned back to Cordell, then noticed Ansara leave the table.

"I can't be in here, sir. I don't do well in tight spaces."

"Nonsense, Victor. We're in this room all the time. Sit down; we have more planning to do." Ansara looked to the door and to Crist, then his shoulders sagged and he returned to the table.

* * *

"Red squadron in position, sir," came the voice of a pilot Wolfe remembered as the most outspoken. *Not surprising that he's a squadron leader.*

"How many squads have you deployed?"

"As we define them, two, with a total of fourteen ships."

"What's the size and capability of your fighters?"

She watched Mr. Blanks's face as he wrestled with what to say. He sighed. "Our fighters are about four gara-tons and have pulse and projectile capability. They are also quite maneuverable, or so my commanders tell me." Wolfe listened and then turned her attention back to the console displays.

"Are you planning to advise me on this?" Mr. Blanks asked.

"I tried that," Wolfe began, "and you ignored—" she stopped, shaking her head. "No. That's not right. You listened half to me and half to your obligation to the collaborative." She turned again to Mr. Blanks. "My advice is for the collaborative to contact the Shan vessel and ask what it wants, then ask them to leave Amaean space. In that way, you've acknowledged you know they're out there. Your fighters are just a show of force."

Mr. Blanks sat for a moment, rubbing his hand back and forth across his bald head. He looked at Wolfe, and then at the command console, turning to a young woman. "Keep the fighters out of offensive range of the Shan vessel. We need to speak again with the planetary collaborative. Contact me if you need me."

The young woman nodded her understanding and began transmitting the message. Mr. Blanks stood and began walking toward the chamber with Wolfe in close pursuit.

* * *

"First, are we better leaving the compound and entering from another arm?" McLeod asked.

Carnahan shook his head. "We're here now, sir. We can't surprise them, but that won't change things very much now."

"Power through?"

"Yes, sir."

"Agreed. Let's go."

* * *

"But what would we say?" Ali asked. "We've never encountered a hostile force like this, and we—"

"And you want us to talk to them before we engage them with our defense forces?" Anoki said. "Why do we continue to listen to this woman?"

"Because she knows what she's talking about," Kyla Crist replied. "Or haven't you figured that out yet?"

Anoki stood. "I know that both of you are without credibility, and I refuse to listen to her advice in these chambers."

"Then don't listen, Ian," Hill said. "But I intend to give a peaceful solution every chance for success, or don't you care about that anymore?" Ali's gavel interrupted Hill, and she looked at the wooden object with scorn. "What?" she asked. "Am I no longer permitted to speak my mind with my fellow ministers?"

"You are, Leyla," Ali said. "But we have work to do here." She faced Mr. Blanks again. "Please tell us how you believe this will aid us, Mr. Blanks."

Mr. Blanks glanced at Wolfe but continued. "We suggest that you speak to the Shan so they know we're aware of their presence. Further, you ask their purpose in our space and ask them to leave. Our show of force through deploying our fighters shows we are serious about our request." Mr. Blanks raised his hand again before continuing. "And since our fighters are already in space and soon will be visible, the Shan vessel can follow our request and leave, avoiding an attack."

"And you believe this to be wise on our part?" Marten asked.

"It takes away their element of surprise," said Mr. Blanks.

"Which only *this woman* says is what the Shan does," Anoki replied.

"That's not true, Minister Anoki," Mr. Blanks countered. "We've researched this: that is how the Shan operates. That is no guarantee they'll do so again, but that's all we have to go on."

The ministers were silentwhile Ali searched their faces. She rapped her gavel on the table again. "Very well. Shall we have a vote?"

Chapter Thirty

"I don't enjoy being out of communication like this," Latimer said as the Shan strike team continued toward the shuttle.

Massi chuckled. "Nor do I, but it can't be helped. Keep monitoring whatever you hear; when *Lance* contacts us, we need to be ready to respond at once."

"Yes, ma'am," Latimer said.

But Massi wasn't as sure as her tone implied. The attack team continued walking toward the point, concerned about the communications blackout and wondering if their attack on the energy storage facility had worked to sway public opinion. They reached the shuttle two hours later, and Massi hustled the team inside.

"How shall we do this, ma'am?" Gwen Tilley asked.

"What do you mean?"

"Well, I thought—" Tilley paused.

"What?" Massi prompted.

"Hold it a minute, ma'am." Tilley listened to a recorded communication from *Lance,* frowning at several points in the recoding. She looked to Massi with concern etched on her face. "There's a small complication, ma'am. There is a Central Federation ship out there."

"Where?" Massi asked. "And how were you able to detect it so easily?"

"I didn't: *Lance* found her." Tilley pointed to her console. "They left us a recorded message. I can play it for you."

"Do it." Massi worked to keep the annoyance out of her voice. "I don't need another complication after walking so long in this godforsaken desert, especially not from the Federation."

* * *

"Is this what commanding officers do: wait around for something to happen?" asked Jarvis. "This is worse than watching paint dry."

"I understand, Drayden," Gattiger said. "And yes, it can be annoying much of the time. But we're not just paid to use our weapons, we're paid to keep and maintain the peace in the galaxy. And for today that means waiting to hear from our partners on the planet."

"What did you think of them?"

"The planetary collaborative members?" Jarvis nodded. Gattiger shook herself. "They're politicians, and they're scared. They've never experienced a Shan attack, and they don't know what to do."

"Then why didn't they accept our offer?"

Gattiger smiled. "*Because* they're politicians. They have to consider more factors in decision making than we do, like how their people will react to Federation intervention in their affairs."

"I don't understand that. It would seem to me that—"

"Nor do I: that's why we're in the military. Things make more sense to me in uniform than trying to do the—" Gattiger struggled for a word, "glad-handing and back room deals politicians have to deal with."

"I understand. It just seems so dirty to me."

"I agree." Gattiger turned to Jarvis and smiled again. "The fact is, we're where we need to be, Drayden. Let's celebrate that."

"Yes, ma'am." Jarvis frowned. "And will we help them if they ask?"

"Count on it."

* * *

"How should we address the Shan in this communication?" Zahara Ali asked, speaking mostly to herself.

"We tell them we're aware of their presence and ask them what they're doing here," Anoki said. "Isn't that what Mr. Blanks said?"

"Of course, Ian. I was just going over it in my mind."

"Well, if you're not going to—"

"I *am*, Ian." Ali turned to Mr. Blanks. His communications technician was opening the connection to *Lance*.

"Do you need to check on the status of the squadron, Mr. Blanks?" Ali asked.

Mr. Blanks didn't move. "They're in position, ma'am, and informed of the collaborative's decision."

Ali sighed. "Open the connection, please."

* * *

An incoming com signal brought *Lance*'s bridge to attention.

"What is it?" Reed asked.

"It's from the planet, sir." Rubinco frowned as he triangulated the signal before turning to Reed and Landau. "It's coming from the planetary collaborative, sir."

Landau turned to Reed. "Well, this is interesting, Jolon. The collaborative wants to talk to us."

"Are we interested in talking to them?"

Landau shrugged. "It doesn't matter. We're here, and they know we're here, so why not?"

"Do you think that's why they're contacting us?"

"To tell us they know we're out here? My sense—"

"Amaean fighters between us and the planet, sir!" Kane said. "They're out of range but in formation."

"That's a little more than a simple greeting, sir," Reed said.

"So it is." Landau nodded, looking up to Rubinco. "Let's see what the collaborative has to say, Cleve. On screen."

Rubinco pressed several buttons. Four faces came to life on the screen. "Keep the focus on me, Cleve."

"Yes, sir." Rubinco turned back to Landau. "Line open, sir."

Landau sat smiling in his chair. "Good day to you. I assume I have the honor of addressing the ministers of the planetary collaborative."

"You do." Ali struggled to keep the nervous quiver from her voice. "I am Minster Zahara Ali, here with my colleagues. What is your purpose in Amaean space?"

Landau smiled as he raised his hands in surrender. "We're just travelers like any other, minister. Our ship, the *Lance,* has no purpose other than that." Leaning forward, he added, "And you have no reason to line up attack fighters against us. It appears you don't want us around."

"And if we don't?"

"We are only travelers," Landau repeated. "And the only way we can travel from place to place is to pass near several planets on the way. We're simply passing through your space."

"But you aren't moving."

"True," Landau agreed. "But every ship's crew deserves to rest." Landau stood moving slowly so the camera could keep the focus on his face. "We have some minor repairs to complete, and it would be—" he paused, "difficult, and perhaps dangerous, for us to be in deliberate motion while we complete those." Landau noticed Ali's eyes move to her left before she turned her attention back to him.

"How long will these repairs take?"

"Not long, I assure you, minister. We need another two or three days, then we'll be away from Amaeus and on toward our destination."

"What is your destination?"

"A star system one hundred seventy mega-clicks from here. That star system contains several worlds that have chosen to affiliate with the Shan Confederacy; something you might consider as well."

"Why would we do that?"

"Perhaps you shouldn't." Landau smiled and shrugged. "We are committed to economic cooperation and maintaining the sovereignty of planets. Not every planet is ready for that or believes that level of economic prosperity to be important."

Ali leaned forward to answer, but thought better of it and sat back. "We will expect you out of Amaean space in no more than three days."

Landau bowed. "As you wish, minister." He nodded to Rubinco, who broke the connection.

"And are we going to leave?" Reed asked.

"Of course we will, when we're finished our work and not before; something the collaborative may find out the hard way."

* * *

In the collaborative chambers, Ali turned to Wolfe with a scowl. "I do not appreciate your distracting me during such a sensitive communication. This was very delicate, and I needed to give him my full attention."

"I understand that, minister," Wolfe said. "And I was trying to make sure you had the entire picture as you spoke to him. He has no intention of leaving in three days."

"Then we will take action at that time."

"Three days will be far too late."

"I will no longer listen to these ravings!" Anoki cried. "We're here to protect this planet and we're listening to someone who—" Anoki broke off, stood, raised his hands in disgust and left the chamber. The other ministers stared as Anoki left, then turned back to Ali, who took a deep breath.

"Even if we've only bought ourselves some time," Ali began, "it's time we can use to develop a stronger plan. We may even choose to communicate with *Pathfinder* so they know what we've done."

The first smart thing you've done on your own since I met you, Wolfe thought.

"Very well, ma'am," Mr. Blanks said. "I will instruct our fighters to run normal maneuvers and sorties in the space between the Shan vessel and the planet so that our presence is constant but in motion."

"Couldn't they just stay where they are?" Marten asked. "That's an awful lot of work for the fighters."

Mr. Blanks smiled. "That's what they enjoy doing, minister. They will appreciate the opportunity." He turned his attention back to Ali. "I should contact our fighters, unless you need me for something else." He shared a glance with Wolfe, who nodded and left the chamber with him.

* * *

"Review that for me again, Julie," Gattiger said.

Beckett looked at her console again. "The planetary collaborative communicated with the Shan vessel, asking their purpose and directing them to leave the area as soon as possible. Sounds like they're leaving within three days."

"They can get into a lot of mischief in three days, ma'am," Jarvis said.

"They can." Gattiger nodded her head. "But the collaborative was smart to contact the Shan vessel."

"Should we announce our presence as well?"

"To the Shan?" Gattiger asked. "They already know we're here; there's no reason to insult their intelligence by announcing ourselves. No; when we need to communicate with the Shan, it will be when we are sure of their purpose here and can do something about it." Gattiger resumed her seat. "And that will happen soon enough."

Chapter Thirty-One

Elvin Cordell advanced toward the western arm with five soldiers, taking his time looking at each door as he walked. He was distracted by the sound of the alarm and the dust from the small arms fire and didn't notice McLeod until it was too late. McLeod shifted the butt of a pulse rifle up to meet Cordell's chin, then swept his legs out from under him as he turned to face the five soldiers. A single shot from Carnahan downed one soldier and stopped the advance of the others.

"You don't want to do that," Ross said, with a larger weapon in her arms. "Rifles down and hands behind your heads!" Ross, Kelly, and Carnahan dashed to the downed soldiers and placed them in restraints.

"Remove their communications devices and get them out of the corridor and into a side room," McLeod said. "We need to get Crist and get out of here."

They moved the soldiers to a side room and placed gags on their mouths before returning to McLeod, who was standing over the groggy, prostrate figure of Elvin Cordell. Cordell's eyes focused on McLeod's as he shook his head to remove the cobwebs. "Who are you?"

"Doesn't matter," McLeod replied. "Just play nice for the moment. Is Crist in his conference room?"

Cordell turned away with a sneer, but McLeod placed his boot on the man's throat and pressed.

"I don't have a lot of time here."

Cordell tried to move his head, but found the boot sinking ever lower, blocking his air. He nodded, hoping that would be enough.

"What does the nod mean?" McLeod asked as he reduced the pressure on Cordell's throat.

"Conference room."

"Good choice." McLeod turned to Kelly. "Virgil, place Mr. Cordell in restraints and get him to his feet; he's going with us." As Ross and Carnahan joined them, McLeod smiled. "They should still be there. If we're lucky, it's just going to be four against four."

Ross smiled. "Nice odds."

* * *

"Prepare for launch," Massi announced, tapping her foot. She turned to her helmsman. "All hands prepared?"

"Yes, ma'am," Latimer said. "We'll be airborne in five minutes."

"Do it. We have work to do." The message from *Lance* bothered Massi. The ship had detected radiation that suggested a Central Federation vessel was in Amaean space, but *Lance* didn't know what ship or why they were there. Massi turned to her communications officer.

"Play the transmission again, from the—" she paused, searching her mind, "thirty second mark."

"Yes, ma'am." Tilley searched the transmission and advanced it to the requested spot. She turned to Massi, who nodded.

"—aware that a Central Federation vessel is also in Amaean space. Vereen has confirmed it through radiation signals and weapons. Class unknown at this time. Unknown why they are in Amaean space. The planetary collaborative may have asked for their assistance. Be cautious in your return to *Lance* and use evasive and non-threatening maneuvers as necessary. Maintain communication silence to avoid detection by Amaean forces."

Massi sat back, only then realizing she had been leaning forward as she listened to the transmission. Landau was not a nervous commander, yet Massi could hear apprehension in his voice. *I'd better watch myself.*

* * *

Gordon Shaw noticed Max Serrano's back straighten and his immediate turn towards Ava Driscoll. "Ava, what kind of chatter are you hearing out there?"

Driscoll turned to Serrano. "If you're asking about the fighters, sir, I just noticed them, too."

"Fighters?" asked Shaw. He left the uncomfortable chair and approached Driscoll and Serrano, who pointed to his display.

"There. I'd estimate about ten in formation and approaching the Shan vessel." He turned again to Driscoll. "What have you heard?"

Driscoll shook her head. "Not much, sir, but what little I could separate from the chatter is that they're the planet's defense forces."

Serrano frowned. "Against a Shan vessel? Are they crazy?"

"I doubt that," said Shaw. "I doubt they've ever encountered the Shan before, and they think somehow this is a good enough show of force."

"In other words," Driscoll said, "they *are* crazy."

Shaw exhaled. "Let's hope they're also damn lucky. Continue monitoring their movements and inform me of any change."

"Aye."

* * *

McLeod led his team down the corridor toward the central hub and the northern arm with as much speed as he dared. The team encountered no resistance in the corridor, which puzzled him. *Does no one else care about this damn alarm?* He stopped and gestured for Ross to come forward. "We need that alarm off, Minty; it's distracting, plus Crist may decide to do something about it. Can you handle it?"

Ross thought for a moment then nodded. She opened a small pack at her waist and removed two devices. She turned on her virtual visor and looked around the corridor, selecting a spot ten meters back the way they had come. McLeod forced himself to look forward to avoiding a surprise, and two minutes later, the sound stopped. He looked back at Ross, first smiling, then frowning.

"What is it?" McLeod asked.

Ross answered by pointing to an area past the conference room. She looked back. "Give me a minute?"

McLeod clenched his jaw. "Time is of—"

"Scout's honor." Ross moved quietly past the conference room, shifting her body back and forth, before using a decoder device to open a small door. She reached inside the compartment and in less than a minute straightened up again. A smiling Ross returned to the extraction team, holding a small device in her hands.

"What is that?"

"The source of the transmission to the Shan," Ross said. "It's a communications node." She pointed down the hallway. "It works on low frequency, but has shielding so it's hard to detect. It was also close enough to the array that someone could transmit at will using it, but nothing else could work properly."

"I'll ask more about that later," McLeod replied. "But for now, let's keep going."

They had advanced to just outside Crist's conference room. Ross joined McLeod at the front. "This is it." McLeod nodded and stepped back from the door. Ross inserted a small device into the door lock, waited two seconds, then smiled as the door whirred. As it opened, Ross nudged Cordell into the room first, then advanced into the room with McLeod, Kelly, and Carnahan behind them to the startled faces of Thorian Crist and four of his senior people.

"Good day, everyone." McLeod smiled. "Sorry for the noise earlier. Shall we talk?"

* * *

"Time to rendezvous with *Lance* is two-and-a-half hours, ma'am."

"Thank you," said Massi, who was still distracted. She faced her attack team leaders. "Are you as concerned as I am about this Federation vessel?"

Latimer nodded. "I am. There's nothing else from *Lance?*"

"We're continuing to check," Massi said. "Apparently, *Lance* is honoring the communications silence as well." She turned again to Tilley at the communications console. "Anything?"

"No, ma'am."

"Continue to monitor. We need to know anything that might impact our return to *Lance*."

"I'll be happier once we're back on board," Tilley said.

"Me too," agreed another team leader, whose name Massi always forgot.

"I'd like to know if our attack was successful," Massi said. "We didn't have time to hear the result."

"Could the planet have asked the Federation for help because of Crist?" Latimer asked.

"Not in the last week." Massi shook her head. "We've been monitoring communications from the planet for weeks."

"So they were already here? That makes no sense."

"It doesn't," Massi said. "And that's what keeps preying on my mind."

Chapter Thirty-Two

"What's the status of the fighters?" Gordon Shaw asked. He tried conveying the confidence that would befit a commanding officer but was finding it difficult to do so.

"They're performing sorties, sir." Driscoll turned to Shaw. "I don't know why they're doing that. Could they be planning an attack?"

"I doubt it. Their positioning hasn't changed in a while. This is a show of force." Shaw turned to Driscoll. "And they don't want to leave the area and be forced to return if the Shan vessel provokes something." Shaw turned his attention away from communications, noticing Max Serrano studying his console. "Something to add, Max?"

"Not as yet, sir."

Shaw smiled and approach Serrano. "But there is something."

"Am I that transparent?"

"If you have to ask—" Shaw began, but Serrano raised his hand.

"I get it. And what I am thinking about is communications."

"What about them?"

"They're a mess. Just ask Ava. We've got signals from the Shan vessel, and from the Federation vessel, and—"

"Anything on the Federation vessel?"

"Oh, yes," Serrano said. "I forgot to tell you about that. Let me retrieve it." Serrano pressed a few buttons and loaded data on the Federation vessel for Shaw to see. "The vessel is *Pathfinder*, a Banti-class vessel. It has a new commanding officer, Su-Captain Lena Gattiger. She's former tactical and executive officer aboard *Pantro*." Serrano looked again to Shaw. "She's spent most of her time in the delta and beta quadrants, sir, so I doubt anyone onboard knows her."

"I do. Not much, mind you, but she's seen as capable." Shaw looked up.

"What?"

"Gattiger is capable as I've said, but I wonder how she'll do handling a Shan Confederacy vessel so early in her first command."

"Does that worry you?"

Shaw started to speak, then glanced to the left. "No. But maybe we can help her pull *Pathfinder* through this mess."

* * *

Thorian Crist spoke through clenched teeth as he rose from his seat. "Who *are* you?" McLeod advanced with his rifle and Crist sat again.

"Thank you." McLeod smiled again. "And who I am doesn't matter. We're here to give you an opportunity, and that applies to all of you." McLeod looked around the room at the faces of Crist's team.

"Elvin?" Maddox asked. "Are you all right?"

Maddox leveled a glare at McLeod, who returned it with a smile. "I assume you want to hear our offer?"

"No," Crist said as he looked around the table. "This is my property; I am the sovereign here, and—"

"You are not a sovereign," McLeod answered. "You are a terrorist standing in the way of this planet's self-determination. And you have to go."

"Go? Go where?"

"You have some choice in the matter, Mr. Crist. We're here to make the transition easier for you."

"I don't understand. Do you dare to take me prisoner? Our forces will—"

"Your forces have been neutralized. With very few shots fired, I might add," McLeod said. "Care to try again?"

McLeod looked as Ross, Kelly, and Carnahan advanced toward the others in the room, looking for weapons.

"Surrender is not an option," Crist said, puffing out his chest. "And we will not stand for—"

"Give it a rest," Carnahan said, who then turned to McLeod. "Shall we just take them all, sir?" Before McLeod could answer, Ansara stood. "Are you with the Shan?"

McLeod and his team exchanged glances, but no one answered. "The Shan Confederacy?" asked McLeod. "Why would you ask that?"

"I, uh, I just thought that—"

Maddox stared. "You thought what, Victor? Is there something you need to tell us?"

"Oh, I imagine Mr. Ansara has a lot to tell us," McLeod replied. "And he'll tell us after we leave this compound."

"I'd prefer to hear it now." Maddox advanced toward Ansara. "What is going on, Victor? And why would you ask these people if they're part of the Shan?"

Ansara stood balancing from one foot to the other. "Well, the Shan are, uh—" Ansara began, but he couldn't string together enough words to soften the stares at him.

McLeod stared again at Ansara. "Ms. Maddox's question is a good one, Mr. Ansara. Why would you assume we were the Shan?" McLeod moved closer to Ansara. "And why do you see them as your savior?"

The room was silent, as Ansara searched the faces and the floor. "I, uh . . . I have nothing to say."

"And that tells me a great deal," Crist said. He turned his attention back to McLeod. "So—are you the Shan? And should we be worried?"

"Concerned, yes," McLeod said. "Worry is something you have to decide for yourself." McLeod smiled. "And I've fought against the Shan enough to resent your comparison, and—"

"Who *are* you?" Crist repeated with a scowl.

"We'll tell you all about that, Mr. Crist," McLeod began, "but it won't be here." He nodded to his team and Carnahan hoisted Cordell. "All of you get up: we have a long walk ahead of us."

* * *

The sound of an alert surprised Massi, who looked to her helm and communications officers. "What is it?"

"Presence of enemy fighters, ma'am," Latimer said. He turned to Massi. "I don't understand it. They aren't from the Federation, so they must be from the planet."

"And Captain Landau didn't think to tell us this beforehand?"

"Well, ma'am, there is the communications—"

A glare from Massi silenced Tilley. "I know about the silence, Tilley, but you'd think something as important as fighting against both Central Federation *and* planetary forces would be worth telling us!"

"Yes, ma'am," the helmsman said, turning back to his console.

Massi turned to her two attack team leaders. "Gentlemen, join me here, please. We have a situation." She pointed. "Check the helm console."

The men walked to the console and looked at the data, then turned back to Massi. "It looks like ten fighters, maybe more, ma'am," Latimer said. "What's their origin?"

Massi appreciated the team leader's calm, deliberate manner. "We are not sure, but we believe they are fighters from the planet itself and not from the Federation."

"That could be good or bad," said the one whose name Massi couldn't remember.

"How so?"

"It may be much easier for us to either evade or neutralize them than if they were Federation fighters."

"I agree," said the other team leader.

"But how could it be bad?" Massi asked.

"That's the tough part, ma'am," said the first team leader. "We don't know what kind of orders the planetary force may have; at least we know how the Federation operates."

"Agreed." Massi rose. "Let's get to *Lance* as quickly as we can; this shuttle is nothing compared to a starship. I don't want to be out here with a minimal weapons array against ten or more enemy fighters, no matter who they are."

The two team leaders looked at each other before the first said, "Got that right."

* * *

Mr. Blanks and Wolfe walked silently back to the control center. They entered, and several people cornered Mr. Blanks, giving him reports. Wolfe listened as best she could without getting in the way. *There's too much to take into account.* She thought about the status of the extraction, and what the Shan vessel, the Amaean fighters, and the Federation ship might do in open space. *The Amaean fighters have more energy than brains, a recipe for disaster.* As Wolfe brought her attention back to the present, she was startled to see Mr. Blanks standing next to her with an expectant look on this face.

"You didn't hear me?"

"Sorry," Wolfe said with a smile. "What were you saying?"

"We have to go back to the chamber."

"Why?"

"Because something else has broken loose and the ministers will call us back, anyway."

Mr. Blanks walked so quickly back to the chamber that Wolfe had difficulty keeping up, a first for her. When they entered the chamber, Zahara Ali was frantic. "Mr. Blanks! Have you heard the news?"

"Yes, minister. We received the communication in the control center a minute ago. We came back to consult with you."

"What are we to do about this?" Marten asked. "Now the public knows everything!"

"Not everything, I am sure, minister," Mr. Blanks replied. "But it makes this part of the operation more difficult. The collaborative may want to broadcast its own message to allay fear or apprehension among the public."

"But what would I say?" asked Ali, drumming her fingers on the table.

Wolfe could see stress on the faces of all the ministers, including Kyla Crist. Taking a risk, she asked, "Mr. Blanks didn't tell me why we returned to the chamber. Can someone tell me?"

"The news services reported that two squadrons of our fighters are now in open space around the planet, which has never happened before," Ali replied. "They've also reported that a Shan Confederacy vessel is in Amaean space. They're asking us what we're going to do."

Wolfe squinted. "Why don't you just tell them you sent the fighters up to investigate? That's what you've done, and it's a plan that makes sense."

"There's more," Ali sighed. "They've also reported that a Central Federation ship is in Amaean space, and they are accusing us of weakness and a lack of leadership. One commentator called for more open communication from the collaborative and full disclosure—but that could cause panic!"

Which is often a risk in a democracy, Wolfe thought. "Have you decided what to tell the press?"

Ali held her head. "I don't know. I just don't know."

Wolfe looked at Mr. Blanks. "The other important question is, how did the news media get its information? They could have noticed the fighter movement; anyone who lives near the base could. But very few people knew about both the Shan *and* Central Federation vessels."

Wolfe was silent as the eyes of the ministers began darting back and forth among their colleagues.

"Exactly," Wolfe said. "And that is a much bigger problem for you to handle."

* * *

After his team placed Crist and his remaining lieutenants in restraints, McLeod gestured with his rifle at the entire group. "Shall we go?" He allowed Maddox to help Cordell walk and accompanied Crist himself. Crist said nothing but walked with an air of superiority about him that McLeod found annoying. Ross led the group outside to the open desert, and after checking on her virtual map, pointed in the direction they should go to reach the pod. McLeod nodded, and they began walking. McLeod placed Carnahan in the lead as he dropped back to confer with Ross.

"Assessment, Minty?"

"It was straightforward, sir, but there may be traps or other hazards in the open desert." She turned to him. "Remember, we didn't come in this way, so we're covering new territory."

McLeod nodded his understanding. "I have nothing in my communicator. How about you?"

"Nothing, sir. But we'll have that capability once we get to the pod and deactivate the jamming device. For right now, though, given the Shan vessel and the possibility of collusion—" Ross frowned and stopped walking. "Wait a minute."

McLeod smiled. "Took you long enough." He inclined his head toward the walking prisoners. "I don't know what kind of deal Ansara was working on, but he was working with the Shan to bring Crist down."

"For personal gain?"

"I don't know and I don't much care. Crist impresses me as someone who wants to do things his way. Like the Shan, Crist preaches self-determination, but he focuses on Amaeus: I doubt Crist wants to affiliate with anyone. He wouldn't be working with the Shan."

"What do we do about Ansara?"

"We'll take them all back to *Raven* and figure it out there. We need Raina's perspective in situations like this."

Something in his face alerted Ross. "Are you worried about her?"

McLeod shook his head. "Just like I told Kyla Crist. Not so much worry as concern." He shook himself. "Let's get back to the pod and return to *Raven*. I want that ship around me again."

* * *

Landau paced on the bridge of the *Lance*, chatting with her personnel as he passed their consoles. Reed noticed the habit and connected it to nervousness. He stopped Landau near his chair. "They're probably in the shuttle now, sir. We can break communications silence."

"Perhaps," said Landau. "And I doubt the planetary forces know enough about our communications to intercept our messages." He looked at the communications console. "But I'm sure the Federation vessel will, and I don't want to give away the shuttle's existence."

Reed searched Landau's face. "They may already be aware of the shuttle, sir."

"True. If they are, I'm hoping they'll leave it alone. And that's more likely if the shuttle doesn't take any aggressive action."

Reed nodded. "That makes sense. The Federation won't like the shuttle being in Amaean space, but they're unlikely to take action against them."

"That's what I'm counting on. What I can't count on are those fighters from the planet."

Reed looked around the cabin. "Should we change our position?"

"For the moment, no. Any movement we take could be considered a provocation. Once the shuttle returns, we can do whatever we want. And then there's—" Landau stopped.

"What, sir?"

Landau looked at Reed, nodded his head, then sat in his command chair. "The other concern is our contact within the Crist compound. We've heard nothing because the signals have been jammed by, well, by the Federation vessel, I assume. Because of that, we don't know if our attacks are having the desired impact, and we also can't determine—"

"Captain," came the voice of Tal Vereen. "There's something else."

"What is it?"

"News reports, sir." Vereen turned to Landau. "They're saying that both a Shan vessel and a Central Federation vessel are in Amaean space along with several fighters from the planet." Vereen frowned.

"What?"

"As far as I can tell, sir, the news reports are talking more about the fact that the collaborative…this doesn't make sense. Hold on." Vereen listened intently again, nodding his head as he gained understanding. "They are calling for open disclosure from the collaborative. They're asking what we're doing here, and why the collaborative would call in the Federation without informing the people." Vereen turned to Landau. "They're more concerned about the collaborative and the Federation vessel than us, sir."

"More important to us, however," Landau said, "is how the news people knew about this. There is a leak somewhere."

"It had to be from a source that knew everything. Who knew everything?"

"We do," Landau said, with a wave of his hand. "Our source in the Crist compound might, and the collaborative knows as well."

"Then who do we target?" Reed asked.

Landau sat back in his chair. "I wish I knew."

Chapter Thirty-Three

The hatch to the pod opened silently as McLeod led his team and Crist's lieutenants inside. "Make yourself at home. With any luck we won't be here too long."

"What will you do with us?" Crist asked. "We have rights on this planet, and unless—"

"I don't have time for you right now, Mr. Crist," McLeod snapped. "We have to contend with a Shan Confederacy ship that's threatening this planet."

"Why do you say they're threatening Amaeus? You only say that because you are an enemy of the Shan."

"Everyone is an enemy of the….you know what? I can't waste time on this right now." McLeod shifted his gaze to Ansara. "Or perhaps Mr. Ansara can tell you about the Shan and their plans for Amaeus. Why don't you do that while we're flying, Mr. Ansara?"

Crist stared at Ansara, a stare that usually made Ansara stand at attention. "Victor?" But Ansara remained silent and looked away from his leader.

Blotting the exchange from his mind, McLeod approached Ross, seated at the helm. "Any more communications from *Raven*, Minty?"

"Just checking that now, sir." Ross stared at the console as she turned on the pod's beacon and scanned the area for signs of *Raven*. She shook her head. "There's something else here, sir."

"Something good or something bad?"

"Good, but unexpected. There's a Federation ship in Amaean space."

"What ship? And what's it doing way out here?"

"Can't give you either answer, sir, just that it's from the Federation. I'll keep looking, but I assume my priority is to contact *Raven*."

"Correct. I don't want to spend any more time in this desert than necessary."

"Beacon activated now, sir." Ross turned to McLeod, and smiled. "We'll be home soon."

* * *

Ava Driscoll smiled as she detected the pod beacon and raised her fist in triumph.

"What happened, Ava?" Shaw asked.

"Beacon, sir. The pod is ready for pickup."

Shaw sat back in the command chair. "And none too soon for my taste. Lily, set course and let's pick up our team."

"Aye. Do you think they succeeded, sir?"

"That's my assumption. I've only worked for Captain McLeod for a short time, but he gets results."

"True. Course set in and engaged."

"Thank you, Lily." Shaw turned again to Driscoll, adding, "Anything from Captain Wolfe?"

"Nothing, sir." She turned to Shaw. "Doesn't mean we have to worry about her, though."

Shaw laughed. "I imagine you're right. Captain Wolfe and Captain McLeod are two of a kind in that regard: you can never count either of them out."

* * *

"We need to prepare a statement for the press," Ali said, looking at her fellow ministers.

"And what is it we're supposed to say, Zahara?" Hill asked. "That the reports are accurate, and we're sorry we didn't tell you sooner?"

Anoki laughed as he turned to Ali. "Any more brilliant ideas, Zahara, because the last few haven't worked out too well."

"If you remember, Ian," Ali began, "we all agreed on our current plan—even you; or did you forget that?"

"I wasn't happy having the Federation here at all, if you—"

"We agreed on a plan!" screamed Marten. "And now we have to agree to our statement. Can we just get to the point?"

Amen, thought Wolfe. She caught the eye of Mr. Blanks and looked toward the door to the chamber. Mr. Blanks nodded and turned to Ali.

"This work is surely more suited for you as ministers, ma'am. I should return to the control room to check on the progress of the operation against the Shan vessel."

"This does not authorize you to call in the Federation, Mr. Blanks," Ali added quickly. "I mean, just check with us if you think it's necessary."

Mr. Blanks bowed. "Of course, minister. If you will excuse me." Ali nodded and Mr. Blanks led Wolfe out of the chamber.

They rushed to the control room, reaching it in minutes. As they entered, they noticed a heightened sense of concern among the staff at the consoles.

"What is it?" Mr. Blanks asked.

"We're not sure, Mr. Blanks," said one. "But—"

"But?"

"There is another smaller ship out there that concerns us."

Mr. Blanks looked at the consoles and the displays. "There are lots of smaller ships out there. Which one are you referring to, and why does it concern you?"

"This one, sir."

"What about it?"

"Well, it's an unusual size; it's bigger than a standard shuttle and much smaller than a transport or freight vessel."

"You didn't call me over here because of this vessel's size."

"No, sir. The fact is that when you asked us to monitor signals and residual radiation, this one came up as very unusual."

"In what way?"

"It has the same or at least a similar signature as the Shan vessels that that woman," she pointed to Wolfe, "told us about." Mr. Blanks turned to Wolfe, who approached the display.

Wolfe leaned in and pressed a few buttons. "Yep. That looks like a pion drive. It's not common around here, but it's classic Shan technology."

Mr. Blanks turned again to the display. "When did this shuttle appear?"

"Recently, sir," the technician said. "Perhaps an hour ago, but we couldn't complete the analysis until just before you arrived. I'm sorry we couldn't do it faster."

"No matter." Mr. Banks waved his hand. "You've completed it now, and that's what matters."

"Wait a minute," Wolfe said. "Let's look at a few more things." She pressed a few more buttons on the console, then looked around. "Can someone here do an emissions analysis on that shuttle?"

A lone voice from the back of the room called out, "Got it." Wolfe and Mr. Blanks walked to the console and examined the display. Wolfe looked it over, then pointed to a series of waves. "There. See it?"

"Those two peaks?" Mr. Blanks asked. "Yes."

"Those are indications of phase weapons and a very large amount of tullarium."

"We mine that on Amaeus all the time."

"But do you often see a concentration this high in one place?" Mr. Blanks shook his head. "Right," Wolfe continued. "They have phase weapons."

"In that little ship? That can't be over seventy-five meters long."

"Doesn't have to be any bigger," Wolfe answered. "Plus no one will be on a ship that size for long. They can be shielded from the radiation long enough to inflict damage, then return to a fighter hold in another ship with superior shielding."

"The other Shan vessel?" Mr. Blanks asked. Wolfe nodded. "So what do you recommend?"

Wolfe hesitated. "Do you trust me?"

"What?"

"Do you trust me?" Wolfe repeated. "You've spent time with me. You know I'm no threat to Amaeus." She closed the distance between her and Mr. Blanks. "Do you trust me to do what's necessary to reduce or eliminate the Shan threat?" Mr. Blanks shuffled Wolfe away from the rest of the technicians in the control room and into a corner.

"What did you have in mind?"

"I need to contact my ship."

"You have a ship?"

Wolfe smiled. "You have no idea, but yes, and I can do more to help you if I'm there rather than here."

"Tell me more."

* * *

McLeod saw Ross's face light up.

"Does that mean?" McLeod asked, but Ross held up her hand, then gave him a headset. McLeod sat and put on the phones.

"—in about thirty-five minutes. Things have been heating up since your departure, and—"

"And we look forward to hearing all about it, Ava," McLeod said. "Patch me through to Commander Shaw." Five seconds later, Shaw's voice came through the headset.

"Captain, good to hear from you."

"Good that we can, commander."

"The mission?"

"Successful as it goes, but we've heard about a few complications in Amaean space."

"Correct, sir," Shaw replied, and McLeod could hear the tension in his voice. "Not only the Shan vessel but another Federation vessel and fighters from the planet."

"Whoa. Are they battling now?"

"Not yet, but I'm not optimistic. Plus, we've not heard from Captain Wolfe for a few hours."

"Any reason for worry?"

Shaw's response was immediate. "None, sir. We're obviously hoping for the best."

"What do you know about the Federation vessel?"

"It's the *Pathfinder*, sir. They have a relatively junior commander, a Su-Captain Lena Gattiger."

"I know her."

Of course you do, thought Shaw. "I'd say she's level-headed."

"I agree. She has a long history at tactical, as I recall, but it's solid experience."

"Think she's up to this challenge?"

"That I can't say, Goody. But she's not really alone out here, is she?"

"My thoughts exactly," said Shaw, whose smile came through the connection.

"Get us onboard as fast as you can, commander." McLeod looked behind him at Crist and his team. "It's a little cramped in here."

* * *

"So you have a plan that will help us?" Mr. Blanks asked.

"I do," Wolfe said. "But I need to contact my ship first."

"Do you need our communications equipment?"

"Maybe. Let me try something else first." Wolfe clicked her jaw and activated the earpiece, shocked at the sounds coming in so close to her inner ear. She raised her hand in reaction and Mr. Blanks flinched.

"It's okay; it's been quiet for a while. Hold on." She made more subtle adjustments, before acknowledging defeat. "I *will* need your equipment. All I'm getting now is static." Mr. Blanks led her to a console and excused the technician. Wolfe hooked up to the console and adjusted the frequencies, pressing a button for a moderate scramble when Mr. Blanks wasn't looking.

"I hope I'm speaking with Enlisted Chief Second Class Ava Driscoll."

"Captain Wolfe!" Driscoll cried. "We've been worried about, I mean, we've—"

"Good to hear your voice too, Ava, but at the moment, I need a pick up from the planet. We have work to do."

"Yes, ma'am." Driscoll turned around. "Here's Commander Shaw." Wolfe smiled at Mr. Blanks and gave him a positive signal.

"Captain Wolfe, this is very welcome."

"Were you all worried about me, Goody?"

"We were getting concerned. But we're better now."

"Good. What's the status on the extraction?" Wolfe noticed Mr. Blanks's eyebrows raise at the word "extraction," but she turned her attention back to Shaw.

"Successful, ma'am. We pick up the pod in ten to fifteen minutes."

"Your next mission is to return to the central city and pick me up at the spaceport coordinates. We need to resolve multiple issues here with the Shan vessel and the Amaean fighters."

"To say nothing about the Shan shuttle out there as well."

"Oh, you know about that?"

"We do."

Wolfe pressed her temples. "Just keeps getting better and better, doesn't it?"

Chapter Thirty-Four

The sorties of the Amaean defense force fighters were running according to plan when communications lit up with a secure transmission from the control room.

"Squadron leaders and fighters," Mr. Blanks's voice rang out. "There is another Shan vessel in your vicinity. It—"

"There are lots of ships in our vicinity, sir," came the voice of one squadron leader. "Can you identify the specific vessel?"

"Shift your sensors to read chromaa engine radiation wave." Mr. Blanks waited for the squadron leaders. "Squadron leaders, report."

"Done, sir," came the voices of both men.

"Good. The ship with highest readings is the one to watch."

"What is the ship, sir?" asked the blue squadron leader.

"We believe it's a Shan shuttle. We don't know its capability." Mr. Blanks turned to look at Wolfe. "But it may have more weapons than you're accustomed to for so small a vessel. Be careful."

"Are we to engage, sir?" Wolfe mouthed the word "no."

"Not at this time," Mr. Blanks said. "Stand by for further instructions."

"Yes, sir."

Mr. Blanks stood and walked closer to Wolfe, directing her to the side again. "I don't like this. I don't like not being able to make definitive decisions."

"Welcome to my world." Wolfe raised her hand again. "That doesn't compensate you for the risk and stress, but it's the truth. The bigger question is, will you allow me to rejoin my ship and crew?"

Mr. Blanks gave a rare smile. "I didn't know I had any choice in the matter."

"Good answer."

* * *

"We must present a united front to the people," said Ali, tapping her gavel again against the table. "This is crucial to our survival, and we can't afford to mess it up."

Kyla Crist was sitting on the table, rather than in her seat, with her arms folded. She was exuding the confidence that had won her leadership in her party and in the southern government. "Full disclosure is our only hope, Zahara. At least then we needn't worry about contradicting ourselves later."

"So you believe the people are prepared for this?" Anoki replied. "A Shan Confederacy vessel in Amaean space, along with an uninvited Central Federation ship?"

"The people are more resilient than you think, Ian," Crist answered. "We have to give them the chance."

"Kyla is right," Hill said. "We've used subterfuge and hiding for too long. We should face the public with our eyes open and tell them what's going on."

"We only have a short time before the news crew arrives for the statement and its release," Ali said. "Let's work on the official statement so we are in agreement when they arrive."

* * *

The klaxon announcing *Raven*'s arrival unsettled the Crist personnel just as it comforted the *Raven* crew. McLeod nodded to Ross, who engaged the pod engines and piloted the pod upwards toward the ship. Its shields on strongest, Ross scanned for anti-aircraft fire from the compound but saw nothing. She contacted Driscoll. "Ava, ask Commander Serrano to keep watch on the compound as we rise. The last thing I want is to be shot out of the sky."

"Aye, ma'am."

"Where are you taking us?" Crist asked no one in particular. Turning to McLeod, he repeated. "Where are you taking us?"

McLeod's turn to Crist was slow and deliberate. "To a place where you can't harm anyone else. Trust me, you're better off with us than on the planet."

"How do you know that?"

McLeod rolled his eyes. "Have you no imagination, Thorian? You were to be sacrificed for the good of the order once the Shan and your friend Ansara here," he said, pointing to Ansara, "got their hooks into Amaeus. He was selling you out, and I doubt you would have survived."

"I don't believe it. Victor was loyal and a good soldier all this time."

McLeod shook his head, then turned to Kelly. "Take Cordell and Maddox to medical when we dock, Virgil. Cordell needs medical attention."

"Aye, sir."

McLeod once again faced Crist. "Mr. Crist, you may as well sit. You won't need to stand like that for quite a while." McLeod turned back to the helm, ignoring Crist, whose breathing he could hear behind him.

"Prepare to dock," came the voice of Ava Driscoll.

"Pod ready."

"Bay is open, commander," said Driscoll. "You're on your own in the final stage."

"Understood, Ava." The pod rose into the interior of *Raven*, enveloped by gray and charcoal metal before the lights in the shuttle's pod bay went on. The sound quality changed as the lower bay doors closed around the shuttle and Ross cut the power. She turned to McLeod with a smile.

"We're home."

* * *

"What do you mean, there's another Shan vessel?" Gattiger asked. "Why didn't we know this before, Tara?"

"Sorry, ma'am. Our focus was on the larger Shan vessel and the fighters, trying to determine how we might intervene."

Gattiger sat in her command chair, her jaw set. *I can't afford incompetence like this in my first command.* "What can you tell me about this Shan vessel?" she asked after a minute.

"Not much, ma'am," Worth replied, turning back to her console. "I believe it's a shuttle. We're sure it's a Shan vessel because of its drive."

"It must be connected to the larger vessel," Jarvis said.

With a quick glance, Gattiger noted, "Agreed. But that's not the whole of the story." She looked again at Jarvis. "We now have to consider not only a larger Shan starship, but a shuttle. And I'm sure that shuttle is well-equipped with weapons." She turned to Worth. "Tara, can you tell if they have phase weapons on board?"

"On it."

"Now Drayden, it's time to contact the collaborative again."

"Why?"

"Because their fighters are no match for the Shan *and* a shuttle," Gattiger answered. "We need to repeat our offer and take a stronger hand in this."

Jarvis smiled and nodded in agreement. This was his first encounter with the Shan, and while he was apprehensive, he preferred to be in command of the situation rather than reacting to it. "I agree, ma'am," he said, turning to Beckett. "Julie, open a channel to the planetary collaborative."

"Aye."

"Let's see if they give us a different answer this time, ma'am."

* * *

McLeod settled into his command chair on *Raven* like it was an old glove. He smiled at the bridge crew, even to Kono's back as she piloted *Raven* through Amaean space in its clumsy freighter configuration. After placing Cordell and Maddox in the medical hold, the crew placed Crist's other lieutenants in isolation and under guard.

"Status and arrival time to central city, Lily."

"Not long now, sir. We're on course."

"Commander Shaw?"

"Sir?"

McLeod pointed to the second command chair. "We need you here, Goody."

"Yes, sir."

"Now," McLeod continued. "What do we do about all these players in Amaean space?"

Shaw frowned. "Captain, do we have to do anything? I care about what's going on, but once we get Thorian Crist off the planet—which we've done—and Captain Wolfe back on board *Raven*, our mission is *technically* over."

McLeod laughed. "I heard the way you said *technically*, Goody. And like all crazy Star Alliance officers, we're going all in." McLeod leaned toward Shaw. "We also have the responsibility to take on the Shan—or at least prevent their expansion when we can. This is an opportunity we should not ignore."

Shaw turned back toward the helm, his face a mask. "Whatever you say, sir." But McLeod could sense the approval in his voice.

* * *

"Therefore," Ali continued, "the planetary collaborative, with the safety of the Amaean people in mind, has authorized a containment operation against the Shan Confederacy vessel. This operation began at 1400 hours today. Further, the Central Federation vessel *Pathfinder* was in the vicinity of Amaeus on the way to another destination and offered its assistance because of the Shan Confederacy vessel's presence in Amaean space." Ali looked up and tried to smile. "The collaborative has declined their generous officer, and we will use our planetary forces for what they are designed to do: defend Amaeus from external enemies." Ali smiled again and turned her head, taking in the other members of the collaborative in the tight shot being broadcast live.

"My fellow ministers and I believed we should start this operation and have it well underway before inciting panic and unease among the Amaean people. If we are at fault for not informing you sooner, we sincerely apologize. We will broadcast more information and status reports as they become available. Please have confidence, as we do, in our planetary defense forces, and thank you for your continued support of the planetary collaborative and our democratic processes." Ali nodded toward the camera, and once the operator nodded back, she exhaled, deflating significantly. She faced her fellow ministers.

"That was fine, Zahara," Marten said. "It couldn't have gone better."

"Unless we could already tell them that we won the battle," Anoki replied.

"I would prefer there not be a battle at all," Crist said.

"Fantasy world," Anoki whispered, before turning away from Crist.

* * *

At the side door to the collaborative, Wolfe stood with Mr. Blanks near a ground transport. "They will be furious with me for letting you go," he said.

Wolfe shook her head. "I think they've rather forgotten about me. The news reports and the Shan shuttle have rattled them. They don't know which end is up."

"That's why I'm worried."

"Don't be," Wolfe offered. "They have you."

Mr. Blanks frowned. "What do you—"

Wolfe smiled. "You're the most level-headed person in that building," she said, pointing to the collaborative with her eyes. "Now if you go inside and take care of your job, I'll rejoin my crew and take care of ours."

"Will I be able to contact you again?"

"That's hard to say, but I know how to contact you." Wolfe entered the transport and turned back to Mr. Blanks. "Good luck."

* * *

"But you must have seen our recent transmission, captain!" Ali cried. She faced the grim and tired face of Lena Gattiger after Gattiger's second offer of help.

"My people told me of the transmission, minister, and I wish you had consulted with us before sending it out. Having a second vessel near your fighters will not end well for you."

Gattiger could see Ian Anoki come into the central picture. "And your presence hasn't helped us, captain," Anoki said. "You were the primary cause of this broadcast."

Patience and deep breathing, Gattiger thought. She forced a smile at Anoki. "Our presence, Minister Anoki, was accidental. We were on the way to another location when we encountered the Shan Confederacy vessel. By statute, we are to protect all Federation affiliated worlds or candidates for membership from the Shan." Noticing Anoki swelling up to talk again, Gattiger quickly went on. "The statute also requires us to contain the Shan Confederacy when they may compromise the self-determination or integrity of any world." Gattiger once more relaxed herself. "And let me be clear to you, ministers: *Pathfinder* is not going anywhere, and whether we engage the Shan for your benefit or stay here as an additional protective force for Amaeus, we're here for the long haul." Gattiger sat back in her chair. "*Pathfinder* out."

Chapter Thirty-Five

Bahira Massi's helmsman directed the shuttle with care, avoiding the Amaean fighters. *How much longer to* Lance? Massi thought. *I don't want to be out here too long.*

"We're receiving a hail from one of the fighters, ma'am," said Tilley.

Massi sat back and thought. "Ensure our shields are up and ready. We have to go into this with our eyes wide open."

"Yes, ma'am," Latimer replied.

Massi shook her head. *What have we gotten ourselves into?*

* * *

Wolfe arrived at the spaceport after *Raven* touched down in her freighter configuration. She strode to the hatch and pressed in her code, touching the hull in a brief caress. The hatch opened, revealing a smiling Tucker McLeod. "I wanted to be the first to greet you."

"Of course you did," Wolfe said, returning the smile. She walked toward him, touching his arm, then approached the ladder. "Is this as complicated and messy as it seems?"

"That's my read of it—and everyone else's. There are too many people on this planet who have no idea what they're doing." He slowed and turned to face Wolfe. "And to be honest, I'm not impressed with the planetary collaborative. Are they showing leadership, or just how to follow?"

"I'm with you. They *need* that Federation vessel's help." Their conversation stopped as they climbed the ladder to the bridge. "I'm still not used to having ladders instead of a lift. I feel like I'm in one of my old trainers at the academy."

"But you love it, don't you?"

"I do." On their final approach to the bridge, Wolfe asked, "What do you know about the Federation vessel?"

"It's *Pathfinder*. A Banti-class vessel on its way to the—"

Wolfe shook her head, impatient. "Right. What I meant was, what crew members do you know, other than the captain?"

"No one, but both Goody and I believe Gattiger is competent, if green."

"I agree. But she has a good head on her shoulders. I think she served under Roanne Sutherland at one time."

"Good experience." Just then, they opened the hatch to the bridge.

"Captains on the bridge!"

"Carry on," Wolfe said. She and McLeod smiled as they regained their command chairs.

"Straight up and to the agreed upon location, Lily," McLeod said.

"Aye, sir. Let me know when we can change into something fiercer."

McLeod smiled and nodded, then turned to Wolfe. "Lily is having too much fun with this ship."

"I can see that. Now, what are we contemplating for this situation?"

"You aren't going to tell me that our mission is over now that we have Crist in custody, are you?"

Wolfe shook her head as she smiled. "I know you better than that, Tucker. Plus, we have unfinished business with this Shan vessel. Which reminds me, have any other messages come through?" Wolfe turned to Driscoll. "Ava, what have you been hearing from planet-side?"

"Not much, ma'am. *Pathfinder* offered her assistance to the collaborative again after the public statement they made; the collaborative declined."

"I was there for the first exchange. Gattiger wasn't happy."

"What else have you heard, Ava?" McLeod asked.

As Driscoll started to speak, she intercepted a signal that surprised her. "Well, until now, nothing, but something's coming through now." Driscoll turned away from McLeod and Wolfe to concentrate on the transmission. "Damn it!" she said without thinking. Driscoll turned to McLeod and Wolfe. "Sorry. But it's not good."

"How not good?" Wolfe asked.

"The fighters have hailed the Shan shuttle, ma'am. They're challenging the shuttle's presence in Amaean space."

McLeod stood. "Under normal circumstances, that isn't so bad. But this is not normal circumstances."

"Which those fighters are likely to find out right now," Wolfe agreed.

* * *

"Identity and purpose in Amaean space," the squadron leader repeated. "We won't ask you again!"

Bahira Massi looked to each of her attack team leaders. "Suggestions, gentlemen? Captain Landau told us not to engage with these fighters, and we're only thirty minutes away from *Lance* at this speed. I don't want to waste time with these idiots."

"How can we avoid them?" Latimer asked. "If we keep ourselves in the proper position relative to *Lance* and these fighters, we'll have the ship as cover soon."

"That depends on what Captain Landau wants *Lance* to do. He'll likely want to fade into the background for now, or at least that's what I think he would say if we could speak with him."

"Is it time for that now?' Tilley asked, who turned, ready to send the transmission.

Massi sat back and took a deep breath. "Let's hold off for now. We may have to call their bluff."

"This is your last opportunity," screamed the Amaean squadron leader. "Identify yourselves and your purpose in Amaean space or risk being fired upon."

Massi looked to her attack team leaders. "Well, I guess that didn't work."

* * *

"Track their movements, Virgil," McLeod said. "We need to know if the shuttle moves into an attack position against the fighters."

"Aye, sir."

McLeod turned to Wolfe. "What's your assessment of the fighters, Raina?"

Wolfe shuddered. "They're young and impulsive—like many fighter pilots. They are way over their heads today, and instead of lying low, which is what I *told* them to do, their fear is sparking this bravado."

"What's their command structure? Is there a way we can contact them to offer more instruction or guidance?"

"A good idea," Wolfe said. "Ava, use the primary frequency for the control room on Amaeus and hail them."

"Aye, ma'am." Driscoll began pressing buttons on her console as Wolfe stood.

"What is it?" McLeod asked.

"What?"

"You're standing; you never do that."

"Sorry. It's just that Mr. Blanks isn't impulsive by nature. I wonder what he's doing, or not doing, on the planet?"

McLeod frowned. "Won't we find that out now?"

"Probably," Wolfe replied. "It's just that—"

"Control room on screen, ma'am."

"Tight on me, Ava." As Wolfe settled back into her command chair, a shot of the control room and the technician she had consulted earlier appeared on the screen.

"Oh," the technician said. "I didn't know it would be you."

"I understand. I was hoping to speak with Mr. Blanks."

"So are we." The technician had a slight tremor in her voice. "He's on his way back from the chamber—they didn't want to let him go."

"My friends and I," Wolfe's eyes tracked around the bridge, "heard the fighters challenging the Shan shuttle. That was a mistake."

"We know. That's why we're trying to contact Mr. Blanks. We don't know what to do."

"Which pilot is hailing the shuttle?"

The technician looked to the side and hesitated. "It's Percy, the red squadron leader. Do you remember him?"

"I remember him. *Well.*" Wolfe rubbed her temples. "Can you get him to stand down?"

"We're trying, ma'am, but once he get's going, he's hard to stop."

"Try *very hard,*" Wolfe said, surprised by her tone. "And when Mr. Blanks returns to the control room, please use this hail frequency and tack to contact us, understood?"

"Yes, ma'am," the technician said, sitting up straighter. "I will."

"Thank you." Wolfe nodded to Driscoll, who broke the connection.

"I thought Mr. Blanks was the easiest one to deal with planet-side," McLeod said.

"He is." Wolfe smiled. "Once you get to know him. And with him absent from the control room, that can only spell bad things."

* * *

Massi watched as the Amaean fighters shifted positions, some to surround her and others to fly in sorties between her and *Lance*. Boxed in, Massi had limited options.

"Open a channel to the—" she began, but before she could respond to the fighters, she heard, "Incoming!" from the tactical console. Massi ran to the console and saw that several missiles had been launched from the fighters to her flank.

"Evasive maneuvers, now! Protect the flank and weapons arrays. Prepare to engage!"

Her attack team leaders looked first to Massi, then shifted to positions on their plasma cannon controls.

"On your mark, ma'am!" one said.

Massi looked to her communications officer. "Open a channel to *Lance*, Tilley. Tell them we have a problem."

"Aye ma'am." Tilley opened the channel as the first missiles glanced off the shuttle shields, throwing people to the deck.

Massi shifted her attention to the tactical console, raising her arm. She tracked the fighters as they moved and pointed. "That one. Percussion missiles to the three fighters to our right. Plasma cannon with emission seeker on that fighter at eighty degrees. Now!"

Tactical complied and seconds later, the fighter erupted in a cloud of gray dust and debris.

Massi collapsed in her chair. "This is not what I wanted to do today."

* * *

"Fire from both the Amaean fighters and the Shan shuttle, ma'am!" Beckett said. "The shuttle refused to answer a hail from the fighters. They opened fire and—"

"I can see that, Julie!" said Gattiger, who regretted her outburst immediately. "But that isn't our concern now." Gattiger turned to Jarvis. "We have to enter this, Drayden." Gattiger turned back to Beckett. "Open a channel to the main Shan vessel, Julie. With any luck we'll stop this mess before it gets any worse." Sitting back and calming herself further, Gattiger faced Tara Worth. "Full alert, Tara. Shields up and prepare to engage."

* * *

"Fools!" Landau screamed. "To engage like this in open space is the height of stupidity. And by someone as experienced as Bahira. It's insane!"

"They pinned her down, sir," Reed said. "She didn't have any other choice."

Landau turned an angry face to Reed. "Then maybe you aren't seeing things as clearly as you should, Jolon."

"Hail from Commander Massi, sir."

"Pull it up." The screen lit up with the face of Bahira Massi, who opened her mouth to speak but Landau cut her off.

"Your orders were not to engage, Bahira. This may cause more reaction than you know!"

"I chose not to die today, captain. I will not allow myself to be fired upon by these idiots!"

"You'd rather countermand my order and bring my wrath down on you? A foolish choice, Bahira! Perform evasive maneuvers and return to *Lance*. Try not to get yourself fired upon on the way."

"Incoming message from the Federation vessel, sir," Vereen said.

"Ignore it."

Vereen turned to Landau. "They're powering up their weapons, sir."

Landau scowled. "We were not prepared for this, Jolon."

"I understand, sir, so should we—"

Landau shook his head and returned to his command chair. "Shields up! Prepare to engage with the Federation vessel."

* * *

Raven gained in height to two thousand kilometers, pulling away from the force of the planet's gravity. As Kono guided the ship toward the fighters and the Shan vessel, Driscoll and Kelly called out.

"What is it, Virgil?" McLeod asked.

"The battle has started, sir. Projectiles from the fighters and then what looked like plasma cannon from the Shan shuttle to one of the fighters." Kelly turned to McLeod and Wolfe. "The fighter is gone."

"So much for patience," McLeod said.

"*Pathfinder* has hailed the Shan vessel; no response as yet." Driscoll's eyes widened. "*Pathfinder* has powered up her weapons, too."

"Shields up and full alert!" Wolfe said as she walked over to Kelly's console, and McLeod turned to Driscoll.

"All-com, Ava," McLeod said. Once on, he said, "All personnel to core positions, prepare to shift to config three on my mark. Report."

"I'm thinking a limited strike to the main Shan vessel," McLeod said. "Enough to get her attention, then a hail to *Pathfinder* to avoid additional engagement. That may defuse the situation."

Wolfe sat, looking first to the floor then at McLeod. "That could work. Which is why I assume you're shifting to config three?"

"That was my thought."

"I just hate being exposed in that configuration on a covert mission."

"True. But I have an idea about that, too."

Wolfe smiled. "Do tell."

Chapter Thirty-Six

Mr. Blanks was hit by the alarm when he reentered the control room. "What's happened?"

The communications officer turned a tearful face to Mr. Blanks. "It's Percy, sir," she said. "He's gone."

Mr. Blanks stopped walking. "What happened?"

"He hailed the shuttle, the one we thought was part of the Shan?"

"Yes."

"He hailed them two or three times, then powered up his weapons. He and two others shot across her flank." The technician looked down. "The shuttle shot him out of the sky. The other fighters have just stopped; the blue squadron leader can't get them together."

"I can do that." Mr. Blanks extended his arm. "Hand me a headset." He sat at the communications console and pressed two buttons. "All fighters, stand down. Maintain shields and power to weapons, but return to containment positions and maneuvers." Mr. Blanks listened for a moment, then added, "Blue squadron leader, acknowledge."

Soon after, he heard a lone voice. "Acknowledged, sir."

"Good. Hagan, acknowledge."

"Yes, sir," Hagan said. "I mean, I acknowledge."

"Good. You are now the red squadron leader. Keep your people in line and disciplined, something your predecessor didn't do."

"Yes, sir. Any other orders, sir?"

"Yes." Mr. Blanks sighed. "Let no more of our people die out there."

* * *

"Fast as you can, Lily," McLeod said. "We need to be in the action."

"Aye, sir."

"Virgil, shift to config three."

"Yes, sir." Kelly pressed a pad, and the ship shuddered as it moved into its starfighter configuration. The favorite of the crew, it offered faster maneuvers, and a more complete weapons array than the other configurations. Its hull also offered the most complete detection avoidance technology of *Raven's* hull forms.

"You mind sharing your plan with me now?" Wolfe asked.

McLeod turned to her, first frowning, then with his characteristic smile. "Sure—but it's changed. Now, I want us in the middle of the action. I want to escort the shuttle to the Shan vessel, taking it out of the equation. With any luck, *Pathfinder* can handle the Shan vessel."

"With or without our help?"

"That's up to Gattiger. We'll make contact with her before we begin escorting the shuttle; she can decide what she wants to do next."

"That's a good plan. It also gives Gattiger the opportunity to make the final decisions on how to handle the Shan overall."

"The question is how well she'll handle that." McLeod turned to Driscoll. "Ava, I'd like you to place a tight communications beam on the shuttle in a few minutes. I want to communicate with them and minimize distortion or bleed to the other vessels. Can you do that?"

"I can try, sir. It's not what I usually do, and I can—"

"No one's asking for guarantees, Ava; focus as much as you can."

Wolfe looked at McLeod. "We communicate with the shuttle, tell them to get their asses back to the mother ship and we'll provide cover, but not to argue?"

"Something like that."

"So, a lot of bluster and posturing—which even Shan commanders fear, am I right?"

McLeod smiled. "That too."

"That's what I thought."

"Shift complete, sir," Kelly said.

"Good," McLeod replied. "Lily, get us into the action, focusing on the fighters and *Pathfinder*. I doubt Gattiger will fire on us without prior warning, and if she objects to our being around, Captain Wolfe will talk to her."

"Why me?"

McLeod waved his hand. "You're much better with the nice talk than I am."

* * *

"Keep both the shuttle and the larger Shan vessel within our field, Darien," Gattiger said, speaking to her helmsman.

"Aye, ma'am."

Gattiger turned to Beckett. "Any response from the Shan, Julie?" Beckett shook her head. Gattiger winced. "Fine. Open a channel to the planetary collaborative." A minute later, Beckett nodded to her commander and opened the communication. Gattiger looked upon the startled and uneasy faces of the five ministers.

"We've come to a new point in this crisis, ministers," Gattiger said. "I assume you don't want to lose any more of your fighters?"

"Of course not, captain," Ali said. "But you must understand—"

Gattiger stood up and strode closer to the camera. "I understand that if we don't take action now, you'll lose more of your fighters unnecessarily. *Pathfinder* is entering into this crisis. *Now.*" She glanced at Beckett, then back to the collaborative. "Your fighters are to stand down and return to containment maneuvers immediately. I will communicate that to your command staff after Ms. Beckett shifts us."

All five ministers looked at each other, but none of them looked up at Gattiger.

"That's what I thought," Gattiger said, her voice weary. "We'll talk later." She nodded again to Beckett, who switched to the control room on Amaeus's planetary collaborative building. Gattiger saw Mr. Blanks seated at a console. She didn't wait. "We have a new crisis, sir, and *Pathfinder* will be taking the lead."

"Understood," Mr. Blanks said. "The ship designations for the squadron leaders are being sent to you now. The fighters are returning to containment positions and maneuvers. However, their shields are on full and their weapons are fully powered."

"I would expect nothing less," Gattiger said with a smile. "We can discuss your ministers later, but for now, please transfer the command codes for your squadrons to *Pathfinder*."

"Consider it done." Mr. Blanks looked up with a grave face. "Help more of my people come home, will you?"

"On it. *Pathfinder* out."

* * *

"Now what?" Latimer asked as he faced his commander. Massi's teeth were grinding as she considered her options: stay here with few weapons or approvals or risk more battles and losses by engaging with more of the fighters. Neither of the options appealed to her. *I don't like being in lose-lose situations.* After a minute, she turned to Latimer. "That's a good question." Massi turned to tactical. "What are we seeing with the Federation vessel?"

"Well, besides her hails to the fighters and powering up her weapons, nothing, except some transmissions to the planet." He turned to Massi. "My guess is they're telling the planet what they're doing."

"Movement?"

"Not much yet, ma'am," he said. "The only thing I'm seeing," he said, turning back to his console, "is that the fighters have changed. They've backed off and are giving us and *Lance* more room."

"They're removing themselves from the fight," said Massi. "That's good." She turned again to her helm. "How is our progress?"

"Steady, ma'am," the helmsman said. "But I've reduced our speed. I thought—"

"No," Massi answered. "That was the right decision. Just keep making that progress and hope the Federation vessel doesn't hail us. I don't want to go up against them."

* * *

"It already feels different." Kono smiled as she turned to McLeod and Wolfe. "Are you sure we can't always be in this configuration?"

"If only, Lily," Wolfe said. "But that isn't the point for *Raven*."

"I understand," said Kono. "I can always hope, can't I?" A sharp noise by the door to the bridge alerted everyone, and they turned to see Mark Carnahan leading Thorian Crist and Victor Ansara onto the bridge. McLeod strode to Carnahan with a questioning look on his face. "There must be a good reason for this, chief."

"Yes, sir." Carnahan said. He motioned to Ansara with his eyes. "This one says he knows more about the Shan vessel and wanted to tell us. I didn't want to do that in isolation."

"And Mr. Crist?" McLeod could see the anger radiating off of Carnahan, and the set to his jaw. "Mr. Crist didn't want to miss anything."

McLeod sighed and pointed to his command chair. "Sit," he said to Crist.

"I'm not going—" Crist began, but McLeod's expression stopped him midsentence. With a huff, Crist sat in McLeod's chair.

"Don't mess up that chair." McLeod turned to Ansara. "You have something to tell us?" Ansara's eyes darted back and forth and he licked his lips.

"If it will help us, Mr. Ansara, we need to know it now."

"Well," Ansara began, "the Shan vessel is *Lance*, and the captain is a man named Landau."

"Tyrus Landau," Wolfe said. "It *would* be him."

"You *know* him?"

"I know a lot of undesirables in this galaxy, Mr. Ansara," Wolfe said, looking at Thorian Crist. "Landau is just another one of them. He's a typical Shan commander: plenty of stealth mixed with a bully who won't engage in a fair fight."

"Assuming any fight can be fair," McLeod said.

"Well, yes," Wolfe conceded.

"Given that," McLeod began, "do you think escorting the shuttle then letting *Pathfinder* take over will work?"

Wolfe hesitated. "It could, but we need a Plan B just in case."

"Don't I always have one?"

* * *

"Shan vessel. This is Captain Lena Gattiger of the Central Federation starship *Pathfinder*. You are intruding into Amaean space, which is under the protection of the Central Federation. You are directed to leave this area immediately. Acknowledge." Gattiger waited, then turned to Beckett.

"No response, ma'am."

"I didn't expect one. Use the command codes to direct the fighters, Tara. Have them continue present positions of containment and await our instructions."

"Aye."

"Inform me once that's complete." Gattiger looked again to Beckett. "Repeat hail, Julie."

"Aye, ma'am."

Gattiger sat down hard.

"Problem, ma'am?" asked Jarvis, smiling. "You sounded confident in your message to the Shan."

Gattiger leaned toward her executive officer. "And that's what I wanted them to hear, Drayden. It wouldn't do to—"

"Captain, there's another vessel out there!" Worth cried.

"What?"

"Another vessel—I can't detect a beacon or determine its type—is placing itself between us and the shuttle."

"On screen." Gattiger turned to the screen and noticed a grayish shadow as it approached the fighters and the shuttle.

"What *is* that?" Jarvis asked.

"I have no idea," Gattiger replied. "Hail it, Julie."

"Aye." Beckett hesitated and turned to Gattiger. "They're hailing us, ma'am; audio only."

"Well, let's listen to what they have to say." Beckett pressed a button.

"This is Captain Lena Gattiger, of the Central Federation starship *Pathfinder*. Please identify—"

"Good day, captain," McLeod said. "Who we are is of no consequence, but we're here to help."

"I don't think you realize what's going on here, sir," said Gattiger, annoyed. "Please identify yourself and—"

"No time for that, captain. We're trying to avoid any more unnecessary loss of life. We also know that the commander of *Lance* is a notorious bully, and we don't want to press his buttons."

"*Lance?*"

"That's the Shan vessel everyone's so worried about. They've been interfering in Amaean politics over the last few days and perhaps months."

"I don't understand what you're staying," Gattiger continued. "But I can't allow a civilian vessel in this sector. Please leave the area immediately."

"That won't do, captain," McLeod replied. "Tell you what: we'll get the shuttle out of here and back to *Lance*, then you can have all the fun you want with her. Fair enough?"

"Whoever you are," Gattiger continued, "We cannot allow you to—" but Beckett interrupted her.

"Connection lost, ma'am."

Jarvis shrugged when Gattiger looked to him. "We don't even know that ship's name," said Jarvis.

"No, we don't. We know nothing about it; and that makes me very nervous."

Chapter Thirty-Seven

"Prepare to come alongside the shuttle," said McLeod. "Steady as she goes, Lily."

"Aye."

"What are you doing?" asked Crist, rising from the chair.

McLeod looked back at him, then at Carnahan. "Keep him away from me, chief."

"Aye, sir." Carnahan nudged Crist with his rifle, forcing him to sit.

"Should we hail the shuttle again?" Driscoll asked. "They never responded to our last transmission." She looked back and forth between Wolfe and McLeod, not knowing who would answer.

"Hail *Lance* instead," Wolfe replied, as she returned to her seat. "Tight on me."

"Does Landau know you by sight?" McLeod asked.

Wolfe shrugged. "I doubt it. We could go with audio rather than full connection to be safe. Let's try that at first, Ava."

"Yes, ma'am." Driscoll made the connection, then turned to Wolfe. "Connection live, ma'am."

"Captain Landau," Wolfe said. "You are in a tough situation and we'd like to help you get out of it." They waited for twenty seconds, before Wolfe spoke again. "We know who you are, captain, and you can see where we are: between you and your shuttle. We also have Thorian Crist and all his people on board our vessel, so that part of your operation has ended. Now, do you want to lower tensions here or risk the alternative?"

McLeod leaned toward Wolfe. "This is your *nice* voice?"

Wolfe waved him away. "Better than yours would be under the circumstances."

A voice interrupted Wolfe. "This is Landau. Who the hell are you?" The anger in Landau's voice was clear.

"We're travelers who hate to see innocent lives destroyed by stupidity and unnecessary posturing. What—"

"That is not an identification!" Landau screamed. "Identify yourselves, or—"

"Shimmer," McLeod said. Virgil Kelly slid a lever down, then returned it to its original position. To outside observers, *Raven* seemed to disappear and become translucent while the lever was depressed.

"Captain, you don't have the time or the guts to out-bluster me," Wolfe continued. "And you have no idea what we can do: that's only a sample. Consider yourself warned. We'll help get your shuttle back to you, and if you're smart, you'll leave Amaean space permanently."

"I'm not going to—" was all Landau got out before Wolfe had Driscoll break the connection.

Wolfe looked to McLeod and grinned. "That was fun."

* * *

"I don't understand that transmission, either," said Gattiger as she looked to Jarvis. "And I can't trust this new vessel to be on our side."

"Agreed. Maintain alert," Jarvis said to the bridge crew. He turned back to Gattiger. "Do we allow this new vessel to escort the shuttle?"

Gattiger sat back in her chair. "Our objective is to get the Shan out of here and defend Amaeus from them. When both ships leave Amaean space, that would be a 'win' in my book."

"Mine, too."

"Though I can't say I'm happy about that other ship's involvement."

"The squadron leaders hailed us, ma'am," Beckett interrupted. "They're asking for instructions about the new vessel." Instead of answering Beckett, Gattiger called Tara Worth. "Tara, have you found an ID beacon for that vessel?"

"The new one?"

"Yes."

Worth shook her head. "I can't break through their shields—there are a *lot* of them." Turning to Gattiger, she added, "They're heavily cloaked; almost as if they aren't there."

"How about drives, weapons?"

"Nothing definitive, ma'am, except that there doesn't seem to be anything off about it, such as a pion drive like the Shan use."

"Thank heavens for small favors," Jarvis said. "What do we tell the fighters?"

"Tell them to continue containment maneuvers, shifting as necessary, but to allow the shuttle to reach the Shan vessel. We won't provoke an unnecessary battle here."

"Yes, ma'am," Beckett replied.

"Thank you, Julie." Gattiger sat back in her chair. "I hope our superiors are okay with this, Drayden."

"The fighter opened fire first without reason, ma'am. That's the responsibility of the Amaean forces and not the shuttle. The shuttle could have opened fire on other fighters, but didn't."

"Agreed."

"Plus, we're not in active war status against the Shan, regardless of our dislike for them. If we can get them out of here without firing a shot, I think we'd be okay."

Gattiger smiled. "Good having you around, Drayden."

* * *

"Continue progress to *Lance*, Bahira," Landau said. "This new vessel may be part of the Amaean arsenal: I didn't know they had ships like this, but I don't feel the need to take chances."

"Should we be prepared to attack her?"

"Not at this time," Landau said. "Once the shuttle is secure in our hold, that will change." As he spoke, the eyes of his bridge crew widened.

"Do you think that's wise, sir?" Reed asked. "We don't know what the new ship can do, and the Federation ship is still out there."

"Wise or unwise doesn't matter, Jolon. I will not allow that woman—or anyone from the Federation—tell me what to do." Reed looked at Landau for a moment, then turned away.

"Awaiting orders, sir." Massi's voice came through the speakers. "Any change in plan?"

"None, Bahira. Continue your progress." Landau straightened himself. "I will deal with the new ship later."

* * *

"What will you do with *Lance*?" Ansara asked. "Captain Landau has a strike team on the planet; I'd bet they're in the shuttle."

"You mean the ones who conducted the attacks on Amaeus over the last few days?" McLeod asked. "*That* attack team?"

"How did—"

Wolfe looked to Crist as she answered. "Neither you nor *Lance* are good at hiding these things, Mr. Ansara. So, you get the public angry at both the collaborative *and* at Thorian Crist and the only way to solve things is to call in the Shan—who won't seem quite so dangerous when they're offering stability and economic prosperity—and *you're* the one who benefits."

"It's a clever plan," McLeod said, "if somebody with more foresight and finesse was carrying it out." Ansara stiffened, looked around, then dropped his head as he relaxed.

"That person would not be you, Mr. Ansara," Wolfe said. "I have to hand it to you, Thorian, at least you were 'keeping your enemies closer'— you just didn't know who they were."

Crist gripped the armrests of the command chair, and McLeod worried he would damage them, but Crist finally sat back, deflated. "All this time," Crist said, as he looked at Ansara then back to the floor. "All this time."

"Yes, and all that time has led to this encounter." McLeod pointed toward the screen. "And we're the ones who have to fix it."

* * *

"What are you thinking?" Reed asked. "Your words to Bahira sounded provocative."

"You heard what I said, Jolon. I told her to return to *Lance*, and that we would take care of the other vessel."

"That's what I mean, sir. With the Federation vessel out there, what are you planning to do?"

"I'm leaving Amaeus with a prize, since our operation here is pretty much over."

"Are you sure Thorian Crist is on board?"

"It doesn't matter. With both the Federation vessel and the planetary collaborative aware of our presence, our efforts are futile for the moment."

"So we wasted our time here over the last few weeks?"

But Landau only shook his head.

* * *

"We counted on you to protect us!" Ian Anoki screamed. Mr. Blanks said nothing. "And you've allowed that woman, the Federation vessel, and who knows who else take over the operation?"

"That's not what he did, Ian," Kyla Crist countered. "How could Mr. Blanks have prevented the Federation vessel from taking over? This is what they do."

"Perhaps we shouldn't have asked to join the Federation," Anoki muttered.

"Ha!" Marten said. "Maybe what you're angry about is you can't come in, push Zahara aside, and become the hero. We all know that's what you want to do."

Anoki started to rise, but Mr. Blanks cleared his throat. "If you would like my resignation, ministers, you may have it now." He stopped and waited for a minute, before continuing. "In the meantime, the Central Federation vessel and another unnamed vessel are in Amaean space trying to defuse the situation. If I may suggest: I will return to the control room to do what I can, while you work on preparing alternative statements for the news reports." Mr. Blanks waited and when no minister stopped him, he bowed and left the room.

"What do we do now?" Leyla Hill asked. And for once, even Ian Anoki had nothing to say.

Chapter Thirty-Eight

McLeod move to stand by Wolfe, ignoring Thorian Crist. "Raina, I don't trust Landau to sit back and let this thing die down without taking action."

"I agree." Wolfe shook her head. "Landau will have something else in mind, probably once the shuttle is back in their shuttle bay."

"Why would they—"

"Mr. Crist," McLeod said. "You're in my chair, but that does not give you the opportunity or right to speak. We're trying to save lives here, something in which you have little to no experience." McLeod gestured toward the screen again. "And while Mr. Ansara was more involved in this escalation, if you had allowed the planet to determine what it wanted through elections rather than playing the savior, none of this would have happened." McLeod saw Crist's jaw tightening and loosening as he considered his options, but he had none. When McLeod saw Crist let go, he smiled, then turned his attention back to Wolfe. "I have my Plan B."

"Will I like it?"

"I think so. We'll maintain a close watch on Landau and *Lance*. If they engage us, *Pathfinder,* or the Amaean forces once their shuttle is on board, we'll engage with a quick strike, then shift to config two while we move out of harm's way."

"So, we'll shift while we're moving and right after firing?"

"Yep."

Wolfe nodded. "You're right: I like it."

"Who *are* you people?" Crist asked, for once not confrontational.

McLeod smiled. "We're the good guys."

* * *

"Track with the shuttle as it nears the larger vessel, Darien," Gattiger instructed. "We need to maintain our relative position."

"Will that throw off the other vessel?" Jarvis asked.

Gattiger looked at him and smiled. "Are you worried about them?"

"No. I'm worried about the potential loss of life." Jarvis sat back in his chair. "Plus that ship is a mystery to us. Could they be as well equipped to take on the Shan as we are?"

"That's what I was trying to get through, Tara," Gattiger replied. "But we couldn't get anything." She leaned toward Jarvis. "Which tells me they may have a lot of firepower that we don't know about. Regardless, maintaining our position relative to the shuttle offers the best possible cover for the planet, so long as the fighters make the proper shifts as well."

"They're tracking fine, ma'am," came the voice of Worth, who turned to Gattiger. "We can hear more than you think."

I hope that's a good thing, Gattiger thought.

* * *

"Check movements of *Pathfinder* and the fighters, Virgil," McLeod said.

"Already monitoring, sir. They're shifting positions to track the shuttle and *Lance*." He turned to the command chairs. "They're doing it well; both the fighters and *Pathfinder*, I mean."

"That's the discipline Mr. Blanks told me about," Wolfe said. "It's a shame the other squadron leader didn't have the same discipline."

McLeod addressed the bridge. "Our plan is simple, people. We don't trust *Lance*, or its commander, so as they bring their shuttle aboard, prepare for a preemptive strike. I'll be counting on you to monitor weapons and *Lance*'s position so our strike is clear and effective."

"Aye, sir," came several voices.

"In addition, prepare for shift to config two right after the attack, so all crew should remain in core positions until further notice."

"Captain?" Kono asked. "Is this going to require some fancy flying?"

McLeod only smiled.

* * *

"Ten minutes to dock, ma'am," Tilley said.

Massi was tense in her seat, watching the consoles of her crew as they moved. "Thank you." Massi turned to her communications officer. "Raise *Lance*."

"Aye, ma'am."

Five seconds later, the face of Tyrus Landau appeared on the screen. He did not look happy.

"You have a reason for breaking communications silence?"

We've already spoken twice, and he still cares about communications silence? "Yes, sir. As you can see, this transmission is scrambled and on a secure channel, so—"

"What do you want, Bahira?"

Massi sat more upright in her chair. "I need to know the plan once the shuttle is secure onboard *Lance*, sir."

Landau waved his hand and turned away from Massi. "That is not your concern, Bahira. If you hadn't destroyed that fighter, we would have more options."

Massi tried hard to smile. "Understood, sir. However, with that unidentified ship in the mix, we don't want to start something we can't finish."

"You dare to suggest that I can't finish something that you so foolishly started? This is the height of insubordination!"

Massi could see a quick move of Jolon Reed's head as Landau spoke, the captain's chest heaving. Massi also saw Reed's face shake back and forth before she answered Landau. Massi sat back in her chair. "Yes, sir. Let us know how we can help." Without answering, Landau gestured to communications, and the connection was closed.

"I've never had reason to doubt Captain Landau," Latimer whispered. "But I don't understand this: how are we going to help if we don't know what he's planning?"

"It doesn't matter." Massi shrugged. "Whatever we do or don't do will count against us, anyway." She smiled at Latimer. "Don't worry. It will come to haunt me first, then dissipate."

"But that's not fair, ma'am. They fired on us first."

"I've endured these situations before. My connections above Captain Landau will protect me, and I doubt he wants to make an example of anybody but me. Just sit back and let's hope his rage doesn't make things worse for everyone."

* * *

"Do we have anything to worry about here, ma'am?" Jarvis asked.

"Such as?"

"The shuttle will be back on that Shan vessel—what did that man call it—*Lance*—in minutes, and I was worried that—"

"You worry too much, Drayden." Gattiger looked at her executive officer, then softened her tone. "We've had a loss of life, Drayden, so the ultimate has already happened. Our priority now is to prevent any further loss of life if we can. So long as we're on alert, we'll be fine." Gattiger turned her attention back to Beckett. "Julie, repeat instructions to the fighters, and engage with the squadron leaders to follow our leads." She turned to Worth. "What did you program through the command codes?"

Worth consulted her console. "Maintain containment and if the Shan vessel attacks, move ahead of *Pathfinder* to surround the Shan."

"Good. Make sure they know that."

"Yes, ma'am."

"What about that other ship?" Jarvis asked.

"What about it?"

"They may get between us and *Lance*. Then what?"

Gattiger's lips tightened. "Then I guess they're on their own."

* * *

McLeod walked to the helm and knelt near Kono. "I think the shuttle is close enough that we can begin changing our position, Lily."

"Aye, sir." McLeod beckoned Wolfe to the helm. "I want to shift slowly to *Lance's* flank while they're distracted with bringing the shuttle on board, so our movements may go unnoticed. That will give *Pathfinder* and the fighters the chance to move into offensive positions."

"A good plan," Wolfe said, looking at McLeod and smiling. "And you want me to stay with Lily as we do that, don't you?"

"If you would." McLeod touched Kono's shoulder. "Not a lack of confidence, Lily. I always want the prime expert in the Central Federation by the helm in times like this."

"But you're in control, Lily," Wolfe said. "Consider me an interested bystander."

Kono shrugged. "Captain McLeod said I could do some fancy flying. I don't care who's watching me."

McLeod shifted to the tactical console and leaned over Kelly. "Be ready for our shift to config two as we leave the area, Virgil. This will require very precise timing."

"Aye."

Chapter Thirty-Nine

"Shuttle almost onboard, ma'am," Worth said.

"Thank you," Gattiger said.

"Wait—" the weapons officer said.

"What is it?"

"One of the fighters, ma'am," Worth said. "He's shifting toward an offensive position too early."

"Reign him in! Get him back in line or he'll be sent to—"

"Moving, ma'am," said Worth.

Gattiger turned to Beckett. "What did you hear?"

"The squadron leader got to him, ma'am, we're good." Gattiger nodded and returned to her chair. *I can't afford to do that again*, she thought. "Very well. Carry on, and Julie?"

"Captain?"

"Confirm our objective with the fighters one more time. If one more of those fighters tries something stupid, they'll answer to me, I don't care what their commander does."

"Yes, ma'am."

Gattiger turned to Jarvis with a smile. "I'm back, Drayden."

"Never doubted it for a moment, ma'am."

* * *

"Bay doors, open, sir," Rubinco said. "Shuttle coming aboard."

"Lock it down quickly," Landau said. "We need to move to an offensive position before that Federation vessel does."

"What's our objective?" Reed asked.

Landau's face was grim. "To leave a lasting impression, Jolon." Landau rose and walked to his helm. "This will be delicate and quick, Tal. We'll unleash a quick salvo at both the Federation vessel and the lead fighters before departing. Lock in a course toward the Parateen system, and be ready on my command, got it?"

"Aye."

"Shuttle locked and bay doors closing, sir," Kane said.

"Good." Landau returned to his chair with an air of confidence. "On my mark."

* * *

McLeod stood at the side of Wolfe's chair. "Su-Commander Kono will have us in position in twenty seconds. We are targeting the secondary weapons array of *Lance*: it won't take out their offensive capability, but it will cripple them and it may compromise their shields in the flank." He turned to Wolfe. "Pulse or plasma?"

"Both. The concussion of the pulse weapons will rock them, but we'll create more damage to the shields with a plasma burst."

McLeod turned to Kelly. "Did you get that, Virgil?"

"Yes, sir."

"Good," McLeod said. "Max, you take over our shift to config two on my mark." He leaned toward Max Serrano as he joined Kelly at tactical. "And we will also shimmer as we begin the shift to config two."

Wolfe turned to McLeod. "Remind me, Tucker: have we ever done that before?"

"No, but Goody told me it should work, and he designed her."

"It's a hell of a time to find out if he's right."

* * *

"Ma'am," Worth said, concern in her voice.

"What is it, Tara?"

Worth pointed to her display. "That other vessel—the unidentified one? It's moved to another position, and—"a burst and cloud on the screen interrupted Worth.

"What the—" Jarvis said.

"Tara?" Gattiger asked.

"That other ship opened fire on the Shan vessel, ma'am."

"On screen!"

A second later, the ship appeared on the screen, as Worth pointed to it.

"There." Worth turned back to Gattiger. "Response?"

As Gattiger and the bridge crew watched the screen, they saw the vessel fade in and out at the edge of the cloud coming from *Lance.* A second later, it was gone.

* * *

"Good shooting, Virgil!" McLeod said. "Shift to config two. Now!"

Raven shuddered and made the shift as McLeod nodded to Lily Kono, who pressed a single pad to pull *Raven* a full click away from the action.

McLeod stood by Wolfe's chair and smiled as he looked around the bridge. "We're all in one piece. Once we return to config two, let's see what's happening with the planetary forces, *Pathfinder,* and *Lance.*"

Wolfe rose from her position next to Kono. "Remain on full alert." She returned to her seat and turned to look at McLeod. "As much fun as you thought?"

* * *

"Was no one tracking that vessel while we pulled in the shuttle?" Landau screamed. "What is our damage?" He glared, standing over his operations officer. "I'm waiting."

"Yes, sir," the young man said. "Shields have held, but they're damaged." He turned to his commanding officer. "The secondary weapons array is severely damaged." The man looked away, not meeting Landau's eyes.

Landau scowled at this, then returned to his chair. "We don't have the luxury of staying here any—"

"Hail from the Federation vessel, sir."

Landau sat in his chair, glancing first to Reed then back to communications. "Connect us."

On the screen appeared the unsmiling face of Lena Gattiger. "Captain," she said.

"Captain."

"We'd like you to leave Amaean space. *Now.* I think we have the advantage at the moment." The fatigue in Gattiger's voice surprised her.

Despite himself, Landau laughed. "And all without firing a single shot. Unless you controlled that other ship."

"That I can't say."

Landau nodded. "That's what I thought. We may meet again, captain, but not here, and not today." Landau turned his eyes away from the screen and nodded, breaking the connection. Seconds later, *Lance* began moving out of Amaean space.

Gattiger sat back in her chair. "And we'll be ready."

* * *

"The collaborative has a lot of work to do to restore public confidence in them," Mr. Blanks said to a smiling Raina Wolfe over the communications link. "They have to explain the loss of a fighter pilot, and that's on top of the previous outcry about not being informed of the Shan vessel and the Federation ship in Amaean space."

"Is Captain Gattiger talking to them?"

Mr. Blanks laughed. "Talking is a nice way of putting it. She's handling it well, but she's making it clear that the outcome might have been different if they had involved her from the beginning, working *with* our fighters rather than coming in after one was destroyed."

"That's a judgment call."

"It is, but that only counts when your decisions work out."

"I can't argue with that." Wolfe looked at Mr. Blanks for a moment, before adding, "We have more people for you to pick up—people associated with Thorian Crist."

Mr. Blanks squinted before he nodded. "I'm sure that's for a good reason."

"We believe so. While Crist is a scoundrel, his enterprises employ tens of thousands of people in the central desert. Without its continued operation, you might have an economic crisis on your hands."

"I'm confused. Why should we—"

"Please, Mr. Blanks. We only have a short time here." Wolfe leaned forward, filling up even more of the screen. "There are three people in Thorian Crist's inner circle who are needed to lead his enterprises: Wen Bokari, Walker Menzel, and Cole Maddox. Maddox is chief engineer, and someone has to run the technical part of Crist's operation, though I have doubts about her character. Bokari and Menzel, on the other hand, had little appetite for violence. We'll return all of them to you: you can decide what to do with them."

"You have them?"

Wolfe ignored his question. "The remaining people associated with Crist who were more complicit in the attacks previous to the housing complex are being returned to you as well, but for judicial action."

"Does that include Crist?"

Wolfe sat back and shook her head. "Call him a casualty of war, Mr. Blanks."

"But we weren't at war."

"You just didn't know you were." Wolfe sat up straighter. "You will have the people you need with detailed instructions within five hours. Have someone at the central space port by that time."

Mr. Blanks looked from side to side, unaccustomed to surprise. "Very well, and—our thanks."

Wolfe smiled. "It was nice meeting you; after we got out of custody, that is."

Mr. Blanks smiled. "Sorry about that."

"Not a problem." Wolfe broke the connection.

* * *

Six hours later, Wolfe leaned back in her chair after handing over the prisoners to the Amaean contingent led by Mr. Blanks.

"Something I should know about you and Mr. Blanks?" McLeod asked.

Wolfe turned to him with a frown. "No. And there's no reason for you to keep bringing it up, either."

"Done." McLeod leaned toward his friend. "Are you sure about leaving Menzel and Bokari to help run Crist Enterprises? They were still associated with Crist all along."

"As confident as you are that we shouldn't return Crist."

McLeod shook his head. "No; he's a bad actor and I don't trust him to reform—at least not here."

"Yet you believe that Amaean authorities should discipline Ansara?"

"As do you. Ansara is a weak behind-the-scenes person. Without someone stronger to hang on to, he's nothing. Tell me you don't agree."

Wolfe put up her hands. "I do. I just don't have confidence in their judicial system."

"Well, on that we agree." McLeod rose. "All com, Ava." After a moment, he said, "Well done, people. Mission accomplished with only a few snags, all of which were handled admirably. Captain Wolfe and I are proud. We will remain in configuration two until we are three clicks away from Amaeus. We'll inform you when to return to core positions for the shift to configuration three. McLeod out." He turned to Kono with a smile. "Take us home, Lily."

Chapter Forty

"All in all," Field Marshall Sinclair said, "I'd say *Raven's* first mission was successful." The older man was smiling as he spoke.

McLeod and Wolfe looked at each before McLeod answered. "We agree, sir. We had no casualties and performed the extraction with minimal difficulty." He looked up. "We also understand Mr. Crist is enjoying his new life."

"That's a surprise," Sinclair replied. "We have no authority over him, but he is relishing the new start we gave him."

"You sound like you're happy with the outcome, sir," Wolfe said. "To be honest, I wasn't sure whether capturing him alive would be the best for us in the long run."

Sinclair raised his hands. "Who knows? People like Thorian Crist enjoy building things from scratch. Plus, they like to be in charge and important. He's content for now." Sinclair paused, then added, "Plus, I believe he's still stinging from the fact that someone so close to him betrayed him so completely."

"What about conditions on Amaeus, sir?" McLeod asked.

Sinclair smiled. "We've spoken with all the ministers from the planetary collaborative since your departure, and they've told us their side of the story."

"They seemed flustered and ineffective when we were there," Wolfe offered. "Is that still the case?"

"I'd say so. We spoke to all of them because the titular head—Ali—has been disgraced, as has Ian Anoki."

"He was," Wolfe searched for a word, "unpleasant, I should say."

"I agree," Sinclair said. "So while Ali is the official head of the collaborative, the leadership has fallen to Kyla Crist, who has become even more popular than before."

"A good choice," McLeod said. "She's level headed and practical."

"She is," Sinclair agreed. "Besides that, the trials for Crist's inner circle are progressing. All of them were charged, even the people you felt were less culpable. I think Menzel and Bokari will come out of this with minimal penalties. Whether the collaborative takes over the Crist Enterprises compound as a government entity is still up in the air."

"I'm surprised," Wolfe began, "given their more caprist leanings, I mean."

"True. But to be honest, that doesn't matter to the Central Federation. What matters is the lack of leadership and the sense that, even with their strong mandate to join the Federation, they are not ready. That's what the latest assessment determined."

"Might we have caused that, Field Marshall?" McLeod asked. "We had to improvise during this mission, so—"

"Not at all, Tucker. *Raven* didn't make our concerns about Amaeus worse; you helped us see them more clearly." Sinclair sat back from the screen. "Perhaps in another couple of years, we will admit Amaeus to membership, but they have to improve their stability before that happens. Fortunately, the Central Federation and the Star Alliance are sending work teams over the next two years to help them, something we should have done in the first place."

"Good to know, sir." McLeod leaned forward, ready to break the connection.

Sinclair smiled. "So tell me, you've been back for two weeks: how would you rate your trainees?"

McLeod and Wolfe looked at each other, sighed, then turned back to the screen. Wolfe smiled. "About that..."

The End